FORGET ME NOT

MIRANDA RIJKS

INKUBATOR
BOOKS

Published by Inkubator Books
www.inkubatorbooks.com

Copyright © 2022 by Miranda Rijks

ISBN (eBook): 978-1-83756-027-1
ISBN (Paperback): 978-1-83756-028-8
ISBN (Hardback): 978-1-83756-029-5

MAP OF THE CANTON OF VALAIS IN SWITZERLAND

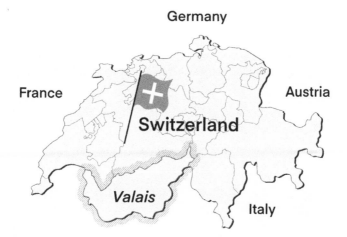

PROLOGUE

I love skiing. It's the speed and the freedom. The feeling of the air rushing past your face, the cold biting your cheeks and stinging your eyes, making you realise how insignificant we all are in the face of the elements. The lovely crunching noise of my skis on the hard packed snow and how the snow flies up behind me like a swirling wave as I carve neatly left and right. I'm in the ski team at school. I thought it would help, help me make friends, gain some respect. It's made no difference. I'm still the idiot who snogged Olivier, whose pictures were circulated all around school. Whom people whisper about and stare at.

But out here I can forget them. I'm free. The mountainside is mine, and I can go wherever I like. I wonder if it's like driving a car. No, probably not. More like riding a motorbike. I might save up for one and ride it when I leave school. I'll be the cool girl then, dressed from head to toe in black leathers.

It's rubbish weather today, but I don't care. I could ski with my eyes shut, just feeling the undulations of the piste through my skis and boots and up through my legs to my hips, relaxing into the regular movements. I'm meant to be practicing today for the giant slalom. Mum is up here with me, but I've left her behind. She keeps on telling me to slow down, to stay in control, but I'm the racer, not her. She just hampers me.

Actually, she hampers me in life. Nag, nag, nag. If she knew half of what I'm going through, she'd be shocked. I can hear the chairlift on my left-hand side, but visibility is so poor I can't see it. But I know where I am. I've been skiing here since I was a tiny kid. I pause at the side of the slope for a moment, leaning onto my sticks, pulling my goggles away from my face, which just makes them steam up even more.

Mum gets angry if I don't stop and wait for her. I think she's worried she'll fall and I won't be there to help her. Despite having grown up on these slopes too, she's not a confident skier, and if it weren't for the fact that I had to practice today, she wouldn't be out in such bad weather. I peer up the piste, but all I can see is dense whiteness. It's totally silent here, and there's no one else skiing. I could be the only person left alive on earth for all I know.

I'm sure Mum's okay, so I remove a ski glove with my teeth and then peer at my mobile phone. They have said nothing crap about me for a few days, but I'm always on the lookout.

BAM!

It comes out of nowhere, this horrendous jolt. I go flying, the phone and my gloves spinning out of my grip, and everything slows right down, as if I'm soaring through the white fog to land in the soft snow. But no.

I gasp as something hard jams into my chest, knocking the breath from me. The pain. I try to call for help, but I can't move. Snow is clogging up my airways. Or is it something else? Metallic. Agony. A flash of colour. Concerned voices. Then silence. I'm dying. What will Mum do? The whiteness fades into black.

1

HELEN – NOW

'Can I play on your iPad?' Emily taps my shoulder and looks at me with her wide blue eyes, her head tilted to one side. I was one of those new mothers who swore that no child of mine would ever get addicted to screens and that playtime would comprise sustainable wooden blocks and crayons and paper. How naïve I was.

'Fifteen minutes only, and then it's bath time.'

She groans but trots off happily with the iPad.

'Dad will be home soon, and he won't want to see you on that thing!' I shout over my shoulder.

Dad is Andrew, yet he isn't Emily's dad. For the first two years of our relationship, even when I realised it was getting serious, both Emily and I called him Andrew. But last year, we moved in together, and when one ordinary Saturday afternoon, four-year-old Emily pirouetted into the living room and asked if she could call Andrew Dad, we were both overwhelmed. Andrew had tears in his eyes when he turned to me and asked if it was alright.

So now we are a little family of three. Andrew, me and Emily. Andrew and I are unofficially engaged because the antiquated legal system says I can't get married for another year and eight months. February isn't the ideal month for a wedding, but we'll marry on the very day we're allowed to. Andrew will adopt Emily on that day too. We've talked about having another child, and although time isn't on my side, I want to wait until everything is official. Some people say that trauma makes you more carefree, that you need to live every day as if it's your last. It hasn't been that way for me. I'm ultra-cautious now, reluctant to commit to anything until I'm positive I'm treading the right path. Although I know without doubt that Andrew loves Emily with all his heart, at the end of the day, she is my responsibility alone. I love that responsibility, but it weighs heavily sometimes.

I respond to an email, double-check the pitch document I'm presenting to a potential new client tomorrow, and turn the computer off. It's been over fifteen minutes, but Emily deserves the odd treat. She's had a long day.

'Right, bath time!' I say as I stride into the living room. Emily is sprawled on the sofa, lying on her stomach, her bare toes wriggling in the air. She groans and clasps the iPad tightly.

And then we both hear the back door open and Andrew's footsteps. 'I'm home! How are my girls?'

Emily drops the iPad onto a cushion, careers off the sofa and hurls herself at Andrew as he walks into the living room.

'Hello, munchkin!' he says as he lifts her up and twirls her around, her feet just millimetres away from swiping the photo of Andrew's parents on the sideboard.

My heart catches, and I know how lucky I am that Andrew and Emily love each other as if they really are related.

. . .

ANDREW PREPARES supper for the two of us while I get Emily ready for bed. I've been lucky in that respect. The important men in my life have both been excellent chefs and willing to carry the load in the kitchen. Just as well, as I'm terrible at cooking, and we'd probably be living off takeaways. He hands me a glass of white wine and instructs me to stir the frying pan while he nips upstairs to give Emily a goodnight kiss.

A few minutes later, we're seated at the small kitchen table, eating a mild chicken curry.

'What are your ideas for a holiday this year?' Andrew asks, taking a sip of wine.

'I haven't given it much thought,' I say. Planning is hard because I am an interior designer, and my work is piecemeal. I bounce from project to project, just hoping that something new will materialise before the end of each assignment. I've been busy the past year, but I can't be complacent about it. That's the stress of being self-employed. So much of my work comes from word of mouth, and it's taken a long time to build up that network. Andrew is a planning officer for the local council, one of those people many love to hate. But he adores his job, and other than being inundated with work and underpaid, he's about as far from being officious as one could imagine. Andrew is the sort of man who likes harmony, and on the odd occasion when he has to propose a ruling that might cause financial or emotional hardship to a homeowner, it eats him up. He leans towards me across the table.

'Well, I was thinking that when we get married next year, I want to take you and Emily somewhere really special. The Maldives or Seychelles perhaps, staying in one of those stilted villas with a glass floor so you can see the fish swimming underneath, so perhaps this year we should take it easy and stay closer to home.'

'You're right,' I say, chewing thoughtfully. Money is tight, and until next year, when I will find out exactly where I stand, it will remain so. The courts allowed me to sell my old home so Andrew and I could pool our funds, but Paul's half of the sale price is now in a bank account, one that I can't access. Our joint home is lovely, but modest. It's a three-bedroom, two-bathroom semi-detached property, one-third of a large cottage that was divided up about fifty years ago. With low ceilings, beams and small rooms, it's quaint but has a sizeable garden that backs onto fields, perfect for Emily. It's also within ten minutes' walking distance of the village primary school, so we have a genuine sense of community, something that was of utmost importance to me. In a year and eight months' time, we will have some more money, but I doubt we'll move. The three of us are content here. In fact, I'm more than content. At long last, I'm happy. And next year, once the long seven years is up, I will be truly settled.

THE NEXT DAY, I drop Emily at school and then get dressed, ready for my pitch for an uber-modern extension of a house in Hove. I've accepted that I look older than my thirty-five years, because tragedy shows in your face however many expensive creams you rub into your skin. Perhaps I would have had fewer grey hairs, but I can't turn the clock back. I'm not one for looking backwards, anyway. There's nothing we can do to change the past. I'm just pulling on my jacket when my work telephone rings.

'Good morning, Helen Sellers speaking.'

'Hello, my name's Camilla Anworth. I've been given your details by Lewis Chen. I was wondering whether you'd consider doing the interior design for a luxury chalet in the Alps.'

'Goodness,' I say, rather taken aback. Lewis Chen was the architect for a lovely renovation project of a converted barn near Pulborough that I did the interior design for last year.

With all of those exposed beams, there was something a little alpine-like about it. In fact, I even sourced a coffee table for the living room that had been a large sleigh in a previous incarnation. For Lewis Chen to recommend me is praise indeed. 'I'm very flattered,' I say. 'Could you tell me a little more?' I glance at my watch and reckon I've got ten minutes before I need to leave.

'It's a chalet my husband and I bought in a small but upcoming resort in Switzerland called Corviez. The renovation and extension work are already under way, but I need someone to oversee the internal decor, soft furnishings and the like. Lewis said you'd be able to put a scheme together for me.'

'Um, yes. I'm sure I could. I'm just about to go to a meeting, but would it be possible for you to email me the details?'

'Of course. I have a healthy budget and no time to do this myself, so you'd have pretty much free rein.'

'It sounds like a marvellous project,' I say.

Camilla Anworth snorts slightly, but says she'll send over some more information shortly. I note down her telephone number and email, and when we hang up, I do a little jig around the room. That is until I remember she said the Alps. As I get in the car and drive down to Hove, I rationalise with myself. The Alps cover a huge area and several countries.

IT'S A BUSY DAY. The pitch goes on for longer than I expected, but I think it went well, and I have to hurry back to collect Emily from school. Back home, I glance at my computer but don't get a chance to study the email that Camilla Anworth has sent me until Andrew is home and Emily is tucked up in bed. The project is amazing, and when Camilla said she had a big budget, she really meant it. I've never pitched for anything this large – monetary-wise, anyway. She's sent me some photos of the chalet, and the place looks delightful, but when I study the plans, my heart really leaps. The architect has been so skilful in harmonising the traditional Swiss chalet with all its wood and large, slate tiled roof with sleek glass that makes the most of the amazing south- and west-facing views. But then I look on the map to see exactly where the chalet is. I groan and bury my face in my hands. Corviez is part of a large ski area linking four resorts together, one of which is Lanvière. I swore to myself five years ago that I would never return there. Never. Not because of Lanvière itself, because the village is delightful and the extensive slopes, a skier's paradise. But because of what happened there. The event that changed my life forever.

'What's up?' Andrew asks as I stride, frowning, into the kitchen and pour myself an extra-large glass of wine.

'I've been asked to pitch for a chalet renovation, but I don't want to go there. It's in the next-door village to Lanvière.'

'Oh,' he says, leaving a wooden spoon in a pan and pulling me into a hug.

'The project is amazing, and it's worth a fortune, but I don't know if I can do it.'

When I tell Andrew how much I'll earn, he releases his grip on me and steps backwards.

'You heard me right,' I say quietly.

He reaches for my hand. 'It's not really something you can turn down if you're offered it.'

'That's the problem.'

'Is it in exactly the same place?' He turns away from me and picks up the wooden spoon in the saucepan. Something I can't quite identify smells good.

'No. On another mountain, but it links in.'

'And when is the project happening?'

'As soon as possible.'

'So in the summer months?'

'Yes.'

Andrew turns to look at me. 'In which case the mountains will seem totally different. You won't recognise the place, darling. The tragedy happened in the snow, but in June and July there won't be any.'

'I suppose you're right.' I sink into my chair at the table.

'Pitch for it, and let's see what happens.'

AND SO I DO. A week later, Camilla Anworth telephones me.

'You've got the job, Helen. How soon can you start?'

2

I think we must be staying in the smallest and cheapest hotel in Lanvière. Paul said it's a three star, but I wouldn't give it much more than a one. I suppose it's clean, at least. There's a small double bed that's built into the wall with wooden cupboards above and to the side of the bed, yet there's barely enough space to manoeuvre around it. The floor, walls and ceiling are all covered in pine, a yellowy-orange colour that clashes with the peach curtains. The en suite shower room is equally small and oppressive, lined with brown and cream tiles and a shower curtain that has mould at the bottom. Unfortunately, Lanvière is one of the more expensive resorts in the Alps, and we couldn't afford anything better. As Paul rightly said, we're not here for the room. We're here for the skiing and the mountains and the après-ski. Not that we've had much of that. The weather has been dreadful, and the hooray Henry types braying at the bars, boasting about the size of their daily trades, are hardly my cup of tea.

I open the peach-coloured curtains, the synthetic fabric feeling slippery, but I'm not sure why I bother. The view is onto a brick wall, and it's dusk, so I can barely make it out. I glance at my watch once again.

It's nearly 5.30 pm, and the lifts shut at 4.40 pm. Paul should have been back ages ago. Even if he'd skied down, which he prefers to do, he would have been back by now. He's not stupid enough to ski in the dark. In fact, Paul is an excellent skier, having been put on the slopes at the age of three and treated to skiing holidays twice yearly throughout his childhood. Our families are very different. He even skied for the university ski team. You might have thought that would make him blasé, but actually it's had the opposite effect. He is ultra safety conscious, always paying attention to avalanche warnings and suggesting that I avoid the slopes when visibility is poor. And that's why it's making me nervous. Paul is never late, not without an explanation, anyway.

I try his mobile again, and once more it rings out. It's hot in our claustrophobic hotel room, but nevertheless, I get togged up once again, pulling on a thick sweater, my red ski jacket, a beanie and my black ski trousers. I've had to leave my waterproof boots along with my skis and ski boots in the hotel locker in the basement. As I take the small lift downstairs, I'm hopeful that Paul's skis might be wedged up against mine, that perhaps he has returned but gone straight out again for a drink. But no. The only skis in our locker are mine.

Outside, it's snowing heavily, and a wind has whipped up. The snow burns my exposed cheeks, and I hurry with my head down, the hood pulled low over my forehead. Snow has frozen on the artificial fur around my hood, creating little icicles that prickle my cheeks and chin.

It's quite a walk to the lift station. I pass skiers strolling in the opposite direction, their voices loud from too much post-ski glühwein. When I reach the main lift station, it's closed and quiet, with not a soul in sight, so different to the morning hustle when everyone is eager to push forward, to get onto the gondolas as quickly as possible. I walk around the exterior, hopeful I might see an official, but the place is deserted. I call Paul's phone again, and this time it goes straight to voicemail. Does that mean he's switched it off? Or has the battery run out? Could he have listened to all of my messages and chosen to ignore them? Surely not.

I hurry back down the main street, where the bars and restaurant windows are glowing and drunken revellers are spilling out onto the pavements despite the blizzard-like weather and the early hour. I catch the scent of cigarettes and cinnamon-spiced red wine. Thumping loud music is barely muffled by the wind. I decide to return to the hotel, and if he's still not there, then I'll have no choice but to scour the bars. Anger chokes my throat. How could Paul be so selfish? He must know that I'm worrying about him, that we're meant to be on this holiday together, enjoying it as a married couple. Perhaps he's done this disappearing act on purpose, to prove a point. If so, that's cruel, and there I was, thinking I was married to a kind man.

I plod up the hill, my face getting battered by the elements, my breath laboured. When I eventually reach the hotel, it's a relief. I remove my boots and walk in my socks to the reception desk, which is a wooden bar built into the corner of the hallway. There's no one there, so I press the little gold bell.

A middle-aged woman appears from behind a door. She's dressed all in mauve, and it makes her face look colourless. 'Yes, how can I help you?' she asks in heavily accented English.

'I was wondering if my husband is back yet?' I ask, glancing at the rack of keys behind her and seeing that the key to room twelve is still hanging there. 'Room twelve.'

'*Non*, I think not. I hope there's no problem?' She glances at her watch. I wonder whether she's looking forward to the end of her shift and can do without any drama.

'He hasn't come back from skiing,' I say, feeling like an idiot.

'He drinking? That's what many of zee Brits like to do, isn't it? Après-ski.'

'Perhaps,' I say. 'Would you mind telephoning me if he returns to the hotel? I'm going to look for him.' I write my mobile phone number out on the back of a ski map, but she tuts when she sees the country code of +44.

'I ask him to call you when he's back,' she says.

I nod, accepting that's the most I can ask for. I just hope he will.

Once I've put my snow boots back on, I stand in the doorway to the hotel and call Gabriella. She's one of Paul's friends from his university days. They're a close bunch, and it's been difficult for me, always feeling on the outside of his friendship group. Most of them seem to have married each other, and I get the sense that there were a few raised eyebrows when Paul announced he was marrying me, the ordinary girl from Horsham without a university degree. I was annoyed when Paul told me that Gabriella and three of her friends would be in Lanvière at the same time as us. This was meant to be our holiday, a time for him and me to reconnect, to get away from our busy working lives, so it was galling when he told me ever so casually at the airport that some of the old crowd would be there too. It felt like a betrayal of sorts, as if he had a fallback plan should things not go too well between us.

Of all them, I like Gabriella the most. She's one of those loud, get-what-you-see type of girls, and the only one who gripped me by the shoulders on our wedding day and told me I was good for Paul. I also like her Australian husband, who prefers sailing to skiing, so has left her to come on this trip without him.

I telephone her. 'Gaby,' I say, 'it's Helen. Have you seen Paul this afternoon?' I can hear loud voices and the beat of a familiar song playing in the background.

'Hi, Helen. No. He didn't ski with us today, and I haven't seen him at all.' She then shouts loudly, 'Billy, have you seen Paul?' I have to hold the phone away to stop my eardrum from being assaulted. 'Sorry, Helen. None of us have seen him. Is there a problem?'

'He hasn't returned from skiing.'

There's a beat of silence, which makes my breath stall.

'Shit. Has something happened?' Gaby asks.

'No, no. I'm sure it's fine,' I say, without much conviction. 'But if you see him, can you get him to call me?'

'Of course. Have you had an argument or something?'

I laugh, but it sounds strained. 'Nothing like that. I'm sure it's fine. Don't worry.'

'Okay,' she says slowly. 'Drop me a text when he gets back to the hotel, won't you?'

'Sure,' I say, silently praying that I'll be doing that very soon.

IF THE WEATHER was bad half an hour ago, now it's much worse. Snow is swirling around biting into my exposed skin, so I have to pull my scarf up to cover my mouth and nose. I wish I'd brought my ski goggles with me, because flakes are settling on my lashes and making it hard to see. I shiver, a mixture of fear and cold. There are fewer people out now, not surprising really, and I slither as I try to walk quickly down the hill towards the centre of town. And that's the problem: Lanvière is a big resort, with a huge ski area and plenty of upmarket shops and bars that attract wealthy tourists from across the globe. Streets meander up and down the mountainside in every direction, and just because I'm searching in the centre of town doesn't mean Paul couldn't be in a bar further out or even having a nightcap with friends I don't know about. I realise I'm probably on a wild goose chase, but I have to do this. I stride into bar after bar, restaurant after restaurant, alternately sweating in my many layers of thermals as I walk into the cosy warmth where tourists and locals alike are enjoying their downtime, and then freezing again as I walk away, with a knot of worry growing increasingly large in my sternum. By 8 pm, I give up. My breathing is laboured and my heartbeat loud in my ears as I trudge back up the hill. Paul is missing, and the chances are he's had an accident up there on that pitch-black mountainside. Has he been rescued, whisked off in a helicopter to the hospital in the valley, or is he still out there, all alone, terrified and suffering from frostbite?

When I arrive back at the hotel, I hurry to the reception desk, peeling off my many layers, steam rising from my clothes. I catch a glimpse of myself in a mirror in the narrow hallway. My nose is scarlet, and my hair wet and plastered to my head. I'm a mess.

'Have you found your husband?' The hotel manager looks up from her slim paperback with a look of concern. I shake my head.

'I think something has happened to him. He hasn't returned from skiing, and I don't know where he is.' I swallow a sob as the woman's eyes widen with concern.

'*Attendez*,' she says and picks up the phone. She speaks rapidly in French, and although my grasp of the language is reasonable, the only thing my addled brain can decipher is Paul's name. '*Oui, oui. Merci.*'

'The gendarmes come,' she says. 'The police.'

I burst into tears, and before I know it, I'm snivelling in this stranger's ample bosom, the unfamiliar scent of her mauve bobbled jumper somehow making it so much worse.

'We have very good mountain rescue here,' she says, which makes me cry even harder. 'But he's probably drinking with friends, no?'

I disentangle myself from her and nod, wiping my nose and eyes with a tissue I extract from my ski jacket.

A FEW MINUTES LATER, I'm sitting in a small office, my icy hands clasping a hot cup of cocoa laced with something alcoholic. A policeman is sitting opposite me, asking lots of questions in fluent English, such as when I last saw Paul, whether he was skiing alone, checking what safety equipment Paul was carrying. None, I think. I give him a photograph of Paul, one that we took a few weeks ago when we were staying with friends, walking their new Labrador puppy along the Littlehampton seafront. And then the policeman is on the telephone, speaking rapid French, and the manageress fires the odd word of English at me. Helicopter. Dogs. Snow plough. Oh sorry, no, no helicopter. The weather is too bad. In the morning, hopefully. But will Paul even be alive in the morning if he's stuck up there on the edge of a mountain? No. I mustn't think like that. I need to stay positive. The policeman's forehead is creased with concern, and I hear the word 'avalanche'. Please no, please not Paul.

'Do you have someone to be with you?' he asks. 'A friend, perhaps?'

I think of Gabriella, the only person I know here, and nod.

'Ask her to come to be with you.' I know then that he's not

hopeful of finding Paul, and something breaks inside me. And then he is gone, and the fate of my husband lies with a bunch of strangers who are prepared to risk their own lives on this most vicious of freezing nights.

Half an hour later Gabriella has arrived. The landlady, who by now has introduced herself as Lucienne, insists that I am upgraded to a room with twin beds and an en suite with a bath so that Gabriella can stay with me and I can have a soak.

'But what if Paul comes back in the night and I'm not in room twelve?' I ask.

'We will tell him where to find you. He has to come through reception to collect his key.' Of course he does; I'm just not thinking straight.

Gabriella doesn't say much, and I fear that she's thinking the same as me. No one can survive a night like tonight, especially someone who might have a broken leg or cracked a few ribs. When we're alone in the room, she runs me a hot bath, and I sink into it, but even so I can't get warm. Still shivering, I get out of the bath and pull on several layers of clothes. When I come out of the bathroom, Gabriella is on the phone.

'Keep me posted, babe,' she says, ending the call when she sees me. 'I've been talking to my friend Orla. Her parents live here, well, part of the time, anyway. Her dad is Swiss, and he knows everyone. She said she'll get her parents onto it and to tell you not to worry too much. The mountain rescue service here is one of the best in the world.'

That doesn't reassure me.

'Should I call Paul's parents, do you think?'

Gabriella pulls a face that suggests that she's met them, beyond the cursory introduction at our wedding. 'Perhaps wait a bit longer. No need to worry them unnecessarily.' She's right of course. 'Look, let's watch some telly or something, anything to take your mind off things.'

I nod, but it's not like I can just switch off. All I can think about is Paul lying frozen in the snow, terrified, in pain and wondering whether he's still alive. What will my life be like without him? What about the future we had planned together? Or am I catastrophising unnecessarily. Will Paul and I laugh about this when we're back home at the weekend?

Gabriella switches on the television, but there are no English channels, so we just watch some wildlife programme with the sound turned down low. All the time, I'm staring at my phone, willing it to ring.

It doesn't.

At 11 pm, I go downstairs, catching Lucienne just as she's about to leave.

'The gendarmes will be in touch when they hear something. Try not to worry,' she says, patting my arm. 'My colleague, Jean, will be in the office. He will wake you if anything happens.'

'Thank you,' I say, but I don't feel I have anything to be thankful for.

Gabriella goes to sleep about midnight. But I lie there all night, my phone on charge next to my pillow, willing it to ring, forcing myself to stay awake just in case I miss something. Even if it's bad news, at least then I will know, and I can stop my imagination from running wild. Anything would be better than this silence. The hours pass so slowly, and the silence is oppressive. It's a relief when the building starts to creak into life, and there are footsteps, doors closing, voices. At 6.30 am, I leave Gabriella sleeping and slip out of the bedroom, joining a couple of early risers in the breakfast room. I drink a black coffee but eat nothing. I wouldn't be able to keep anything down.

At 8 am, my phone rings. With my heart thudding wildly, I answer it.

'Madame, this is Luc Jollien, the policeman. We met

yesterday. I call just to tell you we have no news yet, but the weather forecast is better for this morning, so the helicopter will start the search very soon. We have all the rescue teams out looking. I call you if we find anything.'

'Thank you,' I say. 'I'll be out in the town looking for him.'

'*Non, non.* It's better if you stay in the hotel, please. This is a job for the professionals. Please be confident we will find your husband.'

I HAVE no idea how I get through the next few hours. I tell Gabriella to leave because the sun is shining now and the snow conditions perfect, with several inches of freshly fallen powder. There's no reason her skiing holiday should be ruined. Yet when she leaves, I am bereft and spend hours pacing the hotel corridor.

And then the room phone rings, and with my heart in my mouth, I rush to answer it.

'Madame, Monsieur Jollien is here to see you,' Lucienne says. I can tell from the tone of her voice that there is news, and although this is what I thought I wanted, now I wish I could bury my head under the pillow and stay in this room forever.

'Can Monsieur Jollien come to your room?'

'Yes,' I whisper, because that can only be bad news, can't it? The hotel is quiet, with all the other guests out skiing. How could the sun shine on a day like today? It seems so wrong.

A few moments later I'm opening the door to him. I'm grateful at least that he comes straight to the point. 'Madame, we have found a ski.'

'A ski?'

'It was wedged in a snowdrift at the side of Col de Pavarois.'

'I'm sorry, I–'

'It is not a normal place to find a ski, and we need to check if it belonged to your husband. What skis does your husband use?'

'Um, I'm not sure. I think they were blue, no, red perhaps.'

He throws me a sympathetic smile. 'Did he have his own skis?'

'No, we rented them.'

'From which ski shop?'

'Um, the one up the hill on the right-hand side.'

'And do you have the ticket, so we can check which skis he rented?'

'Yes, I'll find it.' I rummage in my handbag for my wallet and pull out the handwritten receipt with the details of our rented items. The skis, the poles and the helmets.

'Okay. I call the rental shop now, and we can confirm if it is the same ski.'

'And if it is?'

'We worry about that when we have to.' He tilts his head to one side and throws me a sympathetic smile.

Monsieur Jollien leaves the room, but I can hear him in the corridor, his voice low, and then just a few moments later, he knocks on the door again. I know from his face that it's bad news.

'They have confirmed that this ski was rented by your husband.'

'What does that mean?' I ask, feeling my throat choking up.

'I am very sorry, Helen, but we have to presume that your husband had an accident. When he fell, he lost a ski, and just a couple of metres from that location is a sheer drop over the rock face, many hundreds of metres down. If he fell there, then it is not possible to survive. I am very sorry.'

'But we don't know for sure!' I say, my voice high-pitched. 'It's just speculation.'

'Of course, for now, it's just speculation. And we will continue looking for him. But this is an area off-piste, very dangerous and where, unfortunately, several people have lost their lives.'

I sink onto the bed and sob.

3

'Mummy, I don't want you to go!' Emily throws her arms around my legs.

'It's only for a couple of days. You'll have such a lovely time with Aunty Kelly you won't even notice I've gone.'

'I will.' Her little voice cracks, and it makes me feel even worse.

'Come on, munchkin, let's get you ready for school,' Andrew says. 'And when you finish, Aunty Kelly will be there to collect you and take you out for a special meal. We need to let Mummy go; otherwise she'll miss her flight.' Andrew manages to peel Emily away from me, and I feel both grateful and terrible. This is the first time that I have left her overnight with Andrew, and it's a massive step for all of us.

'You take care,' Andrew says, pulling me into a hug. 'Call me and let me know what it's like.' He then whispers into my ear, 'Our imagination is always more dramatic than the reality.'

He's right, and he knows that I've been worrying about this, my first trip to the mountains in five years.

. . .

CAMILLA ANWORTH and I have met twice over the past three weeks, firstly for her to share the renovation plans and to explain her wish list for the interiors of the chalet, and the second time was when I presented my final schemes. I detailed every item on several mood boards, covering the lighting, wall and floor finishes, curtains, headboards and soft furnishings. The costs are enormous, and despite knowing her vast budget, I was still worried when I presented my spreadsheet. She didn't bat an eyelid. Camilla is probably in her late forties, with caramel-coloured hair shot through with blonde highlights that falls gently to her shoulders in what looks like a very expensive style. Her forehead barely moves, and her eyes are slightly cat-like. I think she's had a facelift, or at least a lot of Botox. Both times we've met, she's been head to toe in charcoal grey; perhaps it's her go-to colour, and it certainly fits with the neutral scheme she's requested for the interior of the chalet. We have every conceivable shade of taupe, cream, brown and grey with the odd little pop of red or orange. It's very traditional for a chalet style, with the interest coming from numerous different textures, ranging from felt to fur, and amazing slate walls with wooden parquet floors laid in chevron patterns. It was me who insisted that most of the rooms have a brief nod to colour, and she seems to have bought into the idea, which is hardly radical. Camilla's brief was for traditional yet modern interiors with the focus on the windows. She's shown me a few photographs, and the views are jaw-dropping, so I understand why the focus needs to be on drawing the eye to the outside.

The first time we met, I was on edge. Camilla comes across as super-efficient, one of those boarding-school-educated women who know their place in the world and won't stand for any nonsense. She made it quite clear that any project she works on finishes on time and to budget. I didn't like to ask how many renovations she's done before, but she let slip in conversation that her family owns houses in Majorca, London and Cornwall, so perhaps she's renovated all of those properties too. Her husband, Hugo Anworth, is something big in the city, a hotshot and high-earner.

The second time we met, it was as if I'd passed her test and she'd decided she liked me, because her manner was less brusque. She gushed over my design suggestions, which was a massive relief. Today I am meeting her at Geneva International Airport, and we have our very first site meeting. My stomach is filled with nerves and excitement.

As I step out of the sliding doors and into the arrivals hall, I see her standing to one side, talking into her phone, her arms waving in the air. She's wearing a grey cape with fur around the neck. Real fur, I suppose. When she sees me, she wriggles her perfectly manicured fingers at me and nods. A moment later, her phone is in her Mulberry handbag and we are striding through the hall towards the exit.

'My driver is waiting for me,' she says. 'I hope you had a good flight.'

There I was thinking we'd be getting the train. Andrew had instructed me to sit on the right-hand side of the carriage so I could get the best view of Lake Geneva. Silly me. Of course someone like Camilla has a driver.

We stride over to a shining black Range Rover with Geneva registration plates. A man in a short-sleeved shirt and suit trousers jumps out and takes my small suitcase, placing it in the boot. To my surprise, Camilla hops onto the back seat next to me.

A moment later we are gliding out of the airport and onto

the dual carriageway that takes us through Geneva and out the other side.

'The renovations are going well,' Camilla says, without any small talk. 'You will meet Saskia Berchard. She is our architect. A local woman but very competent. She knows all the best builders and tradespeople. That's the thing with small communities, you need to use the locals and get them onside; otherwise you'll be forever up against bureaucracy and resentment.'

'It's no problem using me, then?'

She laughs. 'The locals are only interested in what they see on the exterior of the property. It's not like many of *them* are going to be invited inside.'

I stare out of the window then because it seems a very snobbish thing to say, as if she can't be bothered to make friends with anyone beyond her closed network. If I was lucky enough to have a holiday home, I'd want to befriend the locals and try to integrate with the community as best I could.

'There's a small cabin adjacent to the chalet, which we haven't bothered to renovate. It's available for your use during the next few weeks of the project. And there's a car that you can use too. An automatic Golf I think it is. You've driven on the right-hand side, I assume?'

'Um, yes,' I say, although it was only the once in Southern Spain, and I hated every moment, trying not to drive the wrong way around roundabouts and hugging the kerb tightly. What worries me is how long Camilla expects me to stay in Switzerland. I thought I'd be in and out either on the same day or just have to stay the odd night. Hopefully, I haven't got that wrong.

Camilla returns to her phone, and I wonder how sending emails and reading things on the small screen doesn't make her carsick. Meanwhile, I'm enjoying the fabulous views. As the motorway climbs up and over Lausanne, the views across Lake Geneva, with the high mountains to the right and in front of us, are staggering. The water is like a silvery-blue mirror, and the mountains, also in hues of dark blue, rise dramatically upwards where the glistening white snow-covered peaks pop against the cerulean blue sky.

'If you glance down to your right, you might get a glimpse of Chateau Chillon,' Camilla says, keeping her eyes on her phone.

'Do you want me to slow down, madame?' her driver asks, the first time he has spoken.

'No, I'm not even sure you can see it from the road,' Camilla says.

I peer downwards and catch a glimpse of the cone-shaped roofs of the castle that juts out on a rock into the lake.

'You should come back sometime and do the sights,' Camilla says. 'The castle in Sion is worth a visit too if you like that kind of thing.'

I lose track of time, enjoying the scenery, but after about an hour and a half, we turn off the motorway and drive through the industrial parts of a town. And then I see the first sign for Corviez, and my heart does a little jump. The road up the mountainside is narrow and winding, yet the driver and this large car make it seem effortless. On the lower slopes we pass acres and acres of vineyards, the spindly plants showing just a hint of green as the leaves start to emerge. A little higher there are orchards of gnarled trees.

'Apricots,' Camilla says. 'They have so many of them, in early summer they roll down the roads like conkers.'

After many more tight turns, the large valley floor seems distant below us, and little clusters of chalets, quaint with red shutters and dark wood, hang onto the hillside. And just when I'm beginning to feel a bit queasy from the winding road, there's another sign for Corviez.

'Nearly there,' Camilla says. 'We're on the edge of the village with the forest behind us.'

The car swings off the road to the left and then climbs steeply up a potted gravel road before coming to a halt next to a van and pickup truck. The chalet in front of us is enormous, bigger than the plans suggested. Perhaps it's because the chalet is built into the hillside, and from this perspective it rises high above us. The chalet is traditional from the exterior, made from larch and stained a mid-brown colour with beautifully carved decorative edging. There are several balconies at different levels, made of the same carved larch inset with glass panels. The base of the building is faced with grey slate, firmly grounding the chalet into the solid mountainside. Scaffolding encases one end and rises around the chimney and the grey slate-covered roof.

'It's beautiful,' I say.

'Better from the inside.'

Camilla gets out of the car, and I follow suit, surprised by the cool fresh air. Camilla inhales deeply and stretches her arms upward.

'Breathe in the mountain air. It's glorious.'

She's right. I catch the scent of pine and burning wood from somewhere in the distance. I've never been to the mountains when there hasn't been a heavy covering of snow, and now in the summer, there is such a different feel. It's a relief.

I follow Camilla inside the chalet, and while the exterior looks finished, the interior is anything but. The place has been gutted, and there are two plasterers in the hallway, working rapidly and chattering away in French.

'As you can see, we have a lot to do. This is still a shell on the inside.'

I smile. This is exactly how I like my buildings – a blank

canvas that I can turn into a home, capturing the feelings that my clients desire.

'Camilla! How are you?' A woman with strawberry blonde hair tied back in a tight ponytail steps out of another room. She's wearing black trousers, a cream silk blouse with a beige blazer, and a scarf tied jauntily around her neck. She's clutching a pile of plans.

The two women give each other air kisses with lots of smooching noises.

'This is Helen Sellers, my interior designer,' Camilla says. 'Helen, meet Saskia Berchard, our wonderful architect.'

Saskia's smile is warm, and I'm immediately drawn to her. We shake hands as she says, '*Enchanté* and welcome to Corviez! I have seen your concepts for the interiors, and they are exquisite.'

'Thank you. It's a pleasure to meet you,' I remark.

Saskia shows us around all the downstairs rooms, blank, empty spaces for now, with views from wide patio doors and windows that are simply jaw-dropping. The chalet faces south and west, and to the west it looks partly over the long, wide valley and partly towards another ski resort where the numerous chalets and apartment blocks look like miniature doll's houses. In every direction, jagged peaks soar upwards, meeting the startling blue sky. We're about to walk up the floating staircase when a man's voice interrupts us.

'*Saskia, tu es la?*'

'*Oui, un moment, Jacques.*'

'Good, it's Jacques Freant, the site manager,' Camilla says. 'He is in charge of all the building works.'

Jacques is a burly man with a shock of dark curly hair and a weathered face. He nods at Camilla and me and launches off into rapid French with Saskia. Camilla quickly loses interest and is once again staring at her phone. I am drawn towards the window in the hallway and that staggering view.

'Jacques, this is Helen, the interior designer from England,' Saskia says. I extend my hand, but he just nods at me and strides away. Charming.

After a tour of the upstairs, where there are five bedrooms, each with an en suite, most of which are yet to be tiled, we return downstairs.

'We will have weekly meetings, and in the final fortnight prior to completion, we will need you to be here on-site all the time,' Saskia says. I glance at Camilla, but she is avoiding my gaze. Nothing had been said about me being here so often. I open and close my mouth. Now isn't the time to voice my concerns. I'm conflicted. I want this job, but to be here so much, that wasn't what I had signed up for. Or was it? I never actually asked how often I was expected to be here. Silently, I curse myself for being naïve.

'Right, ladies,' Camilla says, rotating her shoulders. 'I've got to get a move on. My driver is taking me over to Lanvière for a meeting with an old friend. Saskia, you'll show Helen where she's staying, won't you?'

A COUPLE OF MINUTES LATER, we exit the chalet via the back door and trudge across an area that I assume will be land-scaped but for now is a large mound of mud with some straggly grass either side. I'm glad that I'm wearing a pair of old boots. There's a small hut-like building set backwards into the hillside, the tall pine trees crowding together throwing deep shadows over its roof. I follow Saskia up a path of paving stones, and she turns the front door handle. Inside there is one large room with a kitchenette set into the back wall, an open ladder staircase that leads up to a mezza-nine area and a closed door to the left. The place smells dank and unused, and unlike the chalet, it's dark with a neglected feel. The floor is laid with mottled dark brown and beige ceramic tiles, and there's a large sofa covered with throws in oranges and browns. As I look closer at the brown melamine kitchen units, I see they're worn, and a couple of the handles are hanging off the cupboard doors.

Saskia must notice my look of dismay. 'It's not five stars,' she says, pulling a face to convey sympathy, 'but it's a perfect location. Just behind here is the Bisse.'

'The Bisse?' I ask, frowning.

'The Bisse is a network of irrigation channels that carry glacial waters to fields and vineyards. You can walk alongside them for miles, and it is mostly flat. It is a very lovely walk, several kilometres in either direction, popular with locals and tourists and especially dog walkers.'

'How lovely,' I say. That's about the only thing that is lovely because this place looks like it hasn't been touched since the 1970s, and frankly, it's giving me the creeps. I'm not looking forward to sleeping here.

'Here is the key for the chalet so you can come and go, and the key for the Golf, which is parked at the front. We have a site meeting at 8 am tomorrow morning, so for now I wish you a good evening, and I hope you sleep well.'

I open my mouth to say something, but short of begging Saskia not to leave me or asking her to point me toward the nearest hotel, I'm not sure what to say. Instead, I watch her departing back, and a couple of minutes later I hear a car starting up and the engine noise fading into the distance.

Here I am, all alone, with the choice of staying in a horrible cabin or in a chalet with unplastered walls, no carpets, kitchen or bathrooms. I tell myself to be brave and that this is just for a night. I fling open the windows in the cabin to let in the fresh mountain air; then I turn to inspect the kitchen. The fridge is the first thing I open. To my surprise, there is a shelf full of food: some eggs, dried meat, a bag of cut salad, a carton of milk and a bottle of white wine. I open the cupboard next to the fridge, and there is a bowl of fruit and a loaf of bread. Next to the microwave, someone has left a note written:

Village Shop open 7 am – 7 pm. Two restaurants in the village. Recommend L'Auberge Vue Montagne.

I wonder who Camilla asked to organise this, or perhaps Saskia did. Either way, I'm grateful. Perhaps it won't be so so bad staying here after all.

I walk back along the path and around the front of the chalet, where Camilla's driver has left my suitcase standing in the front porch. Before lugging it back to the cabin, I stand for a moment and drink in the view. It's extraordinary, looking down to the green valley, where the river snakes like a silvery chasm, roads break up rectangular fields and clusters of minuscule buildings form towns and villages. Rising majestically on the other side of the valley is a vast mountain range with jagged peaks highlighted by patches of snow that glisten in the sunlight. The slopes are covered with dark green forests and swathes of lighter green fields broken up by rocky outcrops. Although I thought I was drawn more to the gentle landscapes of beaches, now I wonder. This is true majesty, and it makes me feel insignificant yet grateful to be alive. Taking in another deep breath of air, I turn and trudge back to the cabin.

Despite not doing much today, I don't feel like going out alone, so I make do with the food left in the fridge. After a long phone call with Emily, during which I give her my version of *Heidi* as a bedtime story, followed by a reassuring chat with Andrew, I decide to have an early night. The shower is old but clean, and the water is hot. I find the bed up the precarious wooden ladder staircase, and although the orange and brown bedding is worn and ugly, the mattress is surprisingly comfortable. I lie there in the dark for a long time, listening to a distant owl and trying not to be scared of sleeping here all alone on a mountainside, where I know no one, in a place I promised myself I'd never revisit.

I must drift off to sleep eventually because I awake with a pounding heart, gasping for air, the duvet at my feet. It came again, that recurring nightmare about Paul. That dream that I used to have every night until three years ago. The dream that leaves me a quivering mess.

4

HELEN – THEN

I t has been four days and five nights since I last saw
Paul. They've stopped searching for him now. Even
though I sobbed and begged Monsieur Jollien, telling
him I couldn't live if they called off the search, he just
shrugged, said how very sorry he was, but there was zero
chance of survival out there on the mountainside. Zero. They
had to assume Paul had perished. It's a horrible word,
perished, isn't it? Fruit perishes when it goes off. Is that what
will happen to Paul? I've been reading news stories about
people who disappear in the mountains. Sometimes their
bodies aren't found for decades, centuries even, especially if
they've been entombed in glacial ice for all of those years.

I don't leave the hotel bedroom, as I can't bear the
thought of seeing those happy tourists laughing and joking as
they indulge in their skiing holidays without a care in the
world. Lucienne comes to see me three times a day, bringing
food on a plate that I pick at. I don't feel like eating. I
wondered if I'd start being sick, now that I'm pregnant, but I
feel nothing. Just a hollow loss as if my life is ending before
it's really begun. In the first couple of days Lucienne tried to

give me hope, but now she simply looks at me, her head tilted to one side, as if she can't quite work out what to say. I get the impression she thinks I'm a harbinger of bad luck and wants me to leave; I don't blame her.

There's a knock on the door, and my heart jumps. Is there news?

'Come in!'

The door opens, and I burst into tears when I see my sister, Kelly. Stupid to have hoped for news, I know.

'Oh, Helen,' she says as she rushes towards me and flings her arms around my neck. 'I'm so sorry, darling.' We rock together for a long time until my tears soak through her jumper, and she pulls away.

'I didn't realise you were coming.' The words catch in my throat. Kelly is my older sister, and we're chalk and cheese. She's dark haired and I'm blonde; she's an extrovert and funny, I'm serious and more shy. Perhaps it's our differences that have helped us get along so well. She's my best friend.

'I've come to take you home. I spoke to that police officer and the British consulate, and they said it's better if you come home.'

'I don't want to go.'

'I know,' she says, squeezing my hand. 'Of course you don't. But it will not do you any good staying here.' She glances around the room. 'It's not even a very nice hotel, is it?'

I don't tell her that the previous room was substantially smaller and darker than this one.

'I'm pregnant,' I blurt out.

'Oh, darling!' She hugs me again, but I wriggle out of her grasp. 'Did Paul know before he–'

I can see that there's going to be a whole lexicon of words and phrases that we're going to have to avoid. The before and the after. The tiptoeing around. It's not like anyone can even offer their apologies for my loss or send their condolences because we don't have a body. I guess I'm going to be the awkward pariah, the person people cross the road to avoid because they simply don't know what to say to me.

'He knew I was pregnant,' I mumble.

'Thank goodness. At least he would have been happy.'

I look away from her.

'What is it?'

'I didn't exactly get the reaction I expected.'

'But you've been married for over three years. Didn't he want to have children?'

'I thought he did, but I don't know. The day before he disappeared, I told him I might be pregnant. I hadn't done the test at that point, and well, he seemed shocked. Honestly, I thought we'd be drinking champagne for breakfast – or at least, he would. Instead, he said he wasn't ready for children, and then he said he wasn't that happy in our marriage.'

'What!' Kelly exclaims.

'It was such a shock, Kells. He never said he'd been unhappy or anything before. We've argued quite a bit the last year, but things have been stressful, and all couples argue, don't they? I mean, money-wise, things have been tight, and Paul was worried he was going to be fired from his job. Working in catering is so precarious. But telling me he wasn't happy being married was like this bolt out of the blue. I was so shocked.'

'What happened?' Kelly asks.

'I asked him if he loved me, and he had to think about it for ages, and then eventually he said, "I probably do, but I'm not sure." I asked him if he'd met someone else, but he got all angry and said no. Then he looked at his watch and said he'd be late for skiing. I screamed at him and told him to get the fuck out of the room, and he did. I cried for a bit and then thought, screw you, I'm going to go skiing too, but the weather wasn't great, and I didn't enjoy it, so I came back to the hotel early and just lay on the bed. I wondered if I had overreacted or whether he'd been like that because the pregnancy thing came as a shock. Let's face it, neither of us is exactly in a great place career-wise. We're reliant on my salary mainly, and having a child is so expensive.' I stifle a sob because I am having a child, and I have no idea how he or she and I are going to survive.

'What happened when he came back from skiing?'

'He returned really late and stank of beer. I'd sent him a text apologising, but I hadn't heard back from him. We had another massive argument. I asked him if he wanted to split up, but he simply shrugged his shoulders and said he didn't know. We went for dinner in the hotel and sat there in stony silence like those middle-aged couples who have run out of things to say to each other. I drank way too much and then felt mega guilty in case I was pregnant.' I pause for a moment as I remember that dinner.

One of the waitresses was standing at the side of the room, and she started crying. She was a young girl, sixteen or seventeen probably. Then an older woman joined her, and they both stared at their mobile phones. The news spread quickly after that, and it wasn't long before the couple at the table next to ours turned to us and spoke in English with heavy Dutch accents.

'There's been a terrible accident on the slopes. A young girl was killed skiing today.'

'How awful!' I exclaimed, a shiver running through me. 'Was there an avalanche?'

'No. Someone skied into her, and then she died.'

I've heard of tragedies in the mountains and knew that people had died from skiing into trees or off the sides of a mountain, or being swept away by an avalanche. But to die because someone skied into them, that seemed particularly brutal.

'How is the other person?' I asked.

Our Dutch neighbour shrugged his shoulders. 'The person skied off, apparently. The gendarmes are looking for him.'

'Bloody hell,' I muttered. 'A murder on the slopes! It's awful, isn't it?' I said to Paul.

'Suppose so.' He seemed disinterested, keeping his eyes on his food.

I scowled at him. 'Where's your compassion?'

'It's not our problem, is it? You love other people's gossip, don't you? Why do you always want to get involved?'

'I don't!' I exclaimed. I had no idea what Paul was going on about. It was as if he just wanted to pick a fight.

He drank two glasses of red wine, one after the other, and he seemed restless, as if he wanted to be anywhere other than with me.

'I don't feel very well,' Paul snapped. 'Let's go.'

'I haven't finished my main course.'

'If you don't want to come, fine, stay here. But I'm going back to the room.'

'Paul!' I said, trying to reach across the table to him, but he pushed my hand away and stood up, bolting out of the dining room. If everyone else hadn't been so tied up with discussing the terrible tragedy on the slopes, I suppose we might have been the spectacle for the evening. Small mercies, at least. Perhaps I should have carried on eating, but I didn't. I shoved my chair back and followed him out of the dining room.

'What's going on?' I asked as I caught up with him at the lift.

'I don't want to talk about it.' He crossed his arms and refused to look me in the eye. At the time, I thought it was all about us and our relationship, that perhaps I'd done something wrong. I persisted when we were back in our room.

'Talk to me, please, Paul!' I begged. 'Do you want to call a break on our marriage? Is that it?'

He stormed into the bathroom and turned the shower on full blast. When he eventually emerged, my patience had dissipated, and I was angry.

'There are two of us in this relationship, Paul. Quite possibly three. I deserve to know what is going on with you. If you want to have marriage counselling when we're back home, then that's fine with me.'

'I don't want any bloody marriage counselling!' he exclaimed, getting into bed and turning his back to me.

'Tell me what you want,' I said.

'To go to sleep.'

'No!'

'For God's sake, just leave me alone, Helen. I'm tired. We'll talk about it in the morning.'

I lay there all night, devastated that Paul might no longer love me, terrified what I would do if the pregnancy test was positive. I knew that I had to fight for our marriage. Come what may, I was determined to get through it. In the morning, Paul was up bright and early, only waking me when he was already dressed in his ski clothes.

'I'm skiing with Gaby and the gang today. You've got a lesson, haven't you?' he asked.

'You said we'd talk about us.'

'Later, Helen. I'm going skiing now.'

'Aren't you having breakfast with me?' My words sounded lame and needy, not like me at all.

'I'll pick up something on the slopes. Have a good day.'

He left without kissing me.

An hour or so later, I made my way to the bottom of the lifts. There were police there, talking to skiers, and it reminded me of the tragedy that had taken place the previous day. How awful to go on holiday and never return home! I met up with my ski class. It was the last thing I felt like doing, learning how to carve in the fresh snow. All I could think about was what if I'm pregnant? What if I fall and hurt the baby? I brought up the rear as our snake of ten people curved down the pistes, too tense to try anything new, and when we were on the chairlifts, I chose not to make small talk. I was lost in my own worries, oblivious to the beautiful scenery and near-perfect snow, the cold, fresh air and the warmth of the sun on my face. As soon as the lesson was over, I got the lift back down to Lanvière, not wanting to ski down alone. After dumping my gear, I went straight to the pharmacy in the village and bought a pregnancy test.

I sat in the hotel room and stared at the test. I had always hoped that in this moment, I would be filled with excitement. That Paul would be waiting with me, as eager as me to see the two little lines. I couldn't even bring myself to open the box.

Paul surprised me by returning early. When I heard his key in the lock, I shoved the unopened pregnancy test box under the bed.

'Did you have a good ski?' I asked.

'Okay,' he replied, peeling off his clothes.

'Can we talk?'

'What about?'

'Us?'

'No, Helen. Not now.'

'But I want to!'

'Talk away. I'm having a shower, so I won't be listening.'

'What is it? What's affected you like this? Think about that poor family who lost their child yesterday. Imagine how they're feeling!' I don't know why I said that because, in hindsight, it was a non sequitur, but it had the strangest effect on Paul.

'Don't ever talk to me about that!' he said through gritted teeth. 'It was a fucking accident.'

I froze. How did he know? 'Did you have something to do with it?' I asked, horror filling my veins. Was that why he'd been acting so strangely these past twenty-four hours?

'Of course I didn't!' he said. But then, rather than going to take a shower, he started grabbing clean clothes from the suitcase and pulling them on.

'For God's sake, Paul. Did you ski into her? Was it you?'

'Of course it wasn't bloody me!' He grabbed his wallet, phone and ski jacket and stormed out of the room, letting the door slam behind him.

I sat on the side of the bed, my jaw slack, my stomach curdling with horror. If Paul said he knew nothing about it, then he probably didn't, but for the first time in our relationship, I doubted him. Was he telling me the truth? After a while, I forced myself to remember all the qualities of the man I had married. Paul couldn't kill a fly, let alone hurt another human being. I used to tease him about how he'd switch channels whenever anything particularly gory was showing on television. I liked how he was sensitive, that he embraced both his masculine and feminine sides. No, my Paul could never do something so callous as to ski into someone and leave them for dead.

BUT FOR SOME REASON, I don't tell Kelly any of that. The thought of Paul being involved in a girl's death is simply too horrible to contemplate, so instead I'm focusing on what the future might hold.

'I took a pregnancy test, and it was positive. I'm having a baby, Kells.'

'That's wonderful,' she says, hugging me again.

Except now I'm not sure that it is wonderful. Unless Paul magically reappears, I'm going to be a single mother. In the terrifying depths of the past few nights, I've thought about having an abortion, but immediately dismissed the idea. I want a baby. I've always wanted a baby. It's just I thought my husband did too.

'So when did you tell Paul you were pregnant?'

'I told him a couple of days beforehand that I thought I might be pregnant, but didn't confirm it until the day he disappeared.' What I don't recount to Kelly is the horrendous row we had when he returned late the previous night. Once again, he stank of booze, and there was no way that I was going to tell him about my pregnancy when he was drunk. But I couldn't stop myself from asking what the future held for us, needling him for an answer.

'I still love you, Paul, and I want our marriage to thrive. Please tell me what I've done wrong.'

'It's not you,' he mumbled.

'Then what is it? You've been acting so weird, especially the last couple of days.'

'Perhaps it's you who's been acting weird. You need to let it go, Helen.'

'You owe it to me to let me know what the problem is. You need to be honest with me. Even if you're having an affair or you've done something awful, tell me!'

He sat up in bed, and his eyes were wild in the low light. For the first time ever in our relationship, I wondered if he might hit me. I cowered away from him, almost falling off the side of the bed. He stared at me, and then as if he was coming to his senses, he shook his head, muttered some swear words under his breath and lay back down again, his back towards me. I knew I wasn't going to get anywhere with him.

'How did he react when you told him you are pregnant?' Kelly asks.

'Terribly. He told me I'd need to get an abortion.'

'Shit,' Kelly said under her breath. 'That doesn't sound like Paul, does it?'

'That's what I thought. None of it made any sense. The only thing I can think of is that he panicked because money is so tight. I wonder whether he felt he needed to be the provider and that, as he couldn't do that right now, he felt emasculated in some way.'

'Maybe,' Kelly said. 'But do you think perhaps he met someone else?'

'I asked the question, and he denied it. Just said that he didn't love me anymore.'

'I'm so sorry, Helen. That's terrible. Do you think he really meant it?'

'Honestly, I don't know. I was so angry. I told him I'd tell everyone we knew he was a total bastard, that he wanted me to get an abortion. I asked him what his mother would think. She's been dropping hints about grandchildren ever since we got married. He looked devastated when I said that, but then he left. I haven't seen him since.'

'Oh, my darling.' I get another hug from Kelly, who has always been much more tactile and demonstrative than me. 'I'm sure he regretted what he said.'

'I don't know. I was wondering if perhaps he took his own life,' I suggest.

Kelly looks surprised. 'Did he have mental health problems?'

I sniff. 'I really don't know. I've thought about it, and it makes me feel sick. What if I missed all the signs that he was depressed? What if I pushed him over the edge, literally and metaphorically? I think he might have taken his own life, Kelly, what with the stress of knowing I was pregnant. He probably felt terrible that he couldn't earn enough to support us. I pushed him so hard to tell me what the problem was, and I think I went way too far. I'm going to have to live with that guilt for the rest of my life.'

'It's not your fault. I mean, it's hardly a bolt out of the blue that you got pregnant. You've been married for three years. Besides, he's a great skier, isn't he? Didn't you say he'd been skiing regularly since he was a kid?'

'Yes, but he might have been unnecessarily reckless because he was upset.'

'Whatever happened, Helen, it's not your fault. You need to concentrate on you and your baby now, and I'm going to make damn sure that you're both alright.'

I try to smile at Kelly because she's a wonderful sister and trying so hard to make me feel better. The way I see it, there are two options. Paul is dead either because of an accident or because he took his own life. Except I just can't imagine Paul taking his own life, but on the other hand, I couldn't have imagined my Paul rejecting me when I announced I was pregnant. Either way, it's horrible. I just pray that he didn't suffer, that the end was so quick he didn't realise what happened. Whatever the hell is going on, I'm in a terrible mess.

5

HELEN – NOW

I wake up early to the sound of birdsong and light
flooding in from a small window high up in the eaves,
the sun's rays hitting my bed up on the mezzanine.
After making myself a cup of coffee, I open the front door to
the cabin. The air is chilly, and I shiver, but still I stand there
inhaling the glorious scent of pine and listening to the
chirping birds. At 8 am, the first van arrives, and soon there is
a bustle of activity in the main chalet. I stride through the
garden and say 'bonjour' to the various tradespeople, who
eye me suspiciously while nodding their heads in acknowl-
edgement. It's just as well no one strikes up a conversation, as
my French wouldn't be up to it. Jacques Freant barely looks in
my direction, and I wonder what he has against me. Perhaps
he views me as Camilla's spy, here to keep an eye on things on
her behalf.

Saskia arrives a few minutes later.

'Good morning, Helen. I hope you slept well,' she says
cheerfully, and carries on talking before I can answer. 'So,
after our site meeting, I thought I could show you around the
area and some of the other chalets I have worked on so you

can get some inspiration. We can also visit some showrooms where you can source furniture and furnishings.'

'That's great,' I say, surprised that she is going so far out of her way to help me. I wonder if Camilla has issued instructions.

I have attended many site meetings, but none like this one where I understand perhaps only one word in ten. I simply can't keep up as all the tradespeople – the plumber, electrician, painter and decorator and carpenter – along with Saskia and Jacques, talk rapidly in French. For all I know, they could be talking about me, the useless Englishwoman smiling inanely because she doesn't understand what they're saying. I wish I'd tried harder at French in school. Occasionally, when they're discussing timescales, Saskia does a quick translation for me, and I jot down what is meant to be completed by when. As we walk around the chalet, I give up trying to understand what is being said and concentrate on absorbing the spaces. The longer I spend in each room, the more excited I am by the potential of this project. My initial concept ideas are good enough, but now I understand how important the breathtaking views are and how the light changes throughout the day, I'm forming more and more ideas. I need to cut back on the colour I use and increase the range of textures, bringing tonal variety into each room, creating a modern chalet with nods to the traditional but avoiding alpine clichés.

'Helen?' Saskia startles me. 'We are finished, so shall we leave in the car?'

SASKIA DRIVES A BLACK TESLA. I clutch the passenger seat as she navigates down and around the steep, narrow bends with terrifying speed, all the time chatting to me as if she were on a straight motorway without another car in sight. I reassure myself that she drives these roads every single day. When we meet a big, yellow bus coming up in the opposite direction, she slams on the brakes and laughs.

'Have you been to this area of Switzerland before?' she asks.

'Yes, but a long time ago.'

'What do you think of this place?'

'It's beautiful,' I say, eager to avoid mentioning the terrible trip I try so hard not to think about. 'How did you learn to speak such good English?' I ask, changing the subject.

'I did an exchange with an English family when I was a teenager, and make an effort to watch British or American television. More recently I have had a lot of English clients, so it helps that I practise frequently. Of course, they teach languages very well in schools here.'

'Do you have children?' I ask.

'Yes. Two boys in their late teens, who find their mother very annoying!' She laughs. 'And you?'

'I have a little girl. She's four.'

'Ah, lucky you to have a girl.'

I smile to myself as I think of Emily. I certainly am lucky.

'Does your husband mind looking after her when you're away?' Saskia asks.

'No, Andrew adores Emily.'

'Ah, fathers and their daughters. They often have such a special bond, don't they?'

I smile tightly. 'Andrew's not actually her birth father, but you'd never realise. They adore each other.'

'How lovely. What a lucky girl to have two daddies in her life.'

I frown.

'Oh, sorry.' Saskia glances at me, a look of embarrassment on her face. 'Perhaps your divorce wasn't so amicable?' She keeps her eyes firmly on the road in front of us, but she bites her lower lip.

'Oh, I'm not divorced. My husband, Paul, Emily's father, died.'

If Saskia looked embarrassed before, now she looks mortified. 'It's fine,' I say, reaching across the centre console and patting her hand. 'Andrew and I have been together for three years, and we plan to marry next year.'

'How lovely to plan a wedding. I'm sorry I put my foot in it.'

'Not at all,' I say. But I can tell that we're both relieved when we arrive at a four-storey shop packed full of furniture and homewares.

Several hours later, interspersed only with a cup of strong coffee and a salami sandwich, it feels as if my brain is going to explode with ideas, and my phone overheats with all the notes and photographs I've taken. We visited numerous shops stuffed full of furniture, floor coverings, tiles and fabrics, and also three chalets designed by Saskia. Each chalet was fundamentally different in style and aspect. The first was a traditional wooden chalet, much like Camilla's; the second was a combination of glass and wood, totally open plan; while the third was brutally modern – two adjoined concrete squares, flat roofs covered with plants and shining concrete floors. While I wouldn't choose to live in such an austere place, I couldn't help but admire the minimalist design. I stifle a yawn as we climb back into her Tesla.

'Are you hungry?' Saskia asks.

'Actually, I am.'

'In which case I'll take you for a raclette.'

'Are you sure you have time?' I ask, wondering whether she has to cook for her family.

'I set aside today and this evening for you. We need to

make the most of the window of opportunity before things get too busy.'

'That's very kind. Thank you.'

SASKIA TAKES me to a small restaurant with a wide veranda that hangs over a sheer drop with views to the valley a couple of kilometres down. The interior of the restaurant is simple, with wooden chairs and tables, but as with most places around here, it's the view that's compelling. She obviously knows the owner, as they greet each other with kisses on the cheek, and he then leads us to a table by the window.

'You eat cheese, I hope?'

'Yes, thank you.'

'In which case we will have the local speciality. Have you ever had raclette before?'

I shake my head.

'You'll love it.' She smiles.

'I really appreciate you going out of your way to look after me,' I say. 'This is the largest project I've done abroad, and it's challenging not speaking the language fluently.'

'Camilla is a good client. She says that you worked for Lewis Chen.'

'I didn't work for him. I was employed by his clients, so we worked alongside each other,' I say, recalling the converted barn that I helped renovate last year. Alison and David Chorley were the perfect clients. Relocating from Singapore, they were happy to leave all the decisions to me so long as they had a fully completed, furnished house for their return. That's exactly what they got, on time and to budget. 'Have you known Camilla for long?' I ask.

'About a year. They bought the chalet a couple of years ago, but she and her husband took their time deciding upon the structural renovations they wanted to make. The chalet is very desirable, being right next to the piste. Everyone wants to ski in and ski out these days. Do you ski?'

I shake my head. I might have done, but I won't be skiing again.

'Me neither,' she says.

'I thought everyone here skied!'

'No. You'd be surprised.' We're interrupted by the waiter, who arrives with a large basket lined with red and white gingham fabric, filled to the brim with new potatoes.

'I FEEL SO FULL!' I say eventually, after an excellent but calorie-filled meal of cheese and potatoes.

'You need to take an evening walk. My husband and I try to walk every evening after supper.'

'Good idea,' I say.

'In fact, you should walk back from here to the chalet. It's an easy walk along the Bisse. Just walk up the minor road and turn left.' She points to a track between two chalets just above the main road that runs through the village.

I hesitate, but Saskia doesn't seem to notice. 'Have a pleasant trip back to England, and I'll see you next week. Call me if you need anything.'

Before I can even thank her for supper, she's inside her car and silently driving away, and I'm holding up my hand, waving to someone who isn't looking.

The village feels deserted, with the shutters closed on most of the chalets and not a person in sight. I hear a dog barking in the distance, and it's a welcome sound, reassuring me that there are local inhabitants, and I, along with the restaurant staff, am not the sole survivor in an abandoned village. I climb up the steep hill and then follow Saskia's directions. The Bisse is a long trench with shallow but fast-running water with a footpath that runs alongside it, snaking above the village and through the forest. My sense of direction isn't great at the best of times, and right now I haven't got a clue where I am. I really hope that I recognise Camilla's chalet and my little cabin. Whereas earlier the birds were singing loudly, now the forest is still and quiet. The sun has dipped behind the mountains on the other side of the valley, and it's cold again. I shiver in my lightweight jacket and stride quickly. Long, dark shadows fall across the path, and I hurry, eager to get back to the cabin despite feeling uncomfortable there yesterday. I stumble over a tree root, and my heart thumps. This is ridiculous. I'm scaring myself for no reason. I think of the many times I've walked along the footpaths back in Sussex, through the bluebell woods near where we live, and I never felt like this, as if the forest is oppressive and a terrifying person might be just around the next corner, ready to jump on me. I take some deep breaths. This is because of what happened to Paul, the reason I'm uncomfortable being here. Combined with all the cheese I ate for supper and the red wine and the fact I'm tired, it makes sense that I'm uneasy. And then I screech.

There's a figure just ahead of me, standing stock-still in the shadows of the trees. Why isn't he moving? I gulp and blink a few times, edging forwards. 'Hello?' And then I feel like an idiot. It's not a person but a statue carved out of a tall tree trunk, and a little further on there are more wooden statues of an owl and a fox. I'm being ridiculous. I'm almost jogging now, and then a dog trots into view, a black Labrador followed shortly by its owner, a woman in her sixties.

'*Bonsoir*,' she says, with a smile, walking past me breezily. And I realise that it's my imagination playing stupid tricks.

When I turn the next corner and see the back of the cabin and the yellow digger beyond, I feel a welcome lightness. I hurry through a closed wooden gate and take out the key to the cabin, switching on all the lights as I step inside and locking the door behind me. After drinking two glasses of water, I call Andrew.

'Did you have a good day, darling?' he asks.

I tell him about all the places I visited with Saskia and the delicious meal we ate; what I don't tell him is how scared I was a few moments ago. I remind myself to hang on to the fact that tomorrow night I'll be lying in his arms, with Emily safely asleep in the next-door room.

I climb into the strange bed under the eaves, and, against all odds, I drift off to sleep easily.

It's pitch black when I wake up, sitting bolt upright in bed. What was that?

There's a bang, followed by another crashing sound, so very close. My heart is hammering as I try to make out shapes in the dark. I fumble for the bedside light and switch it on.

Another crash, right outside the window. What the hell?

Holding on tightly to the ladder rail, I make my way downstairs and walk over to the window, pulling back the curtains. I want to sob with relief. There's a howling gale outside, and one shutter has come loose, banging against the side of the cabin.

6

HELEN – THEN

When someone goes missing, you can't have a funeral because there is no body. Of course, missing doesn't mean dead, but in Paul's case, the Swiss mountain rescue and other authorities are utterly positive that my husband died in the mountains. Apparently up to one hundred skiers, climbers and mountain guides lose their lives every year in the Alps, but this is usually the result of avalanches while skiing off-piste. Mostly, the bodies are recovered quickly, but it's not unheard of for someone to disappear. Recently, a body of a skier was found fifty-three years after he vanished. I've been told that Paul may never be found, not in my lifetime at least. So what do you do when your husband is presumed dead and there's no body?

You have to wait seven years. When I was told that, I broke down and sobbed. I will be made to wait seven years before he is legally confirmed dead, before I can properly access his assets, before I can remarry. Not that I could even contemplate being with someone else. But seven years is such a long time, and it feels like I'm being repeatedly punished for something I didn't do.

The first few weeks back at home pass in a blur. Kelly was with me a lot, and the doctor prescribed sleeping pills, which knocked me for six for the first few nights, but now have zero effect. Every night I lie in our big, cold bed, begging the higher powers to give me an answer. I need to know what happened to Paul. Did I miss the signs of a deep depression? Did I somehow contribute to his death, or was it a genuine accident?

Then Paul's parents announced they wanted a memorial service, and while I still wasn't ready to accept he's gone forever, there was a consensus that we all needed some sort of closure.

So there I was, two months after Paul disappeared, dressed in a black dress and a thick woollen coat with a red scarf around my neck, in a tribute to Paul's favourite football team, sitting in the back of a black limousine with Kelly and my parents en route to the very church where Paul and I got married nearly four years ago. I had a small belly, although I was – and still am – so thin, I doubt anyone who didn't know would realise I was pregnant. As Paul died, so our child is burgeoning into life. His parents seem so pathetically grateful that they will get a grandchild. I wonder what they'd think if they knew their son's true reaction to my pregnancy. How would they respond if someone mooted that Paul's cause of death was suicide rather than an accident? I remember one Sunday lunch when Paul talked about a school friend of his who had been diagnosed with bipolar disorder. I was horrified when his mother, Susannah, announced that mental health problems were totally overdiagnosed, that everyone wanted a label for a life problem that her generation would just swallow up and get on with. Paul and Susannah got into quite an argument while his father and I sat there awkwardly, not saying a word. If I suggested that Paul might have died by suicide, I can just imagine Susannah would blame me and feel a sense of shame rather than compassion. It's not on her radar, and I certainly won't be suggesting it to them. I've sworn Kelly to secrecy, and I know my sister will never betray my confidence.

I remember little about the service other than the flowers were blue forget-me-nots and white carnations. The order of service had a blue forget-me-not flower on the front, and I felt resentful that Susannah had chosen everything when it should have been me, Paul's wife. I didn't want the service to be held in the church we married in because now those happy memories are going to be superseded forever, but Mum said Paul's parents were adamant. It's their local church, and as they're the only churchgoers in our joint extended families, and they're Paul's parents, it seemed only right to give in to their wishes. Paul's father gave a reading and then announced to the congregation that they'd paid for a memorial plaque on the last lift that Paul took, at the top of Lanvière. He called it a forget-me-not plaque. They had mooted installing it on the rock next to where Paul's ski was found but reckoned few people would see it there. It was another thing they hadn't bothered to discuss with me.

Everyone was so sympathetic towards me, pitying even, and now I know that there's nothing worse when you're emotionally vulnerable than to have people pity you. I wanted to scream at all of them, 'Piss off home. We don't even know if Paul's dead. He might have survived that blizzard and be on the run somewhere.' That thought gripped my mind like a pair of pincers after the memorial service, and it hasn't let go.

Last week, I put out an appeal online. They say you know, don't they, when a loved one has died, that you have this instinctual sense of finality. Yet I don't have that with Paul. Sometimes, I wonder whether Paul might have chosen to disappear, yet when I mentioned it to the Swiss police, they just looked at me sadly, telling me how denial was a normal reaction. And then I wonder whether he died by suicide, and I question how well I really knew the father of my future child. Of course I can't share my true thoughts with anyone except Kelly because I need to maintain my husband's excellent reputation as the upstanding, honourable and loving son, husband and father-to-be for my in-laws' sake. I'd have to admit that I failed him by not recognising the signs, by pushing him over the edge rather than providing support. I owe our future child an untarnished memory.

I've become obsessed with missing persons forums online. I've joined Facebook groups, added Paul's name to international databases, uploaded his picture just about anywhere that will have it, scoured information on charities websites and all the while acted the grieving widow. Yet even the law says I'm not a widow, not for another seven years. I know it's crazy to imagine he's still on this earth, but without confirmation of his death, I can never know for sure.

Paul and I bought our house last year. The deal was, I'd continue working in my dull office job, earning a good and stable salary, while Paul worked as a chef in a leading five-star hotel. He had always dreamed of owning his own restaurant, and frankly, I think he'd have preferred that to buying our own home. It was me who pushed to have a permanent roof over our heads, and our parents were both generous in assisting with the down payment. I always knew his parents were wealthy; after all, they live in a big former vicarage in the Surrey hills, and his father worked in investment banking for decades. It explains why Paul attended leading private schools and had so many skiing holidays. They never actually articulated it, but I think they were deeply disappointed that their only son's passion was cooking. Once they got their head around it, they ensured Paul had the very best culinary education money could buy, but the reality is, he never earned much money, so it was me who put my dreams on hold so we had a decent joint income. It was me who carried on with the boring job in human resources so Paul could pursue his creative career. But now Paul is gone, and I'm having a baby, and I simply can't bring myself to carry on in that soul-destroying job, but what choice do I have? They gave me compassionate leave – two amazing, generous months of it – but on Monday I have to go back.

There's a knock on the front door, and I'm surprised to see Paul's mother, Susannah.

'How are you?' she asks, giving me a kiss on both cheeks and enveloping me in her cloud of floral perfume. She still speaks with a strong Cheshire accent despite having lived in the south of England for thirty years. Susannah is very proud of her roots, calling herself a northerner and complaining that the weather is too warm in the southeast.

I stand back to let her in and try not to notice the wrinkle of her nose as she surveys my messy kitchen. She turns the kettle on, takes two cups from the cupboard and tells me to sit down.

'I've been thinking,' she says as she places a cup of herbal tea in front of me. 'You shouldn't be going back to work. You're pregnant, and the well-being of your child, and you, of course, is paramount. I quit work when I was pregnant with Paul, and David and I have decided you must do the same.'

I open my mouth in a semi-protest, but she waves my words away.

'David and I are very blessed with money, and we will pay off your mortgage and make sure you have enough money to live off for the next three years, longer if you need it. That will give you enough time to find your feet and get another job when our baby is old enough to go to nursery. What do you think?'

Tears well up in my eyes, and I find myself in a maelstrom

of emotion. I don't want to be Susannah's charity case, but on the other hand, I feel like dancing at the prospect of not having to work in a job I loathe. But what did she mean when she said 'our baby'? It's not hers; this child I'm carrying is mine and mine alone. The other thing their gift will do is allow me to pursue my dream. I want to be an interior designer; it's been my passion for years. However, the training is expensive, and I know it will take a long time to earn as much as I'm currently earning.

'You're all we've got now, Helen,' she says, reaching forwards to hold my hand. 'You and your baby.'

I'm too choked up to say anything other than thank you. I know that Mum and Dad will feel as if their noses have been put out of joint because they can't help me financially, but in some ways I feel as if it's right. Paul said some truly awful things to me, and they were unjustified. The baby I'm carrying is the heir to his wealth.

'I've got to get a move on,' Susannah says, leaving half her tea untouched. 'Let me know what you think, Helen. It's what we'd like, David and me. What is right, after all.'

'I'm blown away, Susannah,' I say. 'I can't begin to tell you what relief I feel not to have to go back to that job.'

'That's marvellous, darling. You concentrate on caring for that little boy in your tummy. You also need to come off those antidepressants. It's not safe for our baby.'

What? How does she know I'm on antidepressants? Has she been riffling in the bathroom cupboard? It's none of her business what medication I'm taking. And a *little boy*? I've chosen not to know the sex of my baby until birth, so how does Susannah know? Then I realise she's looking for a Paul substitute, hoping this new child will fill her chasm of grief. But what if I don't have a boy? Will she still love my daughter?

I stay sitting at the kitchen table for a long time after she's gone, wondering if I've sold out in some way. Will Susannah and David have a hold over me if I accept their money? And if so, how will that play out? After about half an hour, I pick up the phone and call my boss. I feel sick and embarrassed about giving him no notice that I won't be returning, so I apologise profusely, over and over, until he cuts me off and tells me it's absolutely fine, that my health is the most important thing and that I must concentrate on recovering from the terrible tragedy. That makes me cry all over again because he was so nice when he's never been particularly kind before.

A FEW DAYS LATER, I receive a private message from a person on one of the missing persons forums.

I think this man might be your Paul. He's a delivery driver from Amazon, and I've seen him a number of times recently.

I click open the photograph, and it's blurry. The man is wearing a navy baseball cap with the letters MN embroidered on the front. There's something about his profile that does look a little like Paul. I enlarge the photo as much as I can, but it's impossible to tell. Yes, he looks about Paul's height and girth, but I can't make out the features of his face sufficiently or his hair colour.

I send a reply.

Thanks for your message and photo. Where do you live?

I get an immediate response.

Here's my address: 41 Apple Grove, Macclesfield. Let me know if you need any help. My brother went missing fourteen years ago. Still looking. Maria x

I gulp. Isn't Macclesfield where Susannah is from? Could Paul have fled to a place where he has relatives? But I'm sure that Susannah and David have no idea that their son is still alive, assuming this man really is Paul. And would Paul do that to his parents? Could he be so cruel as to pretend that their only son is dead? How would he make sure that his relatives didn't open their mouths and reveal his whereabouts? The trouble is, the more I look at the photograph, the more unsure I become. Perhaps it is Paul. If Maria had spotted him anywhere else, I might have been more cynical, but Macclesfield makes sense. I pick up the phone to Susannah.

'Thank you so much again for your financial support.' This is about the twentieth time I've thanked Susannah verbally, along with the thank-you letter I wrote and a large bouquet of flowers – no forget-me-nots in that on purpose. 'I've a question. Did your family come from Macclesfield?'

'Yes, born and bred. Why?'

'Got a friend up there I might visit, and I was hoping you could recommend where I should stay.'

'Goodness, I wouldn't have a clue. I haven't been back in twenty years.'

'Don't you have any family still there?'

She harrumphs. 'A couple of cousins I never see. It's hard, Helen, when you move up in the world and have to leave family behind. When I married David, my whole life changed. I had money, and well, some relatives were jealous; they wanted a piece of the action. I did what I could, but when we moved away, I had no reason to stay in touch.'

This is the side of Susannah I don't like, the side that Paul was also ashamed of. While she might be right that the world is divided into the haves and have-nots, it doesn't mean that once you're in the 'haves' camp, you can forget about everyone else. In my opinion, I think you would have that added obligation to look out for the people in your old world. Paul loathed his parents' ostentatious wealth. Other than letting them pay for his education and accepting the down payment for the house, which was presented as our wedding gift, he refused to take a penny off his parents. I admired him for that, yet now it feels as if I've sold out by succumbing to their financial help.

'Let me know what you think of Macclesfield.' Susannah laughs as she says goodbye. And before I give it too much thought, I am buying train tickets to take me north.

I BOOK myself into a cheap hotel near Macclesfield station and rent a car. The pregnancy is making me tired, but I need to push through it, and I drive straight to Apple Grove. It's a row of semi-detached houses, all small, red brick and without an apple tree in sight. Now I'm here, I haven't got a clue what I'm meant to do. Sit here all day waiting for someone to receive a delivery? I find a parking space and rub my gritty eyes, finding it hard to keep them open. It's a long half an hour waiting there, but eventually I see a white van pull up on the other side of the road. I hop out of the car and wave my arms at the driver.

'Excuse me, but are you an Amazon delivery driver?'

'Yeah, why?'

This is too easy. 'I'm trying to trace a driver who delivers to this street. Would you know how I can find which drivers are allocated to this patch?'

'Look, if you're wanting to give a driver grief, don't. We're underpaid and overworked, goes for all delivery drivers.'

'No, sorry, it's nothing like that. I'm trying to find this man.' I fumble in my pocket and produce a photograph of Paul. 'Do you recognise him?'

The driver peers at the photo and shakes his head. I show him the blurred photo that Marie sent me.

He laughs then. Actually, he guffaws. 'That's my hat. Do you wanna see it? It's in the van.'

'You think that's you in the photo?' My heart sinks. This man looks absolutely nothing like Paul except he is about six feet tall like my husband.

'Probably. I'm here most days. There are a couple of people who get daily deliveries. So what's up with the geezer you're trying to find?'

'Um, I'm sorry to have bothered you,' I say, backing away from him and heading back to my rental car.

'Oi. I don't like to have me photo taken, okay. Stay away from me, alright?'

'Yes, sorry.' I hurry into the car, and he throws me daggers before heading off in the opposite direction. I slam my fist on the steering wheel. I'm an idiot. Of course the photo isn't of Paul; of course he isn't hiding out in Macclesfield. My husband is dead, his body lost on some icy mountain.

I then have an awful cramping in my stomach and let out a groan. No, I can't be losing the baby. I just can't.

7

HELEN – NOW

In the weeks before Emily was born, I became almost delusional. I know that now with the benefit of hindsight, but at the time I swung between thinking I was the only sane person on the planet, or I was going mad. I couldn't accept Paul was really dead, and I desperately clung onto something that I knew wasn't true. Kelly was my saviour. She was the constant voice telling me I needed to be kind to myself, that denial was all part of the grieving process. Kelly took me to see our GP, who prescribed me pregnancy-safe antidepressants. He was so kind and understanding, explaining the stages of grief, telling me that what I was feeling was totally normal under the terrible circumstances. Those cramps I'd felt in Macclesfield had nothing to do with my pregnancy. I think it was just a physical manifestation of disappointment and grief.

Kelly was right. My denial of Paul's death was all part of the process, and as the medication started to kick in, that fog of desperate misery and denial began to fade. When Emily was born, I had less time for introspection. It was all about survival – her and me. And eventually I started living again, largely because of the phenomenal support of my family and the financial assistance of Paul's parents. After a year, I weaned myself off the medication.

For the first three years after Paul disappeared, Susannah and David were good to their word, and they made sure that Emily and I were well provided for. As his spouse, I had access to Paul's funds and could manage his financial affairs, but I'm just a custodian, like a trustee, and therefore I couldn't go on an extravagant shopping spree with his cards. I'm accountable, apparently. Until he's formerly declared dead, the money isn't really mine.

When Andrew and I first got together, I was very wary about entering a relationship. I didn't want Emily to be introduced to someone she might become attached to, only for him to fall out of our lives, but despite all my reservations, things moved quickly, and within six months he was spending most nights at our house.

One Saturday morning, Susannah arrived unannounced. I was just coming out of the upstairs bathroom, Emily was still in her nightwear, and Andrew answered the door dressed only in his boxer shorts and a T-shirt. Her strident voice carried up the stairs.

'Who are you, dressed like that in my son's house?' Susannah asked, pushing past him and stomping down the hall into the kitchen.

'Hello, Granny,' Emily said. 'This is Andrew, Mummy's boyfriend. He's my friend too.'

'Helen is still married,' Susannah said as I entered the kitchen.

'Andrew knows all about our situation,' I explained.

Susannah stood there with her hands on her hips, her chin trembling. 'You are married, Helen. Your job is to take care of my granddaughter.'

'Emily, sweetheart, you can go and watch telly next door,' I said, shovelling my daughter out into the corridor.

'Probably best if I leave too,' Andrew said, backing out of the room. I reached forward and grabbed his wrist.

'No, please stay.' I held his hand as I turned towards Susannah. 'I'm sorry I didn't tell you sooner, but I deserve to have happiness too. It's good for Emily as well. It doesn't mean Paul is forgotten, but he's gone, Susannah, and I need to live my life. This is Andrew. I wish you hadn't met him for the first time like this, but he's here to stay.'

She stared at me for a long moment and then swivelled around and strode straight out of the front door, leaving the door wide open.

Afterwards, Andrew turned to me, his cheeks flushed. 'Bloody hell, Helen. That was embarrassing.'

'I'm sorry,' I said, standing on tiptoes to kiss him. 'But she's got to realise she can't just turn up here unannounced.'

The following week I received a handwritten letter from Susannah and David explaining they would support their granddaughter as required, but now I had 'moved on', I was no longer in need of their help, and as such, they wouldn't be paying for me anymore. At first I was angry and resentful, but then I mellowed. I could understand their perspective. Besides, I wanted to stand on my own two feet. In a way they helped push Andrew and me together. Not long afterwards, he rented out his apartment and moved in with Emily and me, and we became a family. And we're happy, truly happy. I think about Paul from time to time, and I make every effort to keep his memory alive for Emily, showing her old photos of her birth father, but as far as she's concerned, Andrew is Daddy. She's really not interested in seeing photographs of a strange, dead man.

· · ·

ONCE AGAIN, I'm back in Switzerland for the next site meeting, and once again, Camilla wants to meet me on-site on Friday, but the main site meeting is on Monday, so I'm forced to stay over the weekend. Just because it suits her to come out for her social events over a weekend, it doesn't mean I want to. I wish we had the funds for Emily and Andrew to join me, but for two days, it's just not worth it.

Things have moved on well in the chalet. Many of the decorative items have been ordered, such as the tiles for all the bathrooms, the flooring throughout and the wallpaper for the master bedroom – the only bedroom that won't have painted walls or walls lined in wood.

Camilla and I are perched on a wooden scaffold bench in the soon-to-be living room of the chalet, and I'm flipping through my iPad, showing her photographs of all the lights that I'm proposing for each of the rooms. She seems distant, constantly checking her phone, as if this is all rather boring to her. And perhaps it is.

'Would you like me to email you these so you can choose in your own time?' I suggest.

'No, let's get it over and done with.'

I flick through page after page. 'Yup, that's fine,' she says repeatedly.

It's a bit disheartening that she's displaying so little interest when I've invested hours and hours (admittedly of paid time) to come up with what I hope will be an amazing scheme. When we're finished, it's a relief when Camilla disappears off in her chauffeur-driven Range Rover.

'EVERYTHING ALRIGHT?' Saskia asks. She startles me because I wasn't expecting her on-site today.

'Do you think Camilla is happy with what I'm doing?' I ask. I still lack confidence in my designs, and feedback from my clients is so important that when I don't get it, I tend to flounder.

Saskia laughs. 'Camilla is not an engaged client. She just wants a finished house. I really wouldn't worry. Can we discuss delivery dates? It's probably easier if you share with me, and then I'll tell Jacques just in case there are any language problems.'

'Of course.'

The sun is shining, and it's a beautiful afternoon, so Saskia suggests we sit on the balcony and work through the spreadsheets together prior to Monday's meeting. She finds us a couple of plastic chairs and a table, and I talk her through all the orders I have placed along with the timescales for delivery and installation schedules.

Suddenly there's a loud humming noise, which gets increasingly louder, drowning out our voices. I glance upwards, and a helicopter is coming directly towards us. My heart thumps, and my throat closes up. I feel like I need to run, yet I can't move. Even my fingers have seized up, clutching the pen in the palm of my hand.

'Are you alright?' Saskia peers at me, shouting over the din. 'You've gone white.'

'I... um...' My eyes are transfixed on the helicopter, which is flying at the height of the chalet, so close I can almost see the face of the pilot. I notice there are ropes hanging from the craft's belly, wrapped around something that swings through the air. As the helicopter turns and flies away, I feel some of the tension easing from my body. Saskia is still staring at me, her eyebrows knitted together.

'Sorry, I have a bit of a phobia of helicopters,' I explain.

'Wow, that's a weird one.' Her hand rushes to cover her mouth. 'That was rude of me, sorry. It's just helicopters are very common here.'

I can't help thinking about the helicopters that were

meant to have saved Paul, that low, thrumming sound that once it permeates my head, never seems to go away. It's a horrible flashback, something I thought was in the past. Yet here I am, never far from the memories of what happened back then. As the noise dissipates, I try to focus on the charming sounds of the mountainside, the jingling of the cowbells in the distance, the chirruping of the crickets in the long grass on the steep bank under the chalet, and the occasional cuckoo birdsong from deep in the forest.

'We use helicopters for construction projects, or for moving trees in difficult-to-access places. I even had a client have a grand piano delivered by helicopter in the morning and a hot tub in the afternoon. You can imagine how stressful that was!'

I smile wanly. I suppose I'd thought helicopters were only used in times of emergency, rescuing injured people from the tops of mountainsides. It's reassuring to know they're used for so many other purposes.

I HAVE ANOTHER LONG, empty weekend ahead of me, one where I wish Andrew and Emily could join me. The tradespeople are packing up, even though it's only 3.30 pm, and even Saskia is putting her laptop away.

'Do you have any plans for the weekend?' she asks.

I shake my head.

'Let me think. You could take the lifts to the top of the highest peak here, Mont Charme.'

I can't think of anything I would want to do less. Isn't that where Paul disappeared? The thought of me going up there all by myself fills me with horror.

She types something into her phone. 'Ah, *zut*. The lifts don't open until 1 July, so that's not possible. Silly me! It's the

Inalpe festival this weekend. You should join us. Everyone attends, and it's great fun.'

'What's that?'

'It's when the cows are taken up to the higher pastures for grazing in the summer. They are big cows, heifers with horns, and they jostle for position until one of them is crowned queen. The locals all get together and have picnics. It's very sociable. You must come.'

'It's really kind of you to invite me,' I say.

'Not at all. Everyone will be there. We'll meet you at the top of the lifts at 10 am tomorrow morning.'

I'VE LOCKED up the chalet and am sitting in the cabin with the doors wide open, eating a pizza I've just heated, when my phone rings. It's Camilla. 'Helen,' she barks at me, 'I've just received a fine, and I'm livid.'

I swallow, wondering what it's got to do with me.

'You put your rubbish out in a black bag.'

'Um, yes,' I say hesitantly.

'You didn't use the correct bags bought from the village shop.'

'Does that actually matter?' I ask, glad that we're not in the same room so I can roll my eyes without her seeing. I thought I'd screwed up an order. Is it really necessary to call me at 7.45 pm on a Friday evening about something so trivial?

'Yes, it does matter. I'm livid. I'm trying to be a good citizen in a country where I'm not a native, and your screwing up like that doesn't help me one iota.'

'But–'

'Sorry, Helen, there are no buts. I'll add the fine to your invoice, but it's not the money that concerns me, more the fact that you're not listening to what I'm telling you. I've got to go now.'

I stare at my phone, wondering what the hell that was all about. Camilla hadn't told me anything about using special bags to put my rubbish out, and in the scheme of things, it really can't be that much of a big deal. I take a few deep breaths of fresh alpine air and try to reassure myself that it's nothing personal. Camilla must be having a bad day. I try to let it go and spend too long on the phone to Andrew, talking about nothing in particular. I'm glad I've got something to do tomorrow.

THE NEXT DAY I walk to the lift station and take the gondola. It's a six-seater, and I'm opposite a couple who nod at me and then chat away quietly in Swiss German. I'm facing the valley, and as the gondola rises, the views are fabulous, with numerous craggy mountains reaching high into the sky, little patches of snow glistening on the peaks. Far below us in the valley, a pale grey-blue river snakes as far as the eye can see and the valley floor is sliced up into neat fields in shades of green and beige, interspersed with large conurbations of miniature apartment blocks and houses the size of dots. The sky is a perfect blue without a cloud in sight, and I can't help but smile. All I wish is that Andrew and Emily were here to share this with me.

There is a crowd of people gathered as I step out of the lift station, many carrying picnic hampers or with rucksacks on their backs. I glance around for Saskia and jump when someone places a hand on my shoulder.

'Hey!' she says as I swivel around. Saskia is dressed in blue shorts and a white T-shirt, a baseball cap on her head. 'This is my husband, Matteo Berchard.'

He's a tall and skinny man with thick blond hair and horn-rimmed glasses that sit high on his long but rather distinguished nose.

'*Enchanté*,' he says as we shake hands.

'We're joining friends and neighbours, so I hope you're ready for a good time.'

I smile, feeling awkward and already regretting my decision to come. What will I have to say to these strangers? Will we even be able to talk to each other considering my lack of language skills? We walk down a track and then cross over a pasture full of high grass and stunning wildflowers, varieties I have never seen before in an array of colours: whites, mauves, bright orange, pinks and yellows. If I were here with Emily, I would dance through the meadow with my arms outstretched, singing 'The Hills Are Alive' from *The Sound Of Music*, because they really are. The further downhill we walk, the louder the noise of jangling cowbells, drowning out the sound of the crickets and singing birds. We come to a halt high above an enormous field. It's fenced in, and crowds of people stand around the full perimeter edge of the fence, chattering excitedly as they point at the huge black and dark brown cows in the field.

'They are Herens, these cows,' Saskia explains. They are big, the size of bulls in the UK, and they have horns despite all being female. Each cow has a large number painted on its back, and a bell – some of them vast, the size of a sink – hanging around their necks. A few farmers stand in the field, using their crooks to stop the cows from accidentally charging into the fencing, or to encourage them to fight. I see a couple of cows locking horns, pushing each other, until one concedes and simply ambles away.

'Cow fighting is common for this part of Switzerland,' Saskia explains. 'We call it the *combats de reines*, which means the fight of the queens. The cows push each other until one backs down, and eventually by late afternoon there will be just one winner, the queen of queens.'

From what I can see, the cows don't seem particularly

inclined to fight. They look quite content grazing and using their horns to dig up the dry earth, scattering it far and wide.

We carry on walking down the hillside. Matteo waves at a group of people settled underneath a cluster of pine trees. We make our way towards them. I feel awkward as I stand to one side while there are lots of greetings with kisses on each cheek.

'Everyone, this is Helen,' Saskia says. 'She's the interior designer for the British lady's chalet.'

'Ah yes.' An older woman smiles warmly at me, stands up and extends her hand. 'I'm Manon, and this is my husband, Guillaume. We live next door to Camilla's chalet.' She has short, fine white hair and sparkling blue eyes. Her husband winks at me as he takes a large sip of red wine from a transparent plastic cup.

'Would you like a glass of Fendant?' he asks, holding up a bottle of white wine.

'Um, maybe later,' I say. I'm certainly not used to drinking wine at eleven in the morning.

Saskia takes a blanket out of Matteo's rucksack and indicates for me to sit down. Manon takes a seat next to me.

'How long are you here for?' she asks.

'On and off until the project is finished,' I say. 'Have you lived here long?'

'Oh yes. Thirty-three years, and Guillaume has lived here all his life. We know everyone, and everyone knows us. It's a small, close-knit community.'

'And you all speak such good English. It puts me to shame.'

'Not all of us. My father was a diplomat, so I lived in various African countries as a child, and we were educated in English.'

'Helen, you must have a drink!' Matteo says, holding up two bottles of wine, one white and one red.

It seems rude to decline for the second time, so I accept a glass of white wine and eat a piece of dried sausage that Saskia insists I try. I glance around at the crowd. Everyone looks chilled and happy, laughing and drinking, occasionally pointing at the cows, which seem increasingly inclined to go into combat with their bovine companions.

'Tell me more about what you do,' Manon says.

I smile at her and then glance away, opening my mouth to start speaking.

And then I see him.

The words evaporate on my lips.

I freeze.

Can it be him?

His eyes lock onto mine before he swiftly turns away. I jump up. It's his gait. The way he walks quickly but with a slight stiffness in his right leg, the result of an old rugby injury, unusual in a young man.

'Helen?' Manon says. 'Is everything alright?'

I am trembling, trying to spot the man who has now edged behind a group of people. The man I see in my dreams. The man I thought I was going to spend the rest of my life with. The man who is the father of my child. The man who is dead.

8

PAUL – NOW

It's not really my thing, hanging around with a bunch of people I barely know, struggling to follow what they're saying. But Orla is so happy to be back here, surrounded by the friends she grew up with, friends she hasn't seen in five years. She's beaming, her eyes bright, and little rosy patches highlight her tanned cheeks. If Orla is happy, then I am too. Or at least, that's what I tell myself.

I'm not sure about this cow-fighting thing. It's not like the poor animals want to lock horns. I feel sorry for them with those great big jangling bells around their necks. I stand up and stretch, deciding to go for a wander. There's the scent of a barbecue, and I noticed that various food stands have been set up. I suggested bringing a picnic, even offered to prepare the food, but Orla was dismissive, saying we'd go with the flow. But I'm hungry despite it still being quite early.

I glance around at the huddles of people standing and sitting around the edge of the field. And that's when I see her.

A woman who looks just like Helen. She stares at me, her eyes widening. Widening with recognition?

It can't be. We're, what, a couple of hundred feet away

from each other. It must be someone who looks like her. Her hair is shorter and lighter than it used to be. My eyes are drawn back to her face.

Shit. She looks just like Helen, and now she's getting up, her eyes still focused on me. My heart hammers. What the hell is she doing here?

I've got to get away. Now.

'What's up, hon?' Orla asks, leaning backwards and grabbing my ankle.

'I've got to go,' I say, pulling my leg away from her. I ignore Orla's annoyed mutterings and hurry away, weaving between people, aiming for the dense forest, but first I've got to cross the wide meadow that is one of the main pistes leading down to the village in winter. I stumble, bumping into a man with an enormous belly.

'Sorry, sorry,' I say. He mutters something unintelligible under his breath. I glance back over my shoulder, and Helen is also moving around the edge of the crowd. No, this can't be possible. She shouldn't be here. But I have an advantage. I've been mountain biking down this hillside, and I know the paths. I'll be able to lose her. In the short term, at least.

I stride as quickly as I can across the meadow. It's so tempting to glance backwards, to check if she's following me, but if she sees me looking for her, then she'll know for sure that it's me, so I force myself to focus on moving forwards. I stumble briefly on a tree root and, cursing, carry on towards the welcoming darkness of the forest ahead. The temperature drops immediately, I'm under the cover of the pines. I step away from the path and hide behind an enormous tree trunk, and glance back the way I came. There's no one there.

I lean my head against the sturdy trunk and let out a sigh. This was never meant to happen. Never.

My phone rings. I grab it from my pocket and am relieved when Orla's name pops up.

'Where have you gone?'

'Sorry, love. I've got a bit of a stomach upset. I'm going to head home. Do you mind if I take the car?'

She sighs. Everything is a bit of a problem for Orla these days. 'Okay,' she says with a groan. 'I'll get a lift with friends.'

'See you later,' I say and then end the call.

What am I going to do? And then I reason with myself. I've imagined I've seen Helen on many an occasion over the past five years, and it's never been her. There's no reason to think it's her this time. But that woman, she looked just like Helen. I open up Instagram on my phone, using Orla's login details, and head to Helen's account.

Shit.

I sink down onto my haunches. It's her. Helen is here. She's posted a photograph of a big chalet, one of those that only the rich banker foreigners can afford, and the words next to it say:

Honoured to be working on the interior design of this fabulous chalet. #Corviez #chaletdesign

I bash my head backwards against the tree trunk, welcoming the pain. There is only a handful of people in this world I need to avoid running into, and Helen is at the top of that list. Why did I listen to Orla? We should never have come back here.

I hurry through the forest now, running too fast, stubbing my toe on yet more tree roots, falling and scraping my hands and my knees. It's as if I'm being chased down the hillside by a monster, yet there is no one here. The only noise is the chirping birds and the gentle rustling of the trees, and my ragged breath. What are we going to do?

I let out a cry because I have to tell Orla the truth. What happens if she runs into Helen? How will she react? I stop and let my breathing calm; then I call Orla. She answers eventually.

'Yup,' she says.

'Orla, I need to tell you something. Can you move away from your friends?'

'What? Have you taken something, Paul?' I can hear laughter and cowbells. 'I didn't know you had any drugs.'

'Step away from them, Orla,' I say in a tone of voice I never use with her.

'Keep your hair on,' she says, but I can hear her get up, the grunt as she moves, her heavy breathing as she walks away, the fading voices. 'What is it?'

'She's here.'

'What do you mean, she's here?' Orla asks.

'Helen. She's here, at the Inalpe festival, right here in Corviez.'

There's silence for a moment and then a gasp. 'Are you sure?'

'Of course I'm bloody sure.'

'No!' Orla lets out a low screech.

'Keep your voice down,' I say. 'You need to avoid her at all costs.'

'Did she see you?' Orla asks, panic in her voice.

'No,' I lie. 'Stop stressing. She's no idea I'm here, but we need to be careful.'

'It's you who needs to be careful,' she says. 'Helen and I don't even know each other. Why would she recognise me?'

'She probably wouldn't,' I admit.

'Stop bloody stressing,' Orla says. 'And stay hidden in the chalet.' She ends the call.

9

HELEN – NOW

I lose him. I do my best to follow the man in the khaki trousers and the white T-shirt, the man with that slightly unusual gait just like my Paul, a walk that no one except, perhaps, his parents or closest friends would recognise as being anything out of the ordinary. But there are too many people here. I walk the full circle of the field, my eyes straining to find him, to no avail. The man who might or might not have been Paul has vanished, just like he did five years ago.

I feel ridiculous now. It's not the first time I've thought I've seen him, and I have to admit to myself that it probably won't be the last. It often happens in crowded places; train stations and airports are the worst. And of course, right here in the very place he disappeared, I think I see him the most, in my dreams and now when I'm awake. The man I just saw has much lighter hair than Paul's, and he has a beard and moustache, cropped short. A perfect disguise or just following a trend, a trend that Paul used to mock. I remember how he said he loathed facial hair, that it was itchy and unbecoming, but people change. Especially people who have disappeared.

Even as I think that, I realise how ridiculous I'm being. My brain is playing tricks on me, and it's hardly surprising that it's doing it right here in the mountains. After all, this is the place I last saw him alive. This is exactly what happened in the months after he disappeared. I thought I saw him everywhere. In fact, I saw him nowhere.

I'm halfway around the field now, and I need to get back. Saskia and Manon must think I'm so rude just getting up and hurrying off like that. I make my way back towards them, trying to avoid stepping on picnic rugs and slipping on the steep hillside, trying but failing to stop looking for Paul.

'Sorry,' I say as Saskia looks up at me, frowning. 'I thought I saw someone I knew, but I was mistaken.'

She nods, but her eyes are no longer smiling. She turns back to talk to some other friends, and I'm left alone with my thoughts. He really did look like Paul, the same height, the way he walked, yet of course it wasn't. I'm being stupid. I wonder if I should ask my doctor for another course of antidepressants, yet I don't feel depressed. Of course, I'm more stressed than normal. No, I don't want to go on drugs. I just need to focus on the here and now and remember that our brains can play all sorts of tricks on us.

Matteo fills up my glass with wine, and I gulp it down, the chilled white wine seeping quickly into my veins and calming my thumping heart.

I send Andrew a WhatsApp message along with some photographs of the cows, but he doesn't respond, and the little ticks remain grey. I wonder what he's doing this morning. Kelly will have taken Emily to her Saturday morning music class, and she may well have hung on to Emily so that Andrew could have the day to himself. Perhaps he's at the gym, making the most of a few hours to himself. All the while, I drink. I lose track of time, but the sun is hot now, and I can feel the back of my neck burning. The cows have left the field, yet I don't recall seeing them leave. Saskia stands up and stretches.

'Matteo and I are going to head back. The boys will be home shortly, and I promised to cook supper.'

'Oh yes, fine,' I say. I try to stand up too, but I'm dizzy, and Saskia has to grab my arm to stop me from falling. 'Sorry,' I mumble.

'You don't have to go back yet. You can stay,' she says.

'Um, yes. Probably best if I wander back in my own time.' I'm not sure if my words are coming out correctly. I'm an idiot for drinking too much, and now I can feel the pounding of an oncoming headache. I'll let them stride ahead, and then I'll walk slowly back to the lifts. It's uphill, and I'm feeling very hot, so it'll take me a while.

'Are you sure you're okay?' Saskia asks. 'You look a bit worse for wear.'

'Too much excellent wine and sunshine,' I say, trying to shrug it off and smiling awkwardly.

'It looked like you were rattled by something earlier.'

'I thought I saw my ex-husband, but I was mistaken.'

Saskia grimaces and then whispers to me, 'I often see my ex-husband, and I wish that I didn't! The joys of living in a small community.'

I TAKE MY TIME, trudging back up the hillside, my eyes darting everywhere in the hope of seeing that man again. By the time I've taken the lift back down to the valley and ambled back to the cabin, I have a throbbing headache and a queasy stomach. The local wine might taste delicious, but it's done nothing for my head. I collapse onto the sofa and call Andrew. This time, he answers.

'I think I saw Paul.'

Andrew is silent for a long time. We have had this conversation before. Many times.

'Really?' he asks eventually, his voice flat.

'I don't know, but I think so.'

'Darling, it's the place. Paul is dead. You often think you see him when you're in a crowd of people.'

'You're right,' I say.

'You're under a lot of stress at the moment. You're working on your largest and most lucrative project to date, and you're in the very place he died. It's not surprising that your mind is playing tricks.'

'Yes.'

'I love you, Helen. Just remember that.'

'And I love you too, Andrew,' I say. When I end the call and lean my head back against the sofa, I take several deep breaths, trying hard to get a grip. Of course I'm going to imagine seeing Paul here. There must be thousands of people who walk like he does, and perhaps I've forgotten exactly how he moves. Five years is a long time, a long time to forget things. I remember listening to a podcast where a psychologist explained memories are re-consolidated each time we access them. This very process can alter the memory itself, so repeatedly remembering can actually lead to some details being lost. It's like we're reinforcing a mistake again and again. Perhaps every time I've seen someone walk in the same way I recall Paul walking, I've altered it slightly in my head.

That night I have the recurring nightmare. I'm on a snowy mountainside where it's freezing cold, and the wind is howling, a blizzard whipping around my face. The world is monochrome. I'm trying to trudge through knee-deep snow, but I'm wearing a thin summer dress with bare arms and legs, my feet slipping with every step I take. I can hear Paul screaming for me. 'Helen! Help!' I'm the only person on the mountainside, the only person in the world who can help Paul, and the panic is mounting. Everything is white, the white sky merges with the white snow, and even my limbs are white. Paul screams for me again, but his voice is increasingly muffled. My foot hits something hard, and I stumble. It's Paul. He's in the snow, face down, yet I can hear him gasping for breath. He's suffocating. I try to turn him over, but my hands slip on the ice and snow, and I can't get a grip on him. I'm screaming as I try harder and harder. And then suddenly he turns, and he's an icy statue, totally frozen, his face contorted into a scream, a layer of thick ice distorting his features. I shriek again, and the sun's rays hit him like sabres, and immediately the ice melts until all that's left is a large puddle of water. Paul has gone, and I'm yelling, sitting up in bed, gasping for air.

10

PAUL – THEN

'That was so good,' Orla says, nibbling my neck. I smile, trying to quash the feeling of guilt. 'What are you thinking?' she asks, pressing her hot, sweat-covered body up against mine, making desire surge back through me.

'About you. About how gorgeous you are and how I can't get enough of you.' That's not true. I'm thinking about Helen and how I need to make sure I change my shirt before I go home, dropping the one Orla ripped the button off at the dry cleaners to get it mended.

I visit Orla twice a week before work. Mostly we have passionate sex in a two-hour window between 3 pm and 5 pm, and then I hurry to work, losing myself in my cooking, trying to suppress the feeling of guilt. Occasionally, I stay over at Orla's flat. I tell Helen that we have a late night function and that it's easier for me to stay in town; sometimes it's even true, it's just I don't stay in a cheap hotel. Instead, I lounge about in Orla's luxurious South Kensington maisonette, enjoying her feather-filled bed and cooking her eggs Benedict for breakfast.

It's wrong and I know it. Orla knows it too, but we're addicted to each other, and I don't know how to break this addiction. Helen and I have only been married for three years, and for two of those years, I've been cheating on her with Orla. I didn't mean it to be this way. When I married Helen, I truly believed I would be faithful to her for the rest of my life. What I didn't know is that I would fall for Orla too. It doesn't seem fair that we have to be monogamous. I love two women, and I don't want to have to choose between them. That makes me sound greedy, and I don't think I am; I'm just stuck in a conundrum.

'Imagine if we could do this every night. If you came home to me after your shift in the kitchen, and I gave myself to you in the way you give yourself to your haute cuisine. Don't you want that for us, Paul?' Orla asks, her tongue sliding down my chest.

She wants me to leave Helen, and I keep telling her that I will, but each time I bottle out. How can I break my wife's heart? She's a good, kind woman, the sort of person who will make a great mother and be a steadfast support to me as I rise through the ranks of the kitchen. Helen won't mind when I'm working all hours in my own Michelin-starred restaurant. I can't see Orla being so relaxed about it.

Helen and I bought our first house together last year, the down payment a gift from my parents, topped up by her parents even though I know they couldn't really afford it. Even if I could walk away from Helen, how can I let down both of our families? Yet Orla is electric. Her forceful personality shines, as do her incredible looks. She has that silky black hair and a voluptuous figure along with an insatiable appetite for sex. Every day I have to pinch myself that she's chosen me. Orla is a magnet, not just for me, but for everyone who knows her. She's the sort of woman who attracts everyone's attention and exudes a confidence I've never experienced before. Perhaps it's the confidence that comes with being multilingual, multinational, extraordinarily rich and exquisitely beautiful. And that's why I can't let her go, because she's chosen me. This butterfly has landed on me, a simple, ordinary flower. I'd describe myself as a weed if that word didn't have another negative meaning, because I'm not weak and I'm good enough looking. I know what I want, and I make damned sure I get it. And it's this woman lying with one leg flung over mine.

'What time do you have to go?' Orla asks lazily.

I open my eyes and glance at the clock. 'In half an hour.'

'I'm so tired, I could sleep,' she says, her cheek coming to rest on my stomach.

'Then do so,' I say, stroking her hair.

I met Orla at Gabriella's wedding. Helen and I were engaged and excited to be attending Gaby's marriage together. It was quite the event, held in a quaint English church in a tiny hamlet in Sussex. In fact, it was everything a white wedding should be, with stunning flowers and a big marquee in Gaby's parents' field. The sun shone during the day, and as the light faded, we took our places at large circular tables for supper. I was sat next to Orla, who seemed familiar. I mentioned that we might have met before, and she rolled her eyes as if it was an overly worn chat-up line. But actually we had met before, at one of Gaby's infamous drinks parties. Orla flirted outrageously throughout the wedding supper. Every time she put her hand over mine, I glanced across the marquee, eager to make sure Helen wasn't watching. During the speeches, she put her hand on my thigh, and when her fingers slipped inwards, reluctantly I picked up her hand and placed it back on her lap.

'Don't you feel it?' she whispered, her breath hot in my

ear. I wanted it terribly, but I couldn't. I was due to be married in six months.

'I'm engaged, and I love my fiancée.'

Orla looked furious, and she ignored me for the rest of the evening. But I couldn't ignore her. My eyes constantly sought her out, and that night, when Helen and I made love, I imagined it was Orla's body convulsing under mine.

The next eighteen months were happy ones. Helen and I got married. We were settled and secure, caring with each other, following the expected trajectory for young newly-weds, and everything might have been fine if Orla and I hadn't run into each other once again.

Helen was working long hours, as was I. It was a hot and sticky night, and I needed some fresh air, away from the fiery hot kitchen. I stepped out of the back door, dressed in my chef's whites, and as I was coming back in, I passed the ladies' toilets. Orla walked out of the door. She was wearing a little black dress, her breasts packed in tightly, high heels making her almost as tall as me. My breath caught as I saw her.

'Orla?'

She looked utterly delighted to see me, crushing herself up against me, her lips full on mine.

'I'm on such a boring date,' she whispered. 'Can you rescue me?'

I laughed. 'How?'

'Are you the head chef here?'

'I am tonight,' I said truthfully.

'Come into the restaurant and tell me that I've won a tour of the kitchen. My dreadful date has already said he hates cooking.'

'Really?' I laughed. 'Isn't there an easier way to get rid of him?'

'Maybe, but let's have some fun!' She blew me a kiss and returned up the stairs. I couldn't take my eyes off her.

'What are you doing?' Keiran, the maître d', asked me as I walked into the restaurant a few minutes later.

'There's a guest over there who has asked to talk to me,' I said.

'Says who?' he asked, his nose in the air. Keiran seemed to think he was number one in the restaurant when the owner and principal chef, Giancarlo, wasn't there. I ignored him and walked towards Orla's table, unable to take the smile off my face. Her date did look boring, with his flat combed hair and grey suit.

'Ma'am, as our one hundredth diner of the week, you're eligible for a tour of the kitchen. Is that something that might interest you?'

She clapped her hands together and gasped. 'How amazing! Wow! You don't mind, Neil, do you?'

Neil looked thoroughly annoyed. Orla jumped up. 'Thanks for dinner, but it's probably best if I see myself home.'

He opened and closed his mouth, his eyes wide with shock. I felt a little sorry for him in that moment, but only for a second because Orla was right next to me as we hurried downstairs to the kitchen.

'You're not allowed into the kitchen,' I said. 'Health and safety.'

'That's okay. I'll wait for you here in the hall. When does your shift finish?'

That was the beauty of being in charge for the evening. Even though I'd never done it before, I told the sous chefs to tidy up, and I left with Orla. She hailed a cab, and I didn't even ask where we were going. By the time we pulled up in front of the smart white-painted townhouse with its black railings, I knew that I wouldn't be going home that evening. I sent Helen a quick text apologising. Orla was and is captivating. She's a habit that I crave, a habit that I can't break.

OF COURSE I live in fear that we will be found out. If and when the time comes to tell Helen, I want to do it myself. I can't bear the thought of her finding out through some mutual acquaintance, and that is an acute possibility. Orla and I met through our mutual friend Gabriella, and although Orla and Gaby still see each other, on the whole, our friendship groups don't overlap. Nevertheless, there's still that danger. I wonder whether that adds an extra frisson to our relationship.

She's breathing deeply as I slip out of bed. 'Don't go,' she mumbles, opening her eyes.

'I have to.'

'Have you booked the ski trip?'

'Yes. I'll be able to spend lots of time with you because Helen isn't much of a skier.'

'I wish she weren't coming, that it could just be the two of us. My three favourite things. Sun, skiing and sex. Can't you persuade her not to come?'

'She's my wife, Orla.'

'And I'm your sexy mistress. Oh God, I love you, Paul. I want to be your wife.'

I turn away from her because I don't know how to make that happen, and I don't want to get into an argument before a long shift in the kitchen. 'We'll have a wonderful time. I'm a good skier,' I say, hating myself for being so weak.

'If you ski like you make love, then we're in for the time of our lives,' she says languidly.

'Actually, I do.' I grin at Orla. I'm half dressed now, but I lean over her and kiss her deeply on the lips. I wish I didn't have to go.

11

HELEN – NOW

I t's early evening when I walk around the interior of the chalet, my clipboard in hand, ticking off all the tasks that have been completed. There's still a lot to do, but I'm thrilled with the progress. Most of the bathrooms have been tiled, and I reckon they achieve the perfect balance between style and function. I hope Camilla will be pleased. It's just a shame that some of the scaffolding is up on the rear of the property, particularly around the stone chimney. Outside, it's just the garden that needs landscaping and planting up.

This is the best time of day, when the tradespeople have left and I have the place to myself. The chalet is silent, although outside the crickets are making a cacophony as the sun beats down. The air is still, and the mountains are in a haze, silhouetted in shades of deep blues and purple hues. I lean against the wooden railings on one of the terraces to soak in the view and absorb the sun rays on my pale English skin. This place doesn't freak me out quite as much as it used to, and now, three weeks on from when I thought I spotted Paul, I feel calmer. I know that my mind plays tricks on me, and the reality is, Paul is dead. One day, I will receive a phone call from the Swiss police telling me they have found his remains.

'Cooee!' a female voice says. I glance around, and it takes me a moment to realise it's Manon standing to the side of the chalet, waving.

'Are you here alone again?' she asks.

I redden slightly, remembering my drunken state the last time I saw her at the Inalpe festival, but then I remember how much everyone else was drinking too. Perhaps she didn't realise how inebriated I really was.

'Yes, and enjoying the view.'

'Would you like to come over for an apéritif?' she asks.

I think about the long, lonely evening ahead of me and readily agree.

A FEW MINUTES LATER, I've locked up both the chalet and cabin and have followed Manon's instructions to walk twenty metres along the Bisse and take the wooden steps that peel off to the left. Both Guillaume and Manon are sitting outside the most charming old chalet. It's constructed from a very dark wood, almost black. The small windows are framed with bright red shutters, and underneath each are flower boxes spilling over with geraniums. A well-mown lawn encircles the chalet and gives way to pine trees at the sides.

'Welcome,' Manon says, gesturing for me to sit on a wooden chair next to her. 'Would you like red, white or rosé?' she asks. I promise myself I'll just have one glass this evening.

'Rosé, please.'

As I sit down, I glance to my left and realise how very close Camilla's chalet is to the edge of her neighbour's small plot. The disruption to Manon and Guillaume must have been immense over the past few months. It's not as if there's even a fence dividing the two properties, just a handful of tall pine trees.

'How is the project going?' Manon tips her head towards Camilla's chalet.

'Well, we're on schedule, I hope.'

Guillaume huffs. I raise an eyebrow.

'Ignore him. He's fed up with all the noise and dust.'

'It must be very inconvenient for you to have the works going on so close by.'

'Yes,' Guillaume says, crossing his arms. 'One minute we were hoping to buy the chalet for our son, and the next some millionaire foreigner has swept in, offered crazy money and then doubled its size.'

'Oh, I hadn't realised you wanted to buy it.'

The older man shrugs his shoulders. 'We can't afford what the foreigners can pay.'

'Are there strict planning laws here?' I ask.

A strange look passes between Manon and Guillaume. Before her husband can say anything, Manon changes the subject. 'So how is your little girl?'

'Well, thank you, although I miss her when I'm here.' It isn't until a few minutes later that I realise I don't recall telling Manon about Emily. What I do recall, however, is Saskia saying everyone knows everyone else's business in a small place such as this.

'When will it be finished next door?' Guillaume asks.

'By September, I hope.'

'Everything shuts here in August, anyway,' Manon comments.

I hope not because I have lots of work to be completed in August. I'll need to check on that.

'The problem with madame next door' – Guillaume prods his finger in the direction of Camilla's chalet – 'is that she's made no effort. She didn't come to say hello. She didn't warn us about the building works and the noise and the dust. And when she does visit, her nose is in the air and we're just the silly locals.'

'Oh, Guillaume,' Manon says, trying to wave her husband's words away. 'We don't all have to be friends with our neighbours.'

'There's one thing about being friends and another about human decency,' Guillaume huffs again.

'Your English is amazing,' I say, which it is, but it also gives me the opportunity to steer the conversation away from my client.

'Guillaume used to work for the UN,' Manon says.

'The first member of my extended family to move away. Everyone else works here – the carpenters, electricians, plumbers, shop owners, they're all my cousins.'

'Yet you came back.'

'Ah yes. Once the mountains are in your blood, you can never give them up. Who would want to live in the city if you can wake up to this view every morning? We moved back to Corviez as soon as I retired.'

I smile.

'Sun, snow, fabulous wine and one of the best views in the world.'

'So, tell me more about your work, Helen,' Manon says. 'Have you done the interiors of a chalet before?'

'No, this is my first time. I've helped renovate lots of different styles of houses.'

'Do you have any photos to show me?'

'No, but I have an Instagram page. Would you like to see that?'

'Of course.' She smiles, leaning towards me and peering at my phone. I bring up my Instagram profile and show Manon pictures of the last few houses I've done the interiors for.

'This is exquisite!' Manon exclaims as she sees the living room of a south London townhouse. One wall is covered with bold wallpaper in greens and golds, depicting tropical leaves and the amber eyes of a tiger peeking out behind a palm frond.

'Not to everyone's taste!' I laugh.

'Indeed, no. But I think it's very brave.' She leans back in her chair. 'What do you think, Guillaume? Would you like this design in our house?'

Manon passes my phone to her husband. He peers at the screen for a long time, and I wonder what he thinks. His expression is inscrutable. He then starts swiping up the screen. I'm surprised that he's so technically literate and interested in interior design.

My phone rings, and Guillaume shoves it towards me.

'Sorry,' I say. 'I wasn't expecting anyone to call.'

'It's not a problem.' Manon smiles sweetly.

I assume it's Andrew calling so that Emily can say good-night to me. It isn't. The caller ID is Camilla. Why is she calling me at 7 pm? Again.

'Sorry, do you mind if I take this?' I ask, standing up. I move away from the older couple and stand to the side of their small chalet, adjacent to a raised bed full of ripening vegetables.

'Hello, Camilla. Is everything alright?'

'Yes, and no. I want to bring the completion date forwards. It's my husband's fiftieth birthday in August. I had booked a great big yacht, but the bloody thing has only gone and caught fire, and now they've cancelled on me, and then I thought why not have it at the chalet? We can put up guests in local hotels and christen the new build. What do you say?'

'Um–'

I don't get the chance to answer as Camilla carries on. 'So you'll need to speed everything up. We'll have a party on 15

August, so we're only bringing the completion date forwards by four weeks. And I was thinking it would be best if you stay over there for the final three weeks to oversee everything. I don't want any hiccups.'

'I'm not sure–'

'I'm a yes person, Helen. I employed you because you reassured me you could deliver, and believe me, I have a lot of well-connected friends. You do a good job on my chalet and you'll be inundated with work. Obviously the converse is true too.' She lets her voice fade away as I absorb her threat. I thought Camilla was a pleasant woman when I first met her, but now I'm realising that she is utterly ruthless. Having lots of money doesn't give her the right to be a bitch.

'You still there?' she barks down the phone line.

'Yes. The problem is, I have a young daughter, and you want me to be here in Switzerland during the summer holidays. I haven't got time to organise childcare.' I don't mention that I have no intention of organising childcare. One advantage of being self-employed is that I can choose to spend as much time as I want with my daughter.

'Splash some cash at it, or why don't you bring her over to Corviez with you? There're loads of things for kids to do there in the summer, and the village has a holiday club. Go to the tourist office and sort it out. I'll pay you an additional twenty per cent more to get this done on time, as obviously you won't be able to work on any other client projects during those three weeks. How does that sound?'

I hesitate in answering because on the one hand it sounds great; on the other it fills me with utter panic.

'Make that thirty per cent on top of our agreed payment. Right, I've got dinner at the Ivy tonight so must rush. Cheerio!'

I stare at my phone. She has just bamboozled me into agreeing to stay here for three entire weeks and to finish a job so much faster than we agreed. How the hell am I going to do that? And do I even want to?

'Everything alright?' Manon asks as I trudge back to join them.

'Yes, fine, thank you,' I say.

She peers at me. 'You don't look fine. Is everything alright with the little one?'

'It was Camilla, actually,' I say, immediately feeling bad for talking about my client.

'Now why doesn't that surprise me!' she says, rolling her eyes upwards. 'No doubt with some unreasonable request.'

I smile tightly and finish the last sip of wine. 'If you wouldn't mind excusing me, I need to speak to my partner in England, but thank you so much for the drink and your hospitality.'

'Our pleasure.' Manon smiles. 'If you need anything, don't hesitate to shout. In fact, let me give you our phone number, just in case.'

BACK IN THE CABIN, I call Andrew and explain Camilla's demands.

'I don't think you've got much choice, love,' he says. 'I'm sure Emily will love it out there. Why don't I bring her out at the weekend, and we can all spend a few days together?'

'Really? That would be fabulous.'

That's why I love Andrew. He always sees the bigger picture and does everything in his power to put a positive slant on things. I know I loved Paul for those first few years, but occasionally I feel like I've had a lucky escape. Andrew is so straightforward; Paul definitely had a side to him, a side that I didn't see until it was too late.

. . .

THE NEXT MORNING, I go straight to talk to Jacques Freant, wondering whether Camilla has shared the new timetable with him directly. Clearly not because he lets out a string of French expletives – or words that I assume are expletives.

'*Pas possible!*' he mutters again and again.

'When is the scaffolding going to come down?' I ask, thinking about the ugly tower that is still attached to the side of the chalet.

'Pff!' he says, shrugging his shoulders.

'I can't style the terraces until it's gone,' I say, thinking of all the patio furniture I need to get delivered.

'*Oui, oui!*' he says, throwing his hands up in the air.

I turn away because there's no point in getting angry with Jacques; we have to work together. All the same, I don't like the man.

12

PAUL – THEN

On the one hand, the skiing holiday is going so much better than I could have hoped; on the other it's worse. Orla and I spend our days skiing together. She has a wealthy Swiss father and a Scottish mother. Their main home is somewhere on the banks of Lake Geneva, but they also have a sumptuous chalet where Orla is staying. I see now what a privileged life Orla has led. She went to an international school where the winter sport was skiing, and the summer sport was tennis or wind-surfing on the lake. After a stint at Oxford Brookes University, where she says she became an expert in partying but regressed in studying, she returned to Switzerland, working on and off for her father's business – something in private banking, before relocating to his office in London. I'm not really sure what Orla does. She drifts into the office in London as and when she likes and hops back to Switzerland whenever the snow conditions are good, or in this instance, to enable her to spend some clandestine time with me. It's not like she has a job.

Helen is a beginner skier, which, as selfish as it makes me sound, is ideal, as she and I don't spend the days together. I was fortunate enough to spend most February half-terms skiing with my family, so I'm good at it, competent enough to keep up with Orla, albeit with none of her style.

We're careful not to enter the restaurant on the slopes together, and at lunch, Orla joins her friends while I meet up with Helen. After lunch, we both make our excuses and join up for a quick ski down to the village. We hurry to her parents' chalet – where she's the only person staying – and we make love until I need to go back to Helen and the grimy hotel room.

It's 2 pm on day three of our trip, and Orla and I are on a chairlift, ascending to the top of a particularly challenging black slope. The sky is heavy and low, overcast with thick white-grey clouds, and the light makes it difficult to see the contours of the slope. I fell earlier, and Orla laughed at me.

'You're in a bad mood,' she says, nudging me with her elbow. She's wearing a white ski jacket with fur around the collar and cuffs. I assume it's real fur.

'I'm okay.'

'Don't lie to me. I know you.'

I sigh. 'I had a massive argument with Helen this morning.'

Orla smiles. 'Did you tell her?'

'Yes. No. Sort of.' I look away from her and shiver as the cold, raw air swathes my exposed face.

'What happened?'

'I told her I wasn't happy in our marriage.'

Orla inhales audibly. I don't need to look at her to know that she'll be grinning broadly.

'And?'

'One step at a time,' I say. What I can't tell Orla is the truth. Her heart will shatter into smithereens if she finds out that Helen might be pregnant. It ruins everything because how can I leave my wife if she's really carrying our baby? It's one thing hurting her, quite another destroying the innocent life of my unborn child. I know Helen wants children, and I did too, at the beginning at least. But now I'm not sure. Having children will be such a financial burden and will stop any impulsivity. It will also make it that much harder for me to spend time with Orla. I groan inwardly because I know that if I stay with Helen and we have a baby, I can't continue this affair with Orla. Yet I simply can't imagine my life without her.

I didn't behave well this morning, but it was such a terrible shock. I can't even remember the last time I had sex with Helen, and it simply never crossed my mind that she might fall pregnant. Now I'm totally stuck. All I can do is pray that Helen is wrong, because if she really is carrying a child, it feels as if my life might be over. I can't leave Orla. I just can't. She's my addiction, and I'm infatuated with everything about her. Our thighs are pressed up against each other, and despite the many layers of clothing, I can smell her perfume, and I feel an overwhelming pride that this beautiful woman has chosen me to be her partner.

But Orla shifts away from me.

'What is it?' I ask, alarmed.

'I'm fed up. Actually I'm more than fed up, Paul. I've had enough of being patient, enough of sharing you. You tell me you love me, but you're still with her. I'm going to be thirty soon, and I don't want to waste any more years on you. It's make or break. If you haven't finished with Helen by the end of this week, then it's all over between us.'

'No,' I say, grabbing her arm. 'I love you, Orla.' The thick gloves make it difficult to hold her, and for a moment, I fear I'm going to drop my ski sticks into the whiteness below. We sit in silence for a while, and then when we're approaching the end of the lift, Orla lifts up the bar carelessly. The whole chair jolts violently. She's like that sometimes – volatile and insensitive – but I still love her. Helen would never do anything as stupid or impulsive.

Orla is off the lift even before her skis touch the snow. She's propelling herself forwards with her sticks, leaning into them, pushing her skis away from herself.

'Wait!' I yell, but my voice is lost in the ever-increasing wind.

I catch up with Orla and try to grab her. 'It's your choice, Paul!' she says as she skis away again, out of my grasp. I watch as she points her skis straight down the slope and propels herself, much like ski racers do at the start of a race. I have to hurry myself; otherwise I'll lose her. Orla knows these slopes like the back of her hand; I don't. She's too fast, disappearing over the horizon, her legs bent, her neat backside in the air. I'm a good skier, but I have to carve left and right. My legs simply wouldn't be strong enough for me to go straight downhill.

There's a swirling of snow on the right-hand side of the slope, and then I see Orla further down. I'm going fast myself, too fast to stop, and it's only when I've skied past that I realise there was a person lying crumpled in the snow. By the time I can stop, I'm many metres below the person, and I can see that Orla has also stopped, about fifty metres below me. She's waving her sticks at me.

'Come on!' she yells, her voice faint in the wind. We all make split-second decisions every minute of the day, but we never fully appreciate the consequence of those decisions until it's too late. I carry on skiing, desperate to pacify Orla. I know what she's like when she's in a mood like this: she's reckless, carefree and a little crazy. It's like the time she took a nude selfie and pretended she'd sent the picture to Helen. I was beside myself. Then she started laughing hysterically when she told me she'd sent it to herself instead. There's an edge to Orla, one I'm never quite sure about, but that's what makes her exciting.

'What happened up there?' I ask as I reach her side. The slopes are deserted now the weather is taking a turn for the worse.

'I skied into that idiot girl. Why don't people look where they're going? I mean, the whole slope was empty, but she just cut me off. Stupid cow.'

'You didn't stop,' I say, feeling a bit sick.

'It's fine. We'd both be hurt if there was a problem. Come on, let's get going before the snow comes down heavily. I know what you're like, you wuss.'

'Are you sure she's okay?' I turn to look up the slope, but I'm too low down here, and I can't see her. And then I swing around to speak to Orla, but she's gone, skiing straight down the centre of the piste.

'Shit,' I mutter under my breath. I glance up the piste again, but there's no one coming, so instead I turn around, push myself away and follow Orla.

WE REACH the bottom of the slopes a few minutes later. I'm out of breath and hot, despite the worsening weather. It's hard keeping up with Orla, especially when she's in a mood like today.

'Right, time for drinks,' she says, removing her helmet and unclipping her skis. 'I've agreed with Gaby and the others to meet at Bar Coquette. You can join us.' She fixes those dark eyes onto mine and runs a finger down my cheek, as if our earlier argument has been forgotten.

'Sure,' I say. I've avoided them previously just because it seemed risky. And yes, it's dangerous, me and Orla being around mutual friends, but I don't think Orla will do anything impetuous.

'You promise me you won't do or say anything stupid?' I ask her, my face just centimetres from hers. 'I swear you'll have your answer by the end of the week.'

'Really?' she says, her lips parted and her eyes bright.

'Really.' I smile, but I'm not convinced I'm telling the truth.

Orla's family rent a locker in the basement of the ski station so they don't have to lug their skis back to their chalet, so I follow her down the metal steps and into the concrete basement that smells of sweat and wet dog.

'Do you want to leave your gear here for now?' she asks. I nod. I'll collect it later and take it back to the hotel. I don't want Helen asking questions about where I've dumped my skis.

'Kiss me,' she says, lacing her fingers behind my head.

'Not here!' I whisper, glancing around, but we're all alone. Even so, the risk is too great. Orla has friends here. Gaby, our mutual friend, is skiing in the resort too, and what if Helen decides to come down here right now, not that that's likely?

'If you don't kiss me, it's all over,' she says, her eyes flashing. I know she doesn't mean it. This is just one of Orla's childish games, yet it makes me feel alive. So I kiss her. I pin her up against the bare concrete wall, and I kiss her with a ferocity that even takes me aback. When a door slams, we pull apart, grinning at each other.

We walk side by side, trudging through the blackened slush that's been trodden into the pavement by tired skiers who have walked this path before us, and I try not to think of Helen all alone in our hotel room, my wife who might be pregnant.

The noise of drinkers assaults me as we walk into Bar Coquette. It's packed full of rosy-cheeked people, a little too raucous, sharing their skiing adventures and misfortunes, or braying about the latest deals they've closed. The room is wood panelled, which makes it dark and somewhat oppressive, not helped by the heat – such a contrast to the outside. I follow Orla as she weaves through the tables to the bar, which is already three deep. Gaby is waving from the rear of the room. Orla waves back.

'How's Helen?' Gaby asks as we pull stools over to sit with Gaby and her friends.

'She's good. Finds the skiing a bit tough. This is only her second trip, and she's really exhausted. She sends her apologies,' I lie. I know there's a risk that Gaby might run into Helen and say how sorry she was that Helen couldn't join in the drinks. I'll just be honest with Helen – as honest as I can be – and explain I was still too annoyed with her after our argument to invite her to join us. I take a long sip of beer and try to relax into my chair.

Three beers later, Orla stands up. 'Right, anyone coming to mine for supper? We can pick up pizza on our way back.' Gaby and her friends finish up their drinks and start piling their ski clothes back on, but I just sit there, staring into my almost finished beer.

'You coming too, or do you have to get back to your wife?' Orla asks. Her eyes are narrowed at me.

'Helen is expecting me for supper,' I say, refusing to meet her gaze. And then they're gone. I know I should get up too and go back to the hotel, but I simply can't move.

'Are these chairs being used?' a young woman asks me.

'You can have the table,' I say, grabbing my anorak, gloves, and hat. But I don't head towards the door, and move to the bar instead, where I find a stool at the far end. I order another beer, followed by a whisky, staring into my drinks, hoping for a magical solution to the problems of my heart.

Then I overhear the first conversation. 'It's tragic. I mean,

you don't think you're going to go skiing and die, do you?
Poor girl.'

'Apparently, she was only fifteen. A kid with her whole
life in front of her.'

'Someone said that some shit skied into her and then
skied away. Like a hit-and-run. I mean, that's manslaughter,
isn't it?'

Perhaps it's the alcohol, but my brain doesn't put two and
two together immediately. It's not until a couple of policemen
walk into La Coquette and stride up to the bar, speaking
rapidly in French to the barman, that I gasp, almost choking
on the last sip of whisky.

'You alright, mate?' A British twenty-something on the
adjacent table leans over and half-heartedly pats me on the
back.

'Fine,' I splutter, trying to get the coughing under control.
*A skier died today. A young girl. Someone skied into her and then
skied away.* I remember racing down after Orla, seeing
someone crumpled in the snow. I recall Orla saying she was
fine, so the person she skied into must be too. But what if
Orla was wrong? What if it was my lover who skied into the
girl and killed her? And what if I'm complicit too because I
skied right past her?

I order another double, but then my phone pings with an
incoming text from Helen.

*Are you on your way back; otherwise we'll miss last
orders.*

I swear under my breath, knock back the whisky and
head out of the bar towards the hotel.

13

HELEN – NOW

Emily throws herself at me. 'Mummy! Mummy!' she screeches.

'Welcome to the mountains, munchkin,' I say, hugging her tightly. Andrew leans across and places a kiss on my lips.

'Beautiful setting,' he says, 'but this place...'

'It's temporary accommodation, and honestly I've been fine here. Saskia has loaned me a camp bed, which Emily can sleep on. We'll be alright.'

'You need to show us around.'

I walk Andrew around the chalet, which is looking increasingly like a finished house. Emily trails behind us, talking to her teddy.

'Wouldn't mind living somewhere like this,' Andrew says, leaning his elbows on the windowsill and gazing at the expansive view. 'Not so good if you get vertigo, though.'

'I'm so happy you're here,' I say, putting my arms around him.

'Me too. I miss you when you're not at home,' Andrew says, squeezing me tightly.

. . .

I'VE BOOKED us in for an early supper in one of the restaurants in the village and have pre-ordered a fondue Chinoise for Andrew and myself. Despite going on an airplane for just the second time in her life, Emily is still buzzing with energy. I suggest we walk into the village via the Bisse.

'Can I go in it?' Emily asks as she stands watching the fast-flowing stream.

'No, it's freezing cold water that's come from high up the mountain,' I say.

Andrew finds her a little stick and jams it in a large leaf. 'Do you want to launch your yacht?' he asks Emily, handing it to her.

That's why I love this man. You'd never know that Emily wasn't his own child. He's always looking out for her, acting the perfect father, filling the role I thought Paul would assume.

'Helen!'

I turn around, and Guillaume and Manon are strolling arm in arm towards us.

'This delightful little girl must be your daughter,' Manon says, unlinking herself from her husband and bending down to speak to Emily.

I do the introductions. The men shake hands and immediately engage in conversation.

'We're just off for a fondue,' I explain to Manon.

'We're going in the same direction. Let's walk together.'

We stroll along, with Emily running ahead of us and Guillaume and Andrew deep in conversation bringing up the rear.

. . .

'NICE NEIGHBOURS,' Andrew says as we wave goodbye to them outside the restaurant.

'Yes. They've been very kind to me.'

At the restaurant we're the only guests because it's so early, just gone 6 pm. I order Emily spaghetti bolognaise, and the waiter brings over salads for Andrew and me.

'Is that a witch's cauldron?' Emily asks, staring at the bubbling bowl of broth sitting on top of an open flame.

'No.' I laugh. 'It's for cooking finely sliced meat.'

Emily turns up her nose, and Andrew chuckles.

Over the meal, we talk about the renovation project and witter on about nothing in particular, but there's the unspoken issue of my imaginary sighting of Paul, and I can sense Andrew's eyes on me when I'm not looking at him, and that edge of concern he has. It isn't until much later, when Emily is asleep and I'm lying in his arms in bed, that he broaches the subject that I know has been playing on his mind.

'How are you feeling about being here?' he asks.

'A bit more relaxed than I was when I first arrived.'

'No more sightings of the ghost?'

'Ha ha,' I say.

I've tried not to think about the man at the Inalpe festival who walked like Paul. I haven't seen him again, and I know it was my mind playing tricks. Even so, just by mentioning it, Andrew's stirred something up.

'You're under a lot of stress at the moment,' Andrew says, stroking my hair. 'It's understandable that you're going to be fearing the worst.'

I tense because it's not like Andrew to suggest that I'm imagining things, yet it seems that's exactly what he's suggesting. It's strange because Paul reappearing just hasn't been a consideration since I met Andrew. I wonder what the implications might be if he really was alive. I suppose he'd want to see Emily more often, but it wouldn't change anything regarding my relationship with Andrew. We'd still get married; in fact, we could marry as soon as the divorce comes through. He nuzzles my neck, and I whisper, 'You're right, it was my imagination.' Andrew makes love to me as gently and quietly as possible, conscious that Emily is fast asleep downstairs in this open-plan space. Afterwards, I lie there unable to sleep, remembering how Andrew and I met.

It was my first interior design project working at the tail end of an extension project that involved a new bedroom and en suite upstairs and a study downstairs. As far as I was concerned, I had done my bit. The client was thrilled with the fresh colour schemes and had invited me over for a drink on the day they were to be signed off by building control. What I hadn't expected was to be there while the building control officer was visiting. He was an attractive man, about my age with sandy blond hair and twinkling green eyes. There was something about him that made me smile back when he grinned at me. Unfortunately, there were no smiles a few minutes later when he got out his tape measure and told the house owner that the staircase didn't have sufficient head height and consequently the extension would fail to meet building control standards. She went apoplectic, raging about the architect, the builders and even trying to direct the blame on me. The officer came to my assistance when I exclaimed I was only the interior designer. He calmed her down and got the construction firm boss on the phone, who confirmed he'd come over to make good the next day.

The following evening I was playing in the park with Emily when I saw the building control officer walking a Labrador. I don't know why, but I waved at him, and he strode towards us, that warm smile on his face. Emily threw her arms around his dog, and we got chatting. It turned out that he was caring for his parents' dog, but he lived on the other side of town. He asked me out for a drink. It was only after I'd said yes and he walked away with a spring in his step that I regretted saying yes. There was no way I was ready to date again; besides I wasn't even in a position to do so. My husband might or might not be dead, but I wouldn't be free for another four years. I was a married woman, grieving. And there was Emily. She and I talked a lot about Paul, and I certainly didn't want to confuse her upbringing by introducing another man.

It was my sister, Kelly, who insisted I go on the date. 'What's the harm?' she asked. 'You deserve a good time.'

'I'm not sure.'

'You're never going to be sure, sis. What's the worst that could happen? You'll think he's a prat and never see him again, or perhaps it'll go really well and you'll have the time of your life. If you don't try, you won't know.'

I groaned and agreed to go. Even so, Kelly didn't trust me. She insisted on babysitting and oversaw my preparations for going out, persuading me to wear a dress rather than my normal skinny jeans.

The problem was, we had a lovely first date. And second. And third. It was all going too well, and I got scared. On our fourth date, I told Andrew that I couldn't see him again, but he wasn't going to let me go.

'What's the real problem?' he asked tenderly.

'I'm still married.'

Andrew raised an eyebrow, but he didn't hotfoot it out of the restaurant. 'I assume you're not still living with your husband?'

'He's presumed dead,' I said. I'd given up trying to sugarcoat my reply to the Paul question over the years.

Andrew just sat there and held my hands. Before I knew

it, I had told him everything about Paul's disappearance, and then he knew as much as Kelly.

'I'm so sorry, Helen,' he said. 'I totally understand why dating must feel so weird.'

I felt that I wasn't worthy of a relationship, certainly not with someone as caring as Andrew. I'd goaded a man over the edge once before. Paul's death might well have been my fault, pushing him so hard that he felt he had zero choice but to take his own life. But Andrew isn't Paul. Our relationship progressed slowly, led by me. Andrew never pressed me, never asked for more than I could give; he just listened and held me. He is strong and steadfast.

Andrew has healed so much for me. I trust again, and I never thought I would. Yes, I'm fearful, much more so than I was before, but perhaps that's mainly to do with being a mother.

I might adore the views, but our memories of a place can influence so much. Too much has happened here for me to truly relax. I don't buy into the saying that lightning never strikes twice. If something has happened before, it can happen again. I can't imagine Emily or Andrew disappearing on this mountainside, but other bad things can happen here.

Later, when I'm lying in Andrew's arms, he says, 'I've been thinking. You mentioned that there's a memorial plaque in the lift station near where Paul disappeared. Have you ever visited it?'

I shiver. 'No.'

'I wonder whether it might be a good thing if you did. It could be cathartic. I could go with you if you'd like.'

'No,' I say firmly. 'No.' I can't think of anything I want to do less. I have never had any desire to see the plaque or, as my doctor had recommended five years ago, visit the spot where Paul fell to his death.

'Think about it,' he whispers before kissing my cheek and

turning over. I listen to Andrew's regular, light breathing for a while, and then I gently climb out of bed and, with the light of my phone, tiptoe down the stairs. I stand over Emily like I used to do when she was a baby and hold the back of my hand above her nose. She's breathing. I stroke her hair, kiss her gently on the forehead and tiptoe back upstairs to bed.

14

PAUL – THEN

All the drinking made me late for supper. By the time we were sitting in the hotel restaurant – a cave-like basement painted in white – Helen looked livid, and I was too tired and drunk to make conversation. Actually, I wanted nothing more than to be fast asleep in bed, preferably with Orla, not Helen. My wife went on and on at me, especially after some other diners talked about the girl's death on the slopes. Eventually, I couldn't stand it anymore. I made a scene, but that's just the way it was. I marched out of the dining room. We barely spoke to each other and were still on no-speaking terms the next morning. She went off for her lesson, and I took the lift straight to the glacier and met up with Orla.

Today, Orla's wearing a different outfit – a canary yellow one-piece that would look garish on anybody else but looks chic on her.

'What's going on with all the police?' she whispers to me. There are indeed gendarmes and officials everywhere. I'm surprised she doesn't know.

I don't answer her. 'Shall we ski off-piste today?' I ask.

She frowns at me. 'The weather is crap; of course we can't ski off-piste. You haven't got a clue, have you?'

A policeman walks up to a skier standing next to us who is adjusting his webcam on top of his helmet.

'Excuse me, sir, but were you skiing on the Bleuweiss slope yesterday morning?'

'No, I haven't skied over there in a couple of days. Was thinking about trekking up there later. What's up?'

'We're investigating the death of a young girl yesterday. It's believed someone skied into her and skied off.'

'Goodness,' the man says, a look of horror on his face. 'You're welcome to check out my footage if you want.'

'That won't be necessary, but thank you for your assistance.' The policeman nods.

I turn to Orla and whisper in her ear, 'We need to talk. Start walking now.'

For a woman who spends most of her time joking, Orla looks terrified. She nods at me, her eyes wide. 'Let's take the chairlift. Make sure no one else gets on it. Just follow me.'

I glance back at the policeman, who walks over to another cluster of skiers attaching their skis to their boots.

We queue up for the lift in silence, letting other people through onto the six-person chairlift until it's just the two of us standing side by side, waiting for the next chair.

Once we've risen into the air, without another person in sight, I turn to Orla. 'They're looking for the person who skied into the girl, killed her and fled the scene. That was you, Orla, wasn't it?'

She stares at me, her eyes watery. She looks so small and vulnerable. I never thought Orla could be vulnerable, but now I realise that her outrageous behaviour is a front, that fake bravado just an armour. Orla needs me.

'The police are looking everywhere, studying webcams at

the lifts, asking people for their mobile phone footage. You're not going to get away with this, Orla,' I say softly.

She is still for a moment, and then she turns towards me. 'I'm going to have to disappear. I want you to come with me.'

'What?' I exclaim. 'No, that's ridiculous. It was an accident, and there's no way I can just disappear.'

Orla's eyes harden. 'It's crunch time, Paul. Crunch time for our relationship and how you really feel about me. You need to choose Helen or me, right now, today. If you choose me, we'll go off to Australia and live off my trust fund. I've talked about travelling for ages, so no one will be surprised or suspicious. The only thing that's stopped me from taking off is you. I couldn't bear to be away from you for any length of time. So this is the perfect opportunity. You and me having a wonderful time on the other side of the world.'

'I can't!' I whisper, but even so, I'm imagining Orla and me together, being free in a beautiful country where I speak the language and where the sun shines. Then I imagine being at home, Helen looking bedraggled as she tries to care for a screaming baby. She's yelling at me to get some milk or some new nappies or whatever, and I know I don't want to be there.

'You have to choose, Paul. And remember, you were on that slope yesterday morning too. We are both as guilty as each other.'

I open my mouth to protest, but what's the point? I was there, and I also didn't stop to help. We were both guilty. No, we are both guilty.

Orla is looking at me intently, her lips flat and straight, her eyes holding my gaze, questioning and waiting. It's now or never.

'I'm choosing you,' I say, the words catching in my throat.

Orla throws her arms around my neck, and the chairlift wobbles violently. She places repeated kisses on my lips and mutters, 'You and I will have the most wonderful life together.'

And then we're at the end of the lift, and as Orla is tightening her bindings, she overhears a couple talking. Orla freezes, then hurriedly slips her boots into her skis.

'We need to go now,' she says, pushing herself off from the top of the slope. I hurtle down the piste after her and am relieved she's waiting for me at the side of the piste not far away.

'It was Noemie Moser.'

'Sorry?'

'The girl who died was Noemie Moser. I used to babysit her, Paul! I know her. This is terrible!'

'No one knows it was you.' I grasp Orla's shoulders and blow condensed air into her face. 'You need to stay calm. The best thing is for you to admit you skied into Noemie, that it was a terrible accident, and you had no idea that she was fatally injured. I'm sure they'll look kindly on you.'

'No. That's not how it's going to be, Paul. Don't say a word about this to me or anyone,' she says, pushing away from me. 'I need to think things through.' And then she's off again.

We ski hard for the next few hours, and Orla refuses to talk about the girl's death or the role she played in it. All she does is express how happy she is that I've chosen her and that we'll have a wonderful life together. Perhaps we'll set up a restaurant where I can be the head chef, and she'll entertain the famous guests, or we could have a hotel even, somewhere with a view to the Sydney Opera House. I can't imagine going to Australia let alone setting up a life there, so I say nothing. I'm just relieved that Orla is being her tactile, loving self, and I try to dismiss all the concerns. Suddenly she announces that she needs to get back to the chalet, and I should ski down by myself, and that she may or may not see me later. I worry. Really worry. What if Orla hands herself in before saying goodbye to me, or worse, she disappears. From what she says, it sounds like she has a lot of money. Perhaps she will hire a private jet to get her out of the country, and I might never see her again.

I make my way back to the hotel in a foul mood. I'm worried about Orla, worried about Helen being pregnant and feel like I'm stuck in a vortex, not knowing how to pull myself out of it. My heart and my head are saying such different things.

I walk past a row of bars, and for a moment, I hesitate outside one I haven't visited before. I'm very tempted to go in and have a drink.

'*Vous parlez Francais?*' I jump as a policeman accosts me from behind.

'Not really. I'm English,' I say unnecessarily.

'We are asking everyone, were you skiing yesterday?'

'Um, yes.'

'You're aware of the death of the girl?'

'Yes, it's terrible.'

'Can you tell me where you were skiing between 2 and 4 pm?'

'Um, no, not really. I skied lots of different slopes.'

'Are you a good skier?'

'Reasonably,' I say, wondering why he's asking me that.

'Because the conditions were difficult yesterday. Very challenging.'

'I am a good skier. I've been skiing all my life.' A voice in my head yells at me to shut up.

'Did you see an accident?'

I try to hold the man's gaze, which is difficult because the snow is swirling in my face. 'No, I'm sorry, but I saw nothing. The conditions were bad.'

He narrows his eyes at me, and I wonder for a horrific moment if he can mind read. Then he steps into the doorway, removes his gloves and pulls a small notebook and pen out of his pocket. 'Please, what is your name and telephone number?'

I give him my name, but I change the last two digits of my phone number.

'Thank you, sir,' he says before pushing the door of the bar open and disappearing inside.

Why the hell did I give him a wrong number? That's going to make me look suspicious. I'm such an idiot. I groan as I stomp back to the hotel, any thought of a drink forgotten.

HELEN and I have a terrible argument, which I suppose was inevitable. What makes it worse is it's as if she can read my thoughts. She pushes and needles, asking if it was me who skied into that girl. How could she think I would do that? Surely she knows me better. Yes, I appreciate that I'm judging my behaviour with a different standard to Orla, but Orla is a free spirit. I'm not. If I'd skied into that girl, of course I would have stopped to help. In a perverse way, I'm glad we fight because it makes it easier for me to walk out, to announce I'm off to have a drink, without her. Outside the hotel, I message Orla and ask if we can meet up. To my relief, she responds immediately and suggests I go to her parents' chalet, but first, to make sure I'm not being followed. She makes it sound so clandestine, exciting even, which is ridiculous and just shows how banal my life has become.

I follow Orla's instructions, and I'm not followed, partially because the weather has taken a turn for the worse, and it's snowing heavily. The chalet is huge, with three storeys and lights that throw shadows across the snowy ground. I ring the doorbell, and the door swings open immediately. Orla grabs my arm, pulling me inside. I try to kiss her, but she darts away, telling me to take off my boots. I walk in socked feet into the vast living room. There's a glass cubed fire in the centre of the room and several large, comfy sofas.

'Sit down,' she says, patting the sofa next to her. I'm hoping she'll offer me a drink, but she doesn't. 'Right, here's the plan.'

I stare at the woman I love. I am staggered that she's so resourceful, conniving even, and for a moment I hesitate. Am I that person? Can I really go through with this? But then Orla makes her move on me, and yes, I'm weak. My body yields to her touch, and I just have to have her, my drug. She makes me feel alive, on fire, and I love her.

I RETURN to the hotel even though Orla begs me to stay the night. I need to see Helen one last time. It doesn't go to plan. She goes on and on, asking me if I had something to do with the girl's death, then pushing me to talk about the problems in our marriage. We have another terrible argument, and I know I can't say anything, not now. So I tell her I'm tired and pretend to sleep, but I lie awake most of the night, trying to imagine whether Orla's plan will work, and if it doesn't, what the consequences will be.

The next morning, Helen tells me she's pregnant. Yes, she thought she might be pregnant a couple of days ago, but now she's shown me the pregnancy stick, and it's a certainty. It feels as if my world has just splintered into a million little shards. She screams at me. I scream at her. And then I leave, and it's a relief. There. I've said it out loud. It's a relief.

As I sit alone in the cable car, I reason to myself. Helen is a good person. She'll find someone else and lead a much happier life with him. Perhaps she's faked the pregnancy test and is just saying she's pregnant to persuade me to stay with her. That happened to a mate at work. He married his girl-friend only for her to magically lose the baby some months later. I groan. I've become so cynical. But Helen is stronger than she thinks, and my future lies with Orla. In a very perverse sort of way, perhaps that girl's accident was meant to be. I feel bad about it of course, as I'm sure Orla does, but it's forced me to make my choice, and I've chosen Orla. I'm going to have a life of fun with no money troubles, amazing sex and new adventures. Helen will get everything: our house, my paltry savings, my pension. Even if she has a child, she'll be alright. I just know she will.

15

PAUL – THEN

When I reach the top of the ski lift, I see that quite a few of the lifts further up are closed. It's no surprise. The weather is shocking with a howling wind that's whipping the snow up and making visibility dreadful. Most sensible people will be staying in bed today or drinking glühwien in the resort's bars. I've got layers of thermals and waterproofs on, but still I'm cold, my eyes smarting from the freezing weather. The scarf I've wrapped around my nose and mouth is damp and unpleasant as I inhale minuscule fibres.

Orla waves a stick at me; at least I assume it's her, as the conditions are making her form hard to decipher. I push myself on my skis towards her. She's wearing all white again today, which camouflages her. I assume that was intentional.

'You ready?' she asks. Her words are whisked away by the gale. I nod. She takes her phone out of her pocket and switches it off. I don't need to ask why. She's making sure there'll be no record of her on this mountainside.

'We're going to ski for a bit until the conditions get worse,' she says.

'How do you know they will?'

'There's an amazing weather app that shows you exactly when storms will take place and how quickly the wind will whip up. We've got two hours to kill.'

I nod.

As it turns out, the conditions worsen faster than Orla anticipated, and the slopes are deserted.

'Right, let's do it.'

I recall what Orla told me yesterday.

'My family own an alpine hut. It's where the farmers used to stay in the summers when their cattle were grazing up the mountainside. Dad got it converted years ago, and hardly anyone uses it. It's basically one bedroom and a living area with no mains electricity. Lovely in the summer if you like being cut off in the middle of nowhere but impossible in the winter. It's shut up in the winter, with the shutters closed and taps off, then opened up when the snow has melted, normally in May. You can stay there.'

I look at her in horror.

'Just for two or three days while I get things sorted.'

And now she's going to show it to me for the first time, a 'recce' as she called it. 'Ready?' she asks. I marvel at how Orla can read these mountains even when the visibility is so bad we can barely make each other out in the freezing fog. We take a T-bar upwards, then cut across the mountainside, skiing off-piste between trees and rocks. I stumble a couple of times, but Orla waits for me. Whereas normally she might laugh at my clumsiness, today she's patient and careful.

'It's the second chalet along,' she says as we stand in the shadow of trees, their branches weighed down by inches of fresh snow.

I can barely make out the building, it's so well covered with snow, almost merging into the white hillside.

'I've left some stuff in there for you and turned the taps

on, but you need to make sure they don't freeze up. Are you ready?'

This is the turning point, the point of no return. Right now I could ski away from Orla, straight back to the hotel room, sweep Helen up and tell her I'm thrilled she's pregnant. Or I can accept that I will never see my wife again, that my old life is over and I'm about to embark on a new chapter. I wonder what they'll think at work, whether they'll miss me. I doubt it. I think of my parents, who might have to go on television alongside Helen, urging people to keep a lookout for me. They'll be stoic, maintaining that British stiff upper lip, but what will they be thinking, really?

'Paul?'

'Yes, sorry,' I say. I wriggle my toes inside my ski boots because they're cold and tingly.

'Are you ready?'

She doesn't wait for an answer but pushes herself away, quickly skiing into the murky fog. I have no choice but to follow her. We ski closely together, seeing no one except a ski instructor, his red jacket flashing past us as he skis downwards. We're at the bottom of a two-seater chairlift, about to get on it, when the lift operator waves at us.

He speaks rapidly in French with Orla; her replies lead to a heated exchange at the end of which he shrugs his shoulders dramatically and waves us forwards.

'What was all that about?'

'He wants to close the lift because it's too windy. I had to persuade him not to; otherwise we'd have to walk all the way up the piste.'

I don't say anything, but that conversation worries me. What if the lift attendant remembers seeing us? But then I rationalise. We're both wearing helmets and yellow ski goggles with our noses and mouths covered with fabric. I would defy anyone to recognise us. The chair swings from side to side, making my stomach lurch. It crosses my mind that we might actually die up here on the mountainside and how very ironic that would be, yet no one would be aware of the great irony. Orla leans into me and at one point lays her head on my shoulder. Is this the beginning of our great new adventure or the beginning of the end?

Eventually we get to the top of the lift, and I'm relieved to be off it. It was almost scary the way we were swinging from side to side in the gale. My nose feels as if it's going to drop off, and my fingers are so frozen they're hurting.

'Follow me,' Orla says.

We push ourselves across the mountainside about a hundred metres, and then Orla stops and looks around. She needn't worry. The place is deserted and the snow so heavy it's like someone is shaking out a feather duvet right in front of our noses.

'It's here behind that rock.'

If Orla hadn't pointed it out, I wouldn't have noticed the ten-foot rock. It's just white like everything else here. 'Follow me and be careful,' she says.

She edges forwards, and I keep within her ski tracks, then she disappears around the far side of the rock. I see a few black poles poking up out of the snow and orange netting attached to them, the universal warning sign that there is danger beyond. As I edge around the rock, I glance downwards and gasp. It's hard to make out in these terrible conditions, and although I can't see it properly, I can sense the sheer drop. I lean backwards into the snow-covered rock face.

'What's down there?' I ask.

'Rocks, more rocks, forest. God knows; it's a drop of a thousand metres or so. Anyone who falls here wouldn't survive and would probably be lost for ever. It's inaccessible. Come away from the edge and take your skis off.'

My hands are trembling, and it takes me a couple of

attempts to jam my ski pole into the bindings to release my feet. Orla removes the big rucksack from her back and takes out a pair of ski shoes. Looking at them makes me feel sick. She places them on the ground next to us. They're strange-looking contraptions made from blue and black plastic pieces with buckles to strap around boots. Orla leans down and picks up one of my skis. She lifts it up and, without saying a word, hurls the ski off the side of the mountain. I hold my breath waiting to hear it land, striking the rocks below us, but I hear nothing. Not even a faint thud.

I know now that it's too late. I have committed to a future with Orla.

She takes my second ski and wedges it at a strange angle into the snow.

'Give me your phone,' she says, holding out her white-mittened hands. She's also unclipped her skis.

'What?'

I hesitate, but I know Orla's right. This is the funeral of my old life. I struggle to remove the phone from my pocket, my fingers barely able to move. Once again, Orla is surprisingly patient, almost military in her precision planning, glancing at her watch, double-checking her own phone is still off. I hand her my iPhone.

She takes it from me and switches it off, then drops it onto the snow. She stamps on it with her right ski boot, over and over again, squashing it further into the snow, her right foot now considerably deeper in the snow than her left. Only when she's certain it's smashed up and sufficiently broken does she pick it up and inspect it. The glass front is splintered, making the screen illegible. Then she raises her arm and hurls the phone in the same direction as the ski. All I can think is that I don't even know Helen's mobile number off by heart. My life is stored on that phone, and now my old life is over.

Orla lifts up her skis and, using a little key, adjusts the bindings. 'Try this on for size,' she says, thrusting one ski at me. It amazes me how she's so dexterous in these horrendous conditions, the snow still falling heavily, gusts of wind swirling up clouds of snow, obliterating everything. I step on the ski and push my heel downwards. It clicks into place. She repeats the same with the other ski, and I hand her the snowshoes.

'Can you remember how to get to the cabin?' she asks.

I nod and just pray that the visibility doesn't worsen; otherwise I really may die on this mountain. 'And you, will you be alright?' I ask. She steps towards me, and I envelop her in a hug. Her body warmth reminds me why we're doing this.

'Yes. I know where I'm going, and I've left the snow scooter a bit lower down. I use it all the time, so no one will be suspicious. Honestly, Paul, we're blessed with this weather. The snow will cover up your ski tracks and my footprints in no time. Stay put in the cabin. I've left plenty of food and water, but under no circumstances open the shutters or walk out, and don't light the fire.'

'Stop worrying,' I say, squeezing her tightly. 'I know my instructions.'

'I'll come and get you as soon as I can,' she says. 'Stay inside and stay safe.'

'And you too, darling.'

'I'm so happy, Paul. We're together now. Just you and me against the world, and soon we'll be somewhere hot, having the time of our lives.'

My heart is thudding because this is it. I have made my decision, and I will have to live with the consequences. I'm not stupid. I know what I'm doing, and I keep reminding myself that it's for Orla and me, for a much better future. She pulls away from me.

'Go now,' she says, giving me a slight push. And so I do. I ski down the slope exactly as we practised earlier, and when I see the second pylon of the chairlift, I slow right down, slipping into the forest where we were before. Our tracks are gone now, exactly as Orla predicted. But I'm nervous in the forest. The wind is howling now and the trees creaking. A large section of snow comes loose from a branch and lands just centimetres in front of me. I feel nauseous with terror, a maelstrom of emotions gripping my stomach. I force myself to carry on. When I emerge on the other side, I stay hidden in the trees for several long moments, just to be absolutely sure there's no sign of life, but if visibility was bad before, now it's terrible. I have no choice but to ease myself out of the forest canopy and into the open area, passing the first small cabin. I push myself forwards, sweat gathering on my torso despite the freezing conditions. Orla's cabin is exactly where it was before, but this time I have to let myself in. There's an overhanging area by the back door where a snow shovel is partly covered by snow. I take off Orla's skis and use the shovel to make a clearing so that I can open the door. When the snow is sufficiently cleared, I turn the handle. It's unlocked and opens easily. I slip inside, grabbing my skis and placing them just inside the door, out of view. It's cold and gloomy in here despite it being a wooden cabin. The shutters are closed, and the flat daylight is only coming in through a small window at the side and the large triangular window in the front of the cabin, high up in the roof apex. I take off my ski boots and walk in socked feet into the middle of the space. Orla has done exactly as she promised.

There are two gas fires and several canisters of Calor Gas. I wonder how long each will last and shiver at the thought. I turn both fires on, knowing that I have to get this place warm enough to survive in but not too warm to melt the snow on the roof. It'll be a fine balance. Now I look around. It's basically a large wooden box with a daybed covered in rugs and cushions up against one wall, a sink, hob and under-counter fridge on the back wall, a wooden table and four chairs and two comfy-looking armchairs. At first glance, I can't see a bathroom. I walk to the far wall, and hidden in the darkness is a door. I open it, and there's a toilet and sink but no shower. I remember then that Orla said it had an outdoor shower, which wasn't operational in the winter. I'm going to have to wash in the sink. I turn the tap on, but only a few drops of freezing water come out.

I walk over to the table, where Orla has left me two crates and a typed-out note. The note gives me a long list of instructions as to what I can and can't do. The worst is no hot water for the duration. The only hot water I can have is what I can boil on the stove. The very last point is: Burn this piece of paper. Leave all your rubbish in one of the boxes, and I'll collect it. Use candles only. Make sure you're not seen.

I look in the fridge and see that she's left me some eggs, milk and a couple of carrots – hardly enough to sustain me, but in the cupboard there are numerous cans of food: soups, sauces to add to pasta, and plenty of dried goods like rice, pasta, cereal and bread. I'll survive; for how long, I'm not sure.

The water is slow coming out of the tap, but the longer I leave it running, the more comes out. I count my blessings that at least there is some water. My fear was that the pipes would be completely frozen. There's no kettle, so I find a small saucepan and heat water on the stove. I'm freezing cold and wonder if Orla's left me any additional clothes. There's a small chest of drawers near the daybed, and yes, she really has thought of everything. There is a pile of my boxer shorts, T-shirts, socks and a couple of thick jumpers, including one that seems to have been hand-knitted from extra-chunky yarn. It's not mine. On the daybed there are several rugs, including a sheepskin. After making myself a cup of tea, I sit at one of the chairs and wonder what I'm going to do with myself for the next couple of days. I have no phone, no computer and no television. I glance around and see a few books on a small bookshelf. They're all in French with the exception of *Ulysses* by James Joyce. I never got around to reading it, literature, and the classics especially, not being my thing. I guess I'll be reading it now.

The light is fading fast, so I light a couple of candles, worried that their dim flicker might be seen through the top windows. Orla told me to have no light after 6 pm, as the snow plough operators might see it, and once the emergency services start looking for me, I'll have to be in darkness. I see that she's left me a small torch and a supply of batteries.

IN THE MIDDLE of the night I'm awakened by the loud, incessant whirring of a helicopter. I knew this would happen, but even so, nothing has prepared me for the terror. What if they use heat sensors or see my ski tracks? The police here carry guns, and what if they storm the cabin, multiple rifles pointing at me? I try to stop the negative thoughts; it's not as if I've even done anything wrong. I would never want to point the finger at Orla, but she killed that girl, not me. I'm just acting in my lover's best interests. No, that's a fib. I'm acting in my best interests. I've made my choice now. I lie there, holding my breath, but the helicopter moves away, and the sound fades into the distance. I barely sleep afterwards, thinking about Helen and wondering how soon she will have alerted the emergency services. Perhaps that helicopter wasn't even looking for me. She's probably not even realised I'm missing yet.

The next morning the helicopter is back, approaching nearer and nearer before moving away. I hear skiers shouting, or perhaps they're mountain rescue people, and I think I hear a snowmobile not too far away. But I daren't look. I just imagine that all sorts of people are out there looking for me, and yes, I feel bad about it, wasting their time, causing Helen unnecessary upset, but the circumstances are such that I have no choice. I want Orla, and to have her, I've made some difficult decisions. I know it was the right thing to do.

The hours pass slowly. I sit there, wrapped in blankets, managing to read the odd page of *Ulysses* before my mind wanders off. I eat a lot because there's nothing else to do, and from time to time I do some press-ups to keep my circulation going and to warm myself up. For three days and three nights, I stay in the cabin, locked up like an inmate, wondering what is going on in the outside world, praying that my lover will be back soon.

I'm dozing on the daybed when I'm startled by the creak of the door opening and frigid air blowing through the small space. I jump up, ready to grab a knife from the rack.

'Hey!'

'Oh, Orla!' I say, pulling her towards me and hugging her so tightly that she squeals. I don't care that her ski jacket is wet and her cheeks are cold. I have never been so happy to see her.

'Let me take these off,' she says, wriggling out of my grasp.

'I've missed you so much,' I say.

'I've missed you too, but I've been busy.' She reaches into the inner pocket of her ski jacket.

'Ta-da!' she says, holding out a dark red passport.

I stare at it.

'Take it.' She laughs. 'It's for you, and it's not going to bite.'

I take the passport and flick through to the first page. The photo is of me, although my hair is quite a bit lighter than it is now, and the name says Joel Silver. My date of birth makes me one year older than my actual age.

'Joel? Do I really look like a Joel?'

'I chose names that are phonetically quite similar to yours. If someone asked you what your name was and you answered Paul without thinking, it sounds a bit like Joel.'

'Hmm,' I say, wondering if there's any way we'll actually pull this off. It's all so clandestine, gang-like even, the sort of thing that never happens in real life to an ordinary person like me. This makes me a criminal now, assuming a false identity with a forged passport. I never thought I would turn into a criminal. It's almost laughable.

'How did you know where to get this?' I ask.

'I'm resourceful, Joel.'

'That sounds so weird,' I say. 'And you? What's your new name?'

'I don't need to disappear. I'm not the one who's married and been having an affair!'

I stare at her. That is absolutely not fair. I'm not the one who skied into a teenager and left her to die. We stare at each other, and then it's as if Orla melts.

She collapses against me and mutters, 'I'm so sorry. Forgive me. The past few days have been so stressful, but it's all worth it. Everything's going to be okay now.'

I put my arms around her, and then we're kissing passionately, tugging at each other's clothes. After a few moments, we're on the daybed, and the burning excitement eventually dissolves into the most wonderful sensation of coming home. That is until Orla – ever insatiable – starts trailing her tongue down my neck, and we do it all over again. And again.

We are both exhausted and sleep for hours, only waking when flat, white light pours into the cabin.

'We can't leave until the weather is bad.'

'I wouldn't mind being stuck here with you for days,' I murmur.

Orla kisses me but then rolls out of bed, shivers and pulls

one of the throws around her naked body. She walks to the back window, glancing out of it as I have done for the past three days, standing with my back to the wall and peeking out like a spy.

'It's snowing,' she says. 'Come on, we need to hurry up.'

We dress quickly and then take all of the used tins, trash and burned-down candles and shove them into Orla's backpack. She glances around the cabin with an eagle eye. 'We can't leave any trace of you or an indication someone was staying here.'

'Who might notice?'

'Probably no one because no one uses this place regularly, but better to be safe than sorry.'

'How did you get the fake passport?' I ask again as I fold the throws neatly on the daybed.

'The less you know, the better.' She stands in the middle of the room, her arms crossed, and surveys the cabin, murmuring her checklist under her breath. 'Bathroom and kitchen cleaned, no rubbish anywhere, gas fires back against the wall.'

'All okay?' The nerves are pulsating through me again. I need to stay hidden; otherwise the plan will go haywire.

'Yes. Put on Dad's ski clothes. They'll be a bit big for you, but you can't wear the stuff you went missing in.'

'Are the authorities out looking for me?' What I really want to know is how Helen is coping, but I can't ask Orla that.

She just nods and shoves a navy ski jacket that was hanging from a peg on the wall into my arms. Orla grabs my ski wear and shoves it in another backpack that was behind the door. When we're both fully togged up, she opens the door, and snow blows in. I follow her outside, glad for the fresh air despite the freezing conditions. We slip our boots into our skis, and Orla pushes herself away. I follow as closely as I can, my head down, concentrating on not falling, aware of the heavy rucksack on my back, full of my rubbish.

Before long we're on a slope with other skiers, and now I feel nervous. We take a T-bar up a mountainside I haven't visited before, and about half an hour later, we're skiing down into a small village called Corviez. I follow Orla to the open-air car park, which is half-full. I imagine on a sunny weekend, this place would be heaving. She opens the doors of a silver Kia.

'Whose car is this?' I ask.

'Just get in, Joel.'

I glance around until I realise she's talking to me. I snigger.

'It's not funny. It's your name now, and you can't screw it up.' We fix our skis to the roof rack, and I open the boot of the car to chuck in the rucksacks. There are two suitcases inside – one substantially bigger than the other.

'The small case is yours. You have a completely new wardrobe, Joel. Welcome to your new and better life.'

16

HELEN – NOW

Andrew and Emily had a lovely couple of days playing in the Bisse, even going on a donkey ride. Emily also spent an hour with the local playgroup to see if she liked it and if they liked her. I was worried how she might fit in being the only non-French speaker, but it turns out I needn't have been concerned. At least three of the other kids speak English, and anything as prosaic as language wasn't going to stop Emily from making friends.

Andrew is giving Emily supper, and I'm the last person in Camilla's chalet. Normally, it's my favourite time of day, when the sun's rays hit the front of the building and the little dust motes float in the sun's beams. But this evening, there is no silence and no sun. Vertiginous dark clouds have gathered, obliterating the tops of the mountains, and a pale grey blanket of rain is heading directly towards us. A flash of lightning darts across the sky, and although I'm expecting the clap of thunder, I still physically jump backwards. I've never heard thunder like this, with its deep bass notes that bounce and reverberate across the valleys. A knot settles in my stomach as I hurry around the chalet, making sure that all the windows are bolted shut and the doors are closed. Emily will be scared by this storm. As I glance out of a side window, I see that a tarpaulin covering a pile of bricks has come loose. I'm annoyed because, according to the schedule, the builders should be tidying everything up by now. I dash outside and lock the door behind me. There is a ferocious wind, flapping my hair into my face, the trees groaning and squeaking as they bow ominously above me. It's just a storm, I tell myself, but a storm in the mountains seems so much more dramatic and terrifying than a storm in London. The rain has started now, but it's more like standing underneath a shower on full pressure. Within seconds I'm drenched. I try to pull the tarpaulin back into place, but I'm not strong enough. It might fly away, but the worst that will happen is it'll get wrapped around a tree.

I step backwards and pull my jacket's hood lower over my head, not that it's doing anything to stop me getting soaked through.

Crash!

It's an ear-deafening, splintering sound right next to me.

I scream. I slip as I step backwards, stumbling horribly and landing heavily on the sopping wet paving stones. *What the hell!*

I glance upwards, and for a split second I think I see the shape of a person up on the scaffolding. Is someone there? The wind is too severe, and the rain pierces my eyeballs like miniature darts. I peer around me and realise that a massive slate roof tile the size of an extra-large dinner plate has crashed down and splintered on the ground just centimetres away.

'Who's there?' I shout, trying to peer upwards as my heart hammers in my chest. My words disintegrate in the wind. There's movement again, but this time it's another tarpaulin, a green one that lifts upwards and slams into the side of the building.

'Jacques, is it you?' I yell. But I'm sure I saw Jacques leave earlier. Could he have come back to secure the tarpaulin? Surely it's too dangerous to be up on the roof in a storm like this? I try to get up, but there's a searing pain in my left ankle, and I can't lever myself into a standing position. I'm drenched, and now I'm scared that another tile may come tumbling down.

'Andrew!' I shout, but I know it's futile, as he won't be able to hear me yelling with the noise of the storm. I fumble in my pocket for my phone and am relieved it's not cracked or broken. I dial his number, trying to protect it from the torrential rain.

'Helen?'

'Can you come and get me? I can't move. I'm in between the chalet and cabin.'

As I wait for Andrew, I stare upwards at the scaffolding and the roof. Everything is moving: the trees throwing shadows, the tarpaulin, the heavy rain. My chest constricts as I wonder if I'm a sitting duck, whether another roof tile will fly across the sky and crash into me. I try to shuffle my backside further away from the chalet, but the pain in my leg is excruciating, so much so, I feel nauseous.

'Hey, what's happened?'

Andrew's strong arms wrap around me, and I sob into his chest. He's crouching next to me, and his shirt is already soaked through.

'I've hurt my leg, but if I'd been standing a few centimetres to the left, I'd be dead.'

'What do you mean?'

'Nearly got killed by a slate tile. I told the builders to remove the scaffolding. Can you see anyone up there?' I point towards the scaffolding weaving around the chimney.

'In this weather?' Andrew glances up and then back towards me. 'Do you think you've broken anything?'

'I don't know.' I try to stand up and fail, letting out a yelp. 'It's my ankle,' I say.

'Lean on me.'

More deafening claps of thunder make me freeze. 'Is Emily okay?' I ask, suddenly terrified she'll run out to find out what's going on.

'I told her that the thunder here is what the mountains do when they're laughing, that it's nothing to be afraid of.'

I shake my head in wonder. How does Andrew come up with things like this?

'She's not scared?'

'Nope. She's playing a game on my iPad, and I said I'd be right back.' He feeds his arms under my armpits and helps me to my feet. We're both so wet, it's as if we're stuck to each other. 'Right, you'll need to hop back. Don't put any pressure on your foot.'

I don't because I can't. The pain is searing, and I wonder if I've broken my ankle. By the time we've hobbled to the cabin, I feel almost sick.

Emily laughs when she sees us sodden and bedraggled, but then she rushes to me when she realises I'm hurt.

'It's fine, sweetie,' I say, gritting my teeth and hopping to the sofa.

Andrew strips off and shrugs on a dry T-shirt and trousers and then helps me to undress. Fortunately, Emily seems oblivious to the drama, but my heart simply won't stop racing. He gently undoes my trainers and removes my socks and trousers. Every movement hurts, and I can't stop thinking whether it was an accident or whether I really did see the shadow of a person up on the roof.

'Your ankle is badly swollen already,' Andrew says. 'I'll see if there's any ice in the fridge, but I think we might need to get it looked at in case it's broken.'

This is just what I don't need in the final stages of this renovation project. I can imagine Camilla going apoplectic, and that would be the end of any lucrative overseas jobs.

There's no ice in the little freezer container in the fridge, so Andrew drenches a tea towel in cold water and wraps it around my ankle. I gasp with the pain.

'I think you need to get your ankle scanned at the hospital just in case it's fractured.'

I groan. 'In which case, you need to call the neighbours, Guillaume and Manon, who you met,' I say to Andrew. 'They'll point me in the direction of a doctor. Manon's phone number is on my mobile.'

Andrew fishes my mobile out of my sopping wet jacket pocket and hands me the phone.

'*Oui*,' Manon says, answering on the second ring.

'I'm sorry to disturb you, but this is Helen from next door.'

'Ah, Helen. What do you think of this storm? It's quite impressive, no?'

'Yes, and unfortunately I slipped when I was returning from the chalet, and I've hurt my ankle. I think I need to see a doctor. Is there one in the village?'

'Oh no, you poor thing. No, there's no doctor here. He only works in the mornings. You will have to go to the hospital.'

I pause to think. I doubt Andrew is insured to drive Camilla's car. 'Do you have the phone number for a taxi?'

'Yes, but I'm not giving it to you. Guillaume and I will be with you in five minutes.'

'No – really!' But it's too late, Manon has hung up.

· · ·

FIFTEEN MINUTES LATER, the storm has subsided, and glimpses of sun rays peek out behind distant dark clouds like strobes of light. It's extraordinary how rapidly the weather changes here in the mountains. Guillaume and Andrew support me out to Guillaume's car while Manon watches on with a look of concern on her face. Andrew and Emily stay behind in the cabin.

'Your Andrew is a very good man,' Manon says as Guillaume steers the car down the mountainside.

She's right about that. I lean my head against the back seat, relieved that I'm not driving. Water is pouring off the hillside, and there are branches scattered across the road, mist rising eerily off the tarmac as the sun heats the rainwater.

It takes about half an hour for us to arrive in a big town in the valley, and we pull up outside a large hospital.

'They will help you in the emergency room,' Manon explains. 'It's the only place you will see a doctor this evening.' I nod because it's the same at home.

Guillaume supports me as I hobble into the building, and then a wheelchair is magically produced. Manon wheels me through to the accident and emergency department. I feel like an idiot. I'm the younger woman here, and I'm being pushed by a lady in her seventies, at least.

We wait for over an hour, making small talk where I listen to Manon's stories from having lived abroad, while Guillaume reads the newspaper. Eventually I'm seen by a doctor, who sends me off to get my ankle X-rayed. I suppose if there's anywhere good to break a bone, it would be in the Alps, where the doctors are used to fractures from ski injuries. And then I shiver, thinking that Paul should have been brought here. Perhaps the medical teams in this hospital could have saved him.

After the X-ray, I have to wait in the waiting room for

another long hour, after which the doctor calls me into his cubicle.

'It's good news,' he says with a strong French accent. 'You haven't broken your ankle; it's just badly sprained. We will give you a plastic boot and crutches, and you should keep your weight off it for at least two weeks. Get it checked again when you have finished your holiday. Take ibuprofen and paracetamol for the pain.'

I open my mouth to tell him I'm not here on holiday and then close it again. I'm sure he couldn't care less. I have to focus on the good news: it's not broken. Manon is in the back of the car, and I am sitting in the front passenger seat.

'I'm happy for you it's not broken,' Guillaume says. He drives us back up the mountainside, and we listen to Verdi on his car radio.

'I can't thank you enough,' I say as we arrive at the cabin.

'It's what neighbours are for,' Manon says, helping me out of the car. I hobble to the cabin alongside Manon, who refuses to leave until she's seen me safely inside. Andrew also thanks them profusely, and we both wish them goodnight.

That night, I lie in Andrew's arms and think about what happened. That slate tile could have so easily landed on me, and then what would have happened to Emily? She would be an orphan. Yes, there was a storm, but was it really an accident? Could someone have left that tile in a precarious position in the hope that it would fall? But if so, they couldn't have known who it would hit, so it's unlikely it was left there with the specific aim of landing on me. Although, I'm the only person who walks between the chalet and the cabin after hours. But to also predict the trajectory of a falling tile during a storm seems a bit unlikely. If I really did see a person up there, then the falling slate was no accident. I bury my face in my pillow and groan. I need to stop this negative thinking. Besides, why would anyone want to hurt me? It was an accident, an accident in a storm.

THE NEXT MORNING much of the pain has subsided, and now I'm just angry. I stomp into the chalet with some difficulty, pointing one of my crutches at Jacques.

'We need to talk,' I say.

He raises his eyebrows and crosses his arms. 'Yes?'

'Were you on the roof yesterday evening?'

'*Quoi?*' he asks, his eyebrows raised.

'Were you here?'

'No, Hélène.' He pronounces my name in the French way. 'I was at home with my wife and children, safely out of the storm. I am not an idiot.' He glances down at my foot. 'What happened to you?'

'One of the roof tiles fell off yesterday, and it missed me by centimetres. I already pointed out that the scaffolding should be taken down, and frankly it's dangerous.'

'Ah yes. So now the English interior decorator is telling me how to do my job. Perhaps you would also like to instruct the electrician and the tiler who will be arriving shortly.'

I grit my teeth. 'Did you see the roof tile splintered on the ground at the back?'

'And?'

'It nearly killed me.'

'There was a storm last night, and I can assure you that there are no loose or missing tiles on the roof. I have already been up to check.'

'So how did one nearly land on my head?'

Jacques shrugs and looks at me with an annoying smirk. I have to restrain myself from slapping him.

'Shall I discuss this with Saskia?' I ask.

'Discuss what with me?'

I jump as Saskia strides into the chalet wearing black jeans and a stylish pale grey top.

'Goodness! What happened to you?' she asks, looking at my plastic boot.

'I was nearly killed by a falling roof tile early yesterday evening,' I say, pointing at my foot.

'*Zut alors*,' she says. 'Are you in a lot of pain?'

'It's fine,' I say.

'That's good.' And then she talks in rapid-fire French with Jacques, and there's a lot of hand gesturing and words I don't understand. Jacques throws me a filthy look and stomps away; Saskia turns to me, her hands on her hips.

'He doesn't know where this tile came from. Perhaps you tripped over it?'

I open and close my mouth. Is Saskia choosing not to believe me? Are the locals ganging up against the foreigner? If so, I'm fighting a losing battle.

'Perhaps,' I say through gritted teeth, turning away from her. I hobble to the window as Saskia walks out of the room to speak to someone else. I wonder whether it was a huge mistake coming here. I thought this was an unlucky place for me before, and maybe this is confirmation that I was right. On the one hand, I adore this breathtaking view, the fresh air, and even the people are friendly. The chalet is beautiful and affording me amazing opportunities, not to mention the money. But still. This place haunts me somehow, and right now I wish I were snuggled up on the sofa at home, looking through new sample swatches, drinking tea and moaning about the incessant rain.

I watch as Saskia hops into her car and leaves. Jacques is on his phone, gesticulating wildly and possibly pointing at the scaffolding; meanwhile I have a long list of phone calls I need to make to chase up suppliers. My foot throbs as I think about it. Of course I can't leave now. I have to stay to finish the contract, to take advantage of the bonus Camilla is paying me, to meet the reputation I've gained for myself. But the second this house is completed, I'm out of here.

I HOP BACK to the cabin late afternoon, my heart sinking as I realise tonight is my last night with Andrew. How am I going to manage with Emily when I can't walk properly? How am I going to finish this job and stay sane?

'I wish you weren't leaving,' I say as I wash up the dishes, balancing mainly on one leg.

Andrew puts the tea towel on the counter and turns to face me. 'I've been thinking. I could take a few days off, tell them I'm sick, and then you and I could go and visit the memorial by the ski lift. I can help you walk there.'

'Thank you,' I say gently. 'But no. You're never sick, and you hate dishonesty like that. Don't change for me.' Besides, I have no desire to see the plaque. I don't need to see words on a stone to know that my husband has died. I'm not religious, and I feel no compulsion to leave flowers or any other tribute.

'I'd do anything for you, Helen,' he says, gripping me tightly and kissing me on the lips.

'You need to go back to work, and I need to finish this job. We'll all be together again in three weeks' time.' I try to smile, but I'm sure the corners of my lips are betraying me.

The next morning, Andrew's taxi arrives just before 9 am. Emily and I stand on the doorstep and wave at him. We're still waving when the taxi is out of sight and he's far down the mountainside. 'Do you think I'll see Daddy's train?' Emily asks as she peers towards the valley floor far below us.

'If you look very carefully, maybe,' I say. 'Come on. You need to get ready for playgroup.'

I was worried I wouldn't be able to drive, but as it's only my left foot in a plastic boot and the Golf is automatic, I'm able to control the car without any problems, even though I dislike driving on the right side of the road and hate navigating the tight bends. I drop Emily off and wave goodbye, but she's too excited to see her new-found friends and doesn't even look back at me.

As I turn away, I feel utterly alone. Alone with a horrible sense of foreboding that this place doesn't want me any more than I want to be here.

I am not going to run again. Last time it was a necessity, and it resulted in several glorious years. But I'll never forget the terror of arriving at Geneva airport that first time and handing over my freshly minted passport at security. The guard had deep-set, narrow eyes, and he glanced up at me, then down at the photo and up at me again. I thought I was going to pass out. But then he snapped the passport shut and handed it back to me, wishing me a good flight. That day I knew I was officially Joel Silver, and I would never be ordinary Paul Sellers ever again. I was like a snake shedding off my old skin, and I could step into the future in whatever guise I wanted. It felt wonderfully empowering. It would be a lie to say that I was relaxed when we went through passport control in Brisbane or in the multitude of countries we travelled to thereafter. By the time my new passport was full of stamps and looked battered, I began to accept that we might have gotten away with it, that my metamorphosis into Joel was now fully complete.

For the past couple of years, I'd been thinking it was time we settled down. I didn't care which country we chose; I just wanted a place to call home, a place to persuade Orla we should start a family.

I know it's usually women who get broody; I felt ashamed when I found myself staring at fathers out with their young children. I didn't even know if Helen had given birth to our child, whether I was already a father. But if I was a father, I knew that ship had sailed. I wanted to be a real daddy, to build and care for a family with Orla.

The problem is, I simply can't imagine my crazy, wild, impulsive Orla as a mother. Mothers should be like Helen: stable, sensible, offering security, but could Orla change? I saw how responsible she became within an instant of finding out her father was seriously ill. I have seen multiple times how efficient Orla is, how resourceful she is. She's loving too, towards me and the many people on whom she showers attention. She would be a good mother if only she believed that in herself.

About a year ago, Orla's father became sick, and she flew back to Switzerland.

Her father recovered, and a fortnight later, Orla was back in my arms.

'I want to go home,' she murmured.

'Home as in where?' Because we have been rootless these past years, bouncing from one beautiful villa rental to the next across Australia and Asia. We are free.

She rolls her eyes at me. 'Switzerland. It's where I'm from, where I grew up, where I'll die.'

I shivered.

'Do you want to go back without me?' I wondered if this was it, whether our magical adventures had run their course.

'Of course not!' Orla exclaimed. 'You're Joel Silver now; you have been for years. It's perfectly safe for you to go to Switzerland. You can set up your own restaurant, be that famous chef you've always dreamed of being. We'll be a normal family.'

'Normal, as in having children?' I asked.

'Don't push your luck,' she replied without a hint of irony. I bit my tongue because I knew I would have to be patient. The thing is, I never thought our forever home would be in Switzerland.

'I don't know about Switzerland, Orla. I'm not sure it's safe there.'

'Of course it is. I've already put out some feelers. I've found us a chalet.'

'You've what?'

She glanced at me coyly, twisting a lock of dark hair around her index finger. 'I bought us a house.'

'You what! Don't you think that should be a decision that we make together considering I'm going to be living there too?'

'I thought it would be a lovely surprise.' She looked tearful, and that's the problem with Orla. Her emotions swing wildly, and I'm never quite sure which side of the emotional line I'm treading. Happiness or sadness; tranquillity or anger.

'Can I at least see photos of my future home?' I wondered if it would be sufficiently childproof. Knowing Orla, she would have chosen somewhere with a sheer drop and open staircases.

She passed me her phone and showed me the sales brochure. It's a typical Swiss chalet, with red shutters and a sleek, modern kitchen with white cabinets. It has impressive mountainous views and a decent-sized garage. 'When you see it, you'll love it,' she said with conviction. And she was right, I do love it. The problem isn't the house. The problem is money and children.

Orla hasn't realised that her wild displays of generosity and the way she spends money as if there's a bottomless pit of cash undermines me. I want to be able to afford to buy her nice things, to treat her to things she wants or take her to fancy places she reads about in magazines, but I don't have a trust fund or life savings. My assets are tied up in a house I will never own again and a pension fund I can't access. So Orla holds all the strings. As lovely as this chalet is, will I ever consider it mine?

A few weeks ago, when we were reasonably settled into our new home in Switzerland, I brought up the topic of children once more, but Orla was resolute. She doesn't want a family. Children will tie us down. We're free birds, and if we had a child, we could never have escaped as we did. I accept that, but that was then, and now things are very different.

AND THAT'S ANOTHER PROBLEM. Things haven't been good between Orla and me since we've been back. Unfortunately, meeting her parents didn't help. The first time, I was nervous. Orla introduced me as a Brit she'd met in Brisbane; we fell head over heels in love and got married in Bali. It's true, we did get married, but obviously it's not legal. Unless Helen has obtained a divorce in my absence, I assume I'm still married to her. Emmanuel Sinerre, Orla's father, seemed thoroughly unimpressed with me, and frankly, I don't blame him. I hardly cut the suave successful figure he no doubt hoped his daughter would marry. I'm an out-of-work chef who has been living the good life courtesy of Monsieur Sinerre's wealth. Despite my designer clothes, selected and bought by Orla, it was obvious that he knew I was a fraudster and hanger-on. Heaven forbid he ever finds out the truth of the deception. I've tried to stay out of their way ever since.

The more time I spend alone stuck on this mountain, the more I'm consumed with wanting a family. We used to make love all the time, we just couldn't get enough of each other, and that didn't wear off as it does for so many couples. Up and until we arrived in Switzerland, sex was probably the most important part of us. But over the last few weeks, Orla has been tired or hasn't been in the mood, and I wonder if she senses my desperation for our lovemaking to be more. Orla takes the pill every morning. It's the first thing she does, and I've come to hate that little strip of pills with each day of the week printed on it. Those pills represent a future I don't want. The best hope I have of her accidentally falling pregnant is for us to have sex as often as possible and engineering a situation or two where Orla forgets to take her pill. I haven't quite worked out how to pull that off.

Sex is what binds Orla and me, and I wonder if we can survive without it. It was different with Helen. We were friends first and lovers second; the opposite is true with Orla. What sort of father would I have been? Would I have been a loyal husband if I hadn't met Orla, or am I just one of those guys I despise, ones who think the grass is always greener elsewhere? No, that can't be the case, because I've been totally loyal to Orla. She meets all my needs, and I hope I meet hers. That's the definition of love, isn't it? Wanting to truly commit to one person.

IT'S EARLY EVENING, and I'm sitting at the kitchen table, slowly sipping a beer, staring at the blank screen of my laptop.

'What are you doing?' Orla startles me as she strides into the room wearing navy chinos and a sleeveless white blouse. She seems very underdressed considering the violent storm that has just passed through this valley.

'Just writing up my business plan,' I say. But Orla is too quick and sees that the screen is blank.

She rolls her eyes at me and then pulls out a chair. 'I've done some digging. Yes, Helen is here. She's working on a renovation project for an Englishwoman. Your ex is some sort of interior designer apparently,' Orla says disparagingly. 'You're going to have to disappear for a while until Helen has left.'

I sigh. I feared this was what Orla would suggest. 'Where do you want to go?' I ask wearily. Perhaps we could go back to old Blighty, but then I realise I can never visit my old haunts, see my parents or my old friends. As far as they're concerned, I'm dead.

'I'm not going anywhere. You can go to Istanbul or Tel Aviv. Frankly I don't give a toss where you go; you've just got to get away from here. I'll tell everyone you've gone on a business trip, to do some research for your new restaurant. Whilst you're away, I'll do some more digging and find out how long Helen will be around. The most important thing is that she gets out of here pronto. We cannot have Helen hanging around. Can you imagine, you in your new restaurant and Helen turning up. It would destroy everything. Absolutely everything. I'm going to make sure that this assignment of hers is cut short and she stays well away from Switzerland.'

'I don't want to go away,' I say quietly.

'No bloody choice,' Orla says, standing up and walking to the fridge to take out a bottle of white wine. 'And I don't want to be living with a layabout who can't even put his own bloody washing in the machine!'

'That's not fair!' I say, and it isn't, because I do everything around the house: the cooking, the cleaning; it's only the ironing that Orla sends away to a woman in the village, who returns all of our shirts on wire hangers, perfectly pressed. I'm not even sure Orla knows how to cook or clean considering she's always had someone to do it for her. The most she manages is opening a bottle of wine and pouring herself a glass.

'Pack a bag, and I'll drop you off at the train station,' she says.

'You're not listening to me, Orla. I'm going nowhere. I am not going to go on the run every time we think we see someone who might recognise me as Paul.'

'This isn't a matter of suspecting. We know for sure that Helen is here. You've got no choice but to go underground.'

I shake my head. I can't spend the rest of my life on the run.

'Then what the hell are you going to do? Are you so thick that you don't understand the consequences of you being seen?' She raps her knuckle against her head.

I stand up suddenly, place my palms on the table and lean towards her. 'I am fed up of being your skivvy and your scapegoat, of being bossed around and made to feel bad because you have all the money and I have nothing. You wanted to come back here. You chose this life, not me. I'm doing this because you needed to get away, and you gave me an ultimatum. I'm staying because I love you, Orla, but I'm not going to be shoved around like an idiot. Do you get it?'

She opens and closes her mouth, and then in a very typical Orla way, a smile creeps across her face, and she pulls her sleeveless shirt right up over her head and unclips her bra, then reaches behind my head and pulls me into a deep kiss.

'You're so sexy when you're pissed off,' she murmurs into my lips, and weak as I am, my body yields to hers, and I take her right there on the kitchen table, wondering if this is how best to play it. Make-up sex could just be the answer.

ORLA IS asleep when I wake up the next morning. It's 5.30 am, the sun is throwing orange shadows onto the mountains, and there's nothing more I feel like doing than taking an early morning run. I reckon it'll be another hour or two before Orla stirs, so I pull on a pair of running shorts and top, and then, checking she's still fast asleep, I tiptoe around the bed to her bedside table. I pick up her strip of contraceptive pills, hesitating a moment before dropping them behind the headboard. They make a scratching noise as they fall onto the floor, but Orla doesn't stir. Then I run downstairs and find a baseball cap, which I pull low over my head. I promised Orla that I would stay in the chalet and far away from any prying eyes until Helen left, but I'm damned if I'm going to become a hermit. The chances of Helen being up and out at this early hour are practically zero. I remember how we had to set two alarm clocks to make sure she was up on time for work. Early mornings were never her thing.

I love this time of the new day when the air is totally still and fresh, the sun's rays just beginning to warm the earth, and the clarity of the view suggests a beautiful day ahead. The birdsong is so loud, it's as if they're putting on a vocal show just for me. I run fast, first along the footpath adjacent to the Bisse and then up the mountainside, following a track that weaves into the forest and out the other side. A chamois is standing on a rocky outcrop just metres above me. I stop still. It's goat-like with a white face, short horns and a dark brown stripe along its backbone, a rare and wonderful sight. But then it sees me and hurtles away up the mountainside with impressive dexterity. I've also seen cute marmots on my run, red squirrels that are really black in colour, and the more common antelope, but this is my first sighting of a chamois. I wonder if it is an omen. A good one, I hope.

After stopping to enjoy the view, I head back down towards the village. It's just turned 7 am, and the only establishment open is the bakery. With my baseball hat pulled low, I nip in to buy some croissants for Orla and me.

There's an elderly gentleman in front of me, chatting to

the baker. The gentleman speaks slowly, and I'm able to make out what he's saying.

'She had an accident. That English decorator lady. I took her to the hospital yesterday evening. Yes, it could have been very bad. Much worse. She says that a tile fell from the roof of the chalet and nearly killed her. No, no. She just has a badly sprained ankle. She was very lucky.'

I step out of the bakery. This is a small place, and there can only be one English decorator lady. Helen. What happened to her? Did the tile fall from the roof because of last night's storm, or could it be something much worse? I hate myself for thinking this, but could Orla have had something to do with it?

18

HELEN – NOW

Now that Andrew has left, I have thrown myself into work, determined to get everything done on time. Relations between Jacques and me are strained, but we do our best to avoid each other. I've got used to walking with the plastic boot on and no longer need the crutches. My ankle barely hurts.

Emily has settled in well too and loves her little playgroup. They forage in the forest, play by the Bisse, make tepees under the trees, and when the weather is bad, they paint and make things out of clay. Today she's been there all day, and while this wasn't what I wanted for her summer holidays, at least she's happy, and it means I'm free to concentrate on work.

It's 4 pm, and I'm hobbling up the path to the room next to the church where the playgroup is based. When Emily sees me, she comes running out and grabs my hand, chattering non-stop. We say our goodbyes to the staff, and Emily gives one of the little girls a hug, promising to play with her again tomorrow. She then hops beside me as we walk slowly back up the hill.

'That nice man came to speak to me again,' she says. 'And Thomas poured water all over my painting, and Mademoiselle told him off.'

'What did you just say, darling?' I ask, wondering if I heard Emily correctly.

'That Thomas got into trouble.'

'Before that.'

'Oh, that the nice man came again.'

'What nice man?'

'Ow! You're squeezing my hand too hard,' Emily squeals.

'Sorry, darling.' I release my grip. 'Who is the man?'

'Dunno. He just comes to say hello to me, and he seems nice.'

'Does he work at the playgroup?'

'No,' she says nonchalantly with all the innocence of a four-year-old.

I try to contain the mounting panic. 'But you know you're not meant to speak to strangers, don't you?'

'He's not a stranger. We spoke a few times.'

'What's his name?'

'I don't know.'

'What does he look like, then?'

'He's old. He's a man. Why are you asking these questions, Mummy?'

'Because you shouldn't be speaking to people you don't know.'

Emily sulks as we walk slowly to the cabin. I know I shouldn't be projecting my fears onto her, but this man could be anyone. Just because this is some sweet little Alpine village doesn't mean there aren't any weirdos living here. Or he could be a visitor. Perhaps this person has taken a shine to my pretty little girl. A shudder runs through me. Why would a man be skulking around the playgroup, talking to the children? It's simply wrong. Is someone targeting Emily, planning on abducting her? The very thought sickens and terrifies me. There must be some creep talking to the children. I'm going to have to talk to the staff at the playgroup and make sure they stop any strangers from making conversation. That will be the very first conversation I have in the morning.

My heart sinks slightly when I see Saskia's car parked in front of the chalet. As we walk up the driveway, she appears at the front of the house. She claps her hands together when she sees us.

'You must be Emily!'

Emily smiles coyly.

'Have you got time for a quick word?' Saskia asks.

'Sure.' I turn to Emily. 'Would you like to do some drawing?'

She nods a bit reluctantly. Once we're inside the chalet, I give her a carton of juice and a little cake I picked up from the boulangerie and settle Emily on the floor along with a pad of paper and some felt-tip markers.

'How's your ankle?' Saskia asks.

'Fine now, thank you.'

'Your daughter is adorable!' she says quietly.

I smile. Saskia seems in a good mood today.

'I'm a bit worried because Emily mentioned that a strange man spoke to her a few times when she was at the playgroup.'

Saskia frowns. 'At the playgroup? That's weird. How would a man even get in? Crime here is practically non-existent. Of course, we have lots of visitors staying in resorts like this, but really, I don't think you should worry.'

'I'm sure it's some mix-up. As you say, everyone is so friendly here, saying hello when they pass by. I just thought it was odd.'

'And it is. I'm sure Mademoiselle Marie at the playgroup will sort it out. She's very good.'

We talk through a couple of changes that Camilla has

made to the layout of the master bedroom, which of course has a knock-on effect on everything, and then Saskia leaves.

THE NEXT MORNING, I accompany Emily to the playgroup. She disappears to the back of the hall to play with her friends, but I hang around at the front, eager to speak to Mademoiselle Marie, the thirty-year-old woman who runs the playgroup. She is busy talking to another mum, so I have to wait. Suddenly Emily races towards me, clutching a teddy bear almost as big as she is.

'Who's this?' I ask as Emily squeezes the pale yellow bear.

'He's for me. He's a present for me!' Emily dances around my legs, the bear sweeping against my legs.

'Who gave you the teddy?'

'Mademoiselle Corinne said he was sitting in the doorway, and he's mine!' She darts off to join the other children. That's very strange, and I assume that Emily has somehow got the wrong end of the stick.

Mademoiselle Marie finishes with the other woman and walks towards me with a broad smile on her elfin-like face. 'Your daughter is charming,' she says.

'Thank you. This is slightly awkward, but Emily mentioned she's been speaking to a man a few times.'

Marie scrunches her forehead. 'But we don't have any men who work in the playgroup.'

'I know, and that's what worries me. Could it have been when you were out in the forest?'

Marie swallows hard. I know that the ongoing success of her childcare facility rests upon her reputation for keeping children safe and occupied, and just my suggestion that something isn't right makes Mademoiselle Marie pale.

'This morning, when Corinne opened up, there was a big teddy bear sitting on the doorstep. It had a gift tag attached, and it said, *This bear is for Emily Sellers.* There's no indication who it's from. I checked the application form you filled in for Emily, and it's not her birthday for another four months. I was going to contact you and ask you about it.'

Who would give Emily a big bear like that? Who even knows that we're staying here? And then I relax my shoulders. It's probably from Andrew. It's exactly the sort of thing he would do – sending her a present just because. But why would he get it delivered to the playgroup and not the chalet? And surely he would have told me about it last night when we spoke on the phone? Then I recall Emily saying she had been talking to a man. Could it have been the strange man who left the bear?

'Can I see the gift tag?' I ask. Perhaps there's something attached to the tag saying it's from Andrew.

'Of course.' She strides across the room and disappears behind a door, returning quickly. She walks towards me and hands over a small piece of paper. The words are typed in French, to my surprise. I rather assumed it would be in English. Andrew would have dictated a message in English.

'I just need to make a quick phone call,' I say.

I ring Andrew, and he answers immediately. 'Is everything alright, darling?'

'Yes, fine. Sorry to bother you at work. Did you send Emily a teddy bear?'

There's a beat of silence. 'No. Should I have done?'

'No, no. Just some sort of mix-up. I'll speak to you later. Have a good day.'

'Did you find out who it's from?' Mademoiselle Marie asks.

I shake my head.

'What shall we do with it?' Mademoiselle Marie asks. 'Do you want Emily to keep the bear?'

I try to restrain a shiver. Emily won't understand if a

present is taken away from her, but there's no way I want her to accept a gift from some creep. I'm going to have to spin her a story.

'No, she can't keep it. We don't accept gifts from strangers. Perhaps you could donate it to the hospital or a children's charity.'

'No problem. I can sort that.'

I smile at her. 'Thanks. I'd better break the unhappy news to Emily.' I walk over to where Emily has placed the teddy in a small chair and watch for a moment as she holds an empty plastic beaker in front of its mouth and tells the bear to drink up.

'Darling, we need to talk.'

'With teddy.'

'No, teddy needs to stay here because we're talking about him.'

Emily scowls but follows me across the room away from the other children. I crouch down beside her. 'I know you're going to be very sad, but that teddy bear was meant for another little girl called Emily, so we're going to have to give him back.'

Tears spring to Emily's eyes. 'No,' she says feebly.

'The other little girl is sick, and she needs that teddy bear very badly.' As the lies spill from my tongue, I feel a dart of regret. I hate lying, especially to my daughter, but I've had to do that a lot over the years. Little white lies of convenience to get her to do what I need her to because I'm in a hurry, or bigger societal lies such as Father Christmas, and the biggest lie of all: that her birth father loved her very, very much.

'No,' Emily says, swiping her eyes with the back of her hand. 'This bear is mine. You can give the other Emily another one.'

'I'm sorry, sweetheart, but it doesn't work like that. If you keep this bear, it's stealing.' I feel like a terrible cad and struggle to look Emily in the eyes. 'This other little girl needs the bear so badly. I'll make it up to you some other way.'

Tears spill down Emily's cheeks.

'You're being very brave and very kind,' I say, pulling her towards me and hugging her tightly. 'What special treat would you like for tea?'

THE TEDDY BEAR has freaked me out. For the first time, I'm reluctant to leave Emily at the playgroup despite Mademoiselle Marie making numerous promises that Emily will not be out of her sight for one moment today. Even so, I wish I didn't have to leave my little girl there, but what choice do I have?

Later, when I'm catching up with Saskia, she asks me about the playgroup.

'I'm not happy about leaving Emily there,' I say. 'But a building site is no place for a young child.'

'I had an idea, actually. My friend has a daughter who wants to study childcare, and she would be available to be Emily's nanny for a week or so. What do you think?'

This could be the answer to my prayers. Keep Emily near the chalet and always supervised, and I'll be able to nip back and forth.

'When can I meet her?'

Saskia makes a telephone call, and as normal, I quickly lose track of what she's saying. When Saskia finishes, she turns to me. 'She's called Sylvie, she's sixteen, and she'd like to come over now, if that's convenient?'

'It certainly is!' And then I wonder. Sixteen is terribly young. Is a sixteen-year-old really responsible enough to be looking after a younger child? But then again, surely that's a better choice than keeping Emily at playgroup all day long? Emily will have one-to-one attention, and I'll be around to keep an eye out for her too. Yes. Assuming Sylvie is a sensible young woman, this might be the best solution.

I thank Saskia profusely.

19

I've always dreamed of having my own restaurant, and now it looks as if that might become a reality. Three weeks ago, Orla introduced me to Matteo Berchard, Saskia the architect's husband. He's in private equity and is always looking for schemes to invest in, apparently. When Saskia mentioned to Orla that he'd recently acquired a premises two doors down from the ski lift station right here in Corviez, but wasn't sure what to do with it, Orla came bustling in to see me. Pitch your idea for a restaurant, she exclaimed. I was cynical, but I drafted up a short document with my vision for an Asian-inspired restaurant, outlining my proposed menu and the anticipated financial projections, which Orla sent to Matteo. The next day he invited me to meet him for a coffee. I like him. He worked in banking for years and clearly earned an absolute fortune, and now he's prepared to gamble on start-ups and businesses that need an injection of capital. I think he's keen on owning a restaurant. He seems genuinely interested in my proposal, and this is an opportunity I can't pass by. I would so much rather have an external investor than borrow money from Orla. I've lived off her for the past five years, and the time has come for me to stand on my own two feet. If we hadn't been on the run, I'd have done it sooner, but Orla convinced me that life is for living not working. It's easy for her to say that when money is no object, but that simply isn't real life. I crave normalcy now. I want a family, a business, to be the man of the house and the provider. She'll never understand that, but I have to do this for me. For my own self-respect if nothing else.

I think seeing Emily has shifted something inside me. If I'd stayed with Helen, life would have been undoubtedly harder, but I would have roots and a sense of purpose and fulfilment. But then again I wouldn't have had the excitement of the past five years. Anyway, now I'm sitting at the round kitchen table, working on my business plan, and it's shaping up pretty well. I have to admit though that Helen being here and working with Saskia is a massive spanner in the works. It's definitely too close for comfort.

Something broke inside me when I saw Helen and Emily walking together. Helen was struggling a bit, shuffling with a plastic boot on her left foot, but Emily was dancing backwards and forwards, chatting to her mother, her face aglow with happiness. I knew she was my child the moment I set eyes upon her. She looks like Mum did when she was young, and I think one just knows. It's a primeval thing. I have this overwhelming urge to get to know Emily, but that's not easy when you're meant to be dead.

I followed them. I'm not proud of it, but what else could I do? I wore glasses and a bike helmet and kept my head down low. When I saw Helen drop our daughter off at the playgroup, it was easy enough for me to engineer an opportunity to talk to Emily.

They take the kids out every morning. A group of ten of them wander into the forest to play. Dressed in running gear, I waited until the two members of staff were otherwise occupied and bent down to do up my shoelace exactly where Emily was playing with a little boy.

'Hello,' I said.

She glanced at me and ignored me.

'What's your name?' I asked.

She hesitated for a moment, so I smiled broadly at her. I could tell that she was conflicted between conversing with a stranger and not being rude. What a darling girl. 'Emily,' she said eventually.

My daughter is called Emily. It's a sweet name and suits her well.

And then one of the teachers looked up, so I whispered goodbye to my daughter and carried on my way. For the next three mornings, I engineered an opportunity to say a word or two to Emily. Once I helped catch her little boat in the Bisse, and I waved at the young teacher, gesticulating that I was just helping. Everyone laughed. I wanted to say she's my daughter and look how bright and bubbly she is! But I couldn't. Two days ago, before Orla's pronouncement that I was to stay hidden, I was in the valley doing a grocery shop, because Orla would never deign to do something as prosaic. But I also enjoyed it, spending time selecting the best produce, pretending that I was buying for my own restaurant. I walked past a toy shop, and a large teddy sat in the window. I strode straight in and bought it, along with a few other bits and pieces, toys I hoped Emily might like. Of course I couldn't give the bear to her in person, so I left it on the doorstep of the playgroup. What else could I do?

I feel desperate, guilty and confused, but I can't stay away from my daughter. She has my eyes and my mother's lips and is utterly adorable. But how can I make myself known? I'm a criminal, living on a forged passport, and if it came down to it, I know Orla would make me carry the blame for skiing into that young girl. So for now, all I can do is admire my daughter from a distance, snatching the occasional word with her.

I TRY to switch off from thinking about Emily and refocus on the Excel spreadsheet detailing the restaurant's projections. Orla walks into the room.

'What's this?' she asks, her eyes flashing with anger. She's holding up a game for four-to six-year-olds and a dressing-up outfit in the style of some Disney character the lady in the shop said was all the rage with four-year-old girls at the moment. I hid the items I bought for Emily at the back of the wardrobe in the spare room, but it seems that Orla has found them.

I open and close my mouth. Orla steps closer to me and chucks both onto the table.

'You bought them to give to Helen's daughter, didn't you?'

'She's my daughter too, Orla.'

Tears spring to Orla's eyes, and she trembles. In an instant, she has gone from strong, carefree Orla to the woman whose confidence is all a big facade. I jump up and pull her to me. I get no resistance.

'Your life is with me, Joel,' Orla sobs, and then she pulls away from me, eyes furious again. That's what she's like, mercurial, swinging from one emotion to another. 'You need to stay away from Helen and the child! Do you get it? That child isn't yours.'

'She's called Emily,' I say, which infuriates Orla even more.

'You gave her up when you became Joel Silver. You gave her up when you chose me, and you don't get to change your mind over something like that!' Orla paces up and down the kitchen, running her fingers through her hair. 'Think of the implications. We'll both go to prison if Helen finds out you're alive and discovers what we did. I think we need to move away again.'

'No,' I say. 'Things are starting to come together for us. I want to stay here now. Besides, Matteo is about to invest in the restaurant. I can't walk away from that.'

I've been stupid. Really stupid. I should never have left that bag in the wardrobe.

I walk over to Orla again and throw my arms around her. I then lift her up onto the island unit and kiss her deeply. 'I'm sorry, I've been an idiot,' I say.

'You are an idiot,' Orla moans, 'but I love you.'

I whisper into her hair. 'I promise to stay hidden. I don't want to jeopardise us.' But the truth is, I wonder if I can keep that promise. Perhaps if I get Orla to agree to have a baby, then I'll find it easier to let Emily go. Does it work like that? Can one child substitute for another?

AFTER LUNCH I try to concentrate on my business plan again. I've done as Orla suggested, stayed at home, worked on my business proposal, kept my head down, but this afternoon it's glorious weather, and I'm feeling claustrophobic. The urge to see Emily is monumental. Knowing that she's only here for a finite amount of time, and that once she and Helen have returned to England I may never get the chance to see them again, is stressing me.

'I'm going out to see a friend,' Orla says. She doesn't wait for a response, and I feel a welling up of resentment. Orla is free to do whatever she wants, yet I'm the one suffering for what she did. I just have to go for a run. I tell myself that I'll go in the opposite direction to where Helen is staying, that I won't be actively looking out for my daughter. I slip on my running gear and am just tying up the laces on my running shoes when the door opens.

'What are you doing?' Orla says, her mouth set in a straight line.

Why is she back so soon? I feel like I've been caught out like a naughty child. 'I'm going for a quick run. I need fresh air.'

'No you're not. We discussed that you cannot leave the house.'

'Orla, I'm going to be careful. I'm going in the opposite direction.'

'Don't push me, Joel.'

'What?' I say, my foot hovering in the air.

'Don't make me do something I might regret.' She then runs upstairs, returning with her wallet a couple of seconds later, pushing past me in the hallway. When she leaves the house, she slams the door so hard, the whole chalet reverberates.

I stand there for a moment, frozen. What does Orla mean, that she might do something she'll later regret? Is she implying that she was responsible for Helen's accident? And does it mean that Helen and Emily might be in danger? Surely not.

Camilla is on the phone to me several times a day now, and the pressure is mounting. But at least the childcare situation is sorted, for now. Sylvie is a sweet girl who looks younger than sixteen but speaks with a confidence greater than her years. Her English is excellent, but I've asked her to speak French with Emily. It's never too young to learn a new language.

'There was a strange man talking to Emily when she was at playgroup,' I explain to Sylvie. 'I'm sure it's nothing to worry about, but I need you to be extra careful with her. Please watch her all the time.' I decide not to tell her about the teddy bear incident so as not to scare her off.

'Of course, Mrs Sellers,' Sylvie says, with a seriousness that fills me with confidence. 'I will watch her all the time, and any problems I will call for you or telephone you. Emily is adorable, and I am very happy to be looking after her.'

The feeling seems to be mutual, so despite my initial misgivings about her young age, I leave Emily happily playing with Sylvie in the garden.

.   .   .

THE WOODEN FLOORS are looking beautiful throughout the chalet, although mostly they've been covered with a foam sheeting to protect them. However, I'm still waiting for the bathroom fittings for three of the bathrooms, and if they don't arrive in the next forty-eight hours, it's going to throw our scheduling. I telephone Clesaux, the bathroom supplies company, and give the customer service lady the order number and other details, asking her to check when the items are going to be delivered on-site.

'Ah yes, I've found the account. This is strange. We received a telephone call from you last week cancelling the order.'

'No, that's not right,' I say, trying to quell the panic. 'I haven't telephoned.'

'Let me check, one moment, please.' She disappears, and I have to listen to some electronic music. After a couple of minutes, she returns. 'I've checked, and my colleague received the phone call. It was from a lady called Helen Sellers.' She reads out my telephone number.

I didn't make that call. Of course I didn't, so who the hell did? Who knew my telephone number, and who would knowingly do something to undercut me like that? Or have the suppliers just made a mistake and got our order mixed up with another one?

'When will everything be available again?'

'I will have to check and get back to you. I shall call you back.'

I pace the room. This is something I'm going to have to tell Camilla because it could throw the whole installation schedule. She might have to choose different bathroom fittings, and I can just imagine how that will go down. I hold my breath as I dial her number.

'There's been a problem with the delivery of some of the baths, sinks and toilets,' I explain.

'I'm busy. I don't want to know about it. That's your job, so just sort it.' She hangs up on me.

Wow! And to think I liked Camilla the first time we met. Instead I call Saskia, but I don't get much support from her either. 'I'm sorry, Helen, but I'm really busy. I have to leave the interiors to you.'

And of course she's right. That's what Camilla is paying me to do, but it's hard being all alone with a young child in a foreign country where you don't speak the language. I stride back to the cabin, make myself a strong cup of coffee and watch Emily and Sylvie playing with Emily's dolls. Then I pull myself together, sit down at the small table and go online, searching for other sanitary-ware suppliers, in case the original company can't deliver in the timescale.

And then the lady from Clesaux calls. 'I can get the items delivered to you a week today,' she says.

'That's too late. I need them tomorrow.'

She tuts. 'We have to charge a lot extra for expedited delivery. You will have to cover the cost.'

When she tells me the sum, I nearly choke. That's equivalent to a day and a half of my time, but what choice do I have? If I'm lucky, Camilla will cover the cost. If not, then I'll just have to take the hit personally.

'Okay,' I say, thinking how hectic it'll be tomorrow having both the bathroom fittings and kitchen units delivered on the same day. I'm not looking forward to breaking the news to Jacques.

THE NEXT MORNING I ask Jacques to get the driveway cleared of all vehicles – always a challenge here in the mountains, where there seems to be more houses than parking spaces and garages. He does his normal eye roll and shrugging of shoulders, as if I've requested something totally unreasonable, but at least he sorts it. The kitchen is spotless, ready for the units, and Jacques paces the chalet. He's not the only one who is getting impatient. I glance at my watch every couple of minutes, but the promised 8 am start is already over half an hour delayed. At 9 am, I telephone the kitchen company.

There's a long silence on the phone when I ask where our units have got to.

'But you rang me and asked for the installation to be delayed by one month!' the account manager exclaims.

'No,' I say, crouching down with my back against the wall. 'I was expecting them this morning.'

'I have it in my diary, Ms Sellers. You telephoned the day before yesterday, gave your name and your telephone number, and then you followed it up by email. We replied confirming the future date.'

'It wasn't me,' I murmur as my stomach cramps. 'What's the email you have for me?' I ask.

'Helensellers23@gmail.co.uk.'

'That's not my email. Someone has pretended to be me!' Someone is trying to undermine me.

The man tuts, and I've no doubt that he thinks I'm some crazy English lady. I need to pull myself together and focus on getting out of this mess.

'How soon can you deliver and install the kitchen? We can't wait another month. I was expecting you today.'

He huffs and puffs down the end of the phone, but eventually we negotiate that they will be here in three days' time. It totally throws the schedule, but it could be so much worse. Jacques is livid, and I don't blame him. It's messed up his planning too. He throws his hands up in the air and mutters away to himself.

I don't have much time to think about this until later because the bathroom units arrive mid-morning, and the chalet is bustling with activity. When I eventually return to the cabin, I take stock. I can't understand who would want me to fail on this job. Who, other than Jacques, Saskia and Camilla even know which contractors I've been dealing with? Unless he's using some voice app to pretend to be female, I have to discount Jacques. Camilla isn't going to stop the units from arriving on time because that would derail her own tight schedule, so the only person left is Saskia. But why would Saskia want me to look like an idiot? If I don't complete on time, then she's also tainted. It really doesn't make any sense.

BY EARLY EVENING the weather has cooled off, and Emily is restless. I suggest we play boats in the Bisse and go out for a wander. Emily finds a big pine cone and runs after it as it floats along the stream.

'Shall we have a race?' I suggest, improvising two little boats from pine cones and sticks. Mine has the lighter coloured spindly stick.

'One, two, three, go!' Emily says excitedly. We release our cones, and as she runs off after them, something makes me stand still. I shiver. I get the feeling that I'm being watched. I swivel around very slowly, but there's no one on the Bisse. I glance around the forest, but anyone could be hiding either up or downhill from us in the shadows of the trees. Or perhaps it's a wild animal, hiding behind a bush, waiting for us to leave its territory.

'Mummy, I'm winning!' Emily shouts, bouncing up and down excitedly. I hurry to catch up with her, but it's hard moving quickly with this damned boot on. I don't want my daughter to be out of my sight for one moment. What if it isn't an animal? What if that man is here? Could he be planning to abduct Emily?

'I think we should go back,' I say as I eventually catch up with her.

'No!' Emily wails. 'We've only just started playing.'

She's right of course, and no doubt contrary to every parenting manual there is, I relent. 'Alright, we'll stay for a little while, but make sure you're right next to me all the time. Mummy can't move quickly with her hurt ankle.' I groan to myself. I hate talking to Emily in the third person and only ever slip into the way that my mother spoke to me when I'm stressed or tired.

Emily chooses to ignore the second part of that sentence because she's already running off along the footpath. I hurry to keep up but still get the sense that there's someone else here. Emily stops, crouches down and leans into the stream.

'It's freezing!' she says as she fishes out her cone that has got stuck in some fronds on the side.

'The water comes from melting glaciers,' I say.

And then I hear the crack of a branch.

'Who's there?' I shout, trying to work out which direction the noise came from. 'I know you're there, so just show yourself!'

Then there's another crack, and I hear running feet crunching on pine cones and fallen twigs, but the person doesn't emerge onto the Bisse until a few seconds later, and then he's running, fast, away from us. The way he runs, the way his right foot seems to lag slightly behind, makes my throat close up. That gait is so familiar, just like the man I saw at the Inalpe festival. Just the way Paul used to run.

'Wait!' I yell, hobbling forwards as quickly as I can. 'Who are you?' I rack my brains for the correct phrase in French. '*Qui êtes vous?*' I shout.

But the person just disappears around the corner without once glancing backwards. In the shadows of the trees and the bokeh light caused by the sinking sun, I can't see properly.

There's nothing I can do but lean my hands against my knees and groan. The question is, was he following us? Was he standing in the shadows of the trees, breathing in the same pine-scented air as us, waiting? But if so, waiting for what? Could it be Paul? Is it possible that he's alive and well and living here? Does he want to snatch Emily? Is that what it's all been about? Does he want to hurt my beautiful daughter? Is Emily really in danger?

I shake my head. I'm being stupid. Paul is dead. I think of the plaque by the ski lift that Andrew wanted me to visit. Perhaps that's what I need to do. Perhaps all these imaginary sightings of Paul are because I've had no closure. Seeing a memorial plate might just be the resolution I need.

21

I hurry Emily back to the cabin and lock the door behind us. She's bolshy with me, and I don't blame her, what with my questioning as to whether she'd seen 'that' man again and trying to get her to give me a better description. I sit her down in front of my iPad and make myself a cup of tea.

I'm sure I didn't imagine the person in the woods. I heard the footsteps; I had that horrible, tingling sensation that we were being watched. Could it really have been Paul in the woods? No, it's a ridiculous thought. Even thinking that makes me question my own sanity, but on the other hand, the similarities between his stature and that limping gait are just too great to ignore. Should I seriously consider it was Paul? Does the very thought make me crazy? But what if he really is alive and living here? What if he's following us? And then I remember my conversations with Andrew. It's been immensely stressful for me, particularly the last few days with the order cancellations. Could my mind be playing tricks on me? Am I mentally unwell? I know people crack under pressure, and the past few years have been far from easy. All things considered, I coped pretty well after Paul's disappearance, but perhaps it's catching up with me now. Maybe the mountains are closing in, cracking my mind, making me fearful and delusional. I groan out loud. Although it's going to be emotionally hard, I resolve to visit Paul's plaque. I need to do that for my sake and that of my family. With my foot in a boot, I can't hike up to the spot where Paul disappeared, so all I can do is visit the lift station, assuming I can get there easily.

'What is it, Mummy?' Emily asks.

'Nothing, sweetheart. I'm just tired. Would you like to do some colouring?'

'No.' Emily stamps her feet, and I know she's just picking up on my unease.

'You can watch a video on my iPad,' I say, and immediately she perks up.

When she's settled and likely to not listen to my conversation, I telephone the tourist office.

'Which is the main lift station to get to Col de Pavarois?'

'You take the gondola up to La Carousselle and then a chairlift to Col de Pavarois. From there follow the path signed to Lac de Pavarois. Your hike will take you through Col de Pavarois.'

'Um, I don't actually want to hike. Actually I can't, because my foot is in a boot. But would I be able to take the gondola and then the chairlift if I can't walk properly?'

'Yes, but you need to be able to walk to get on and off the chairlift.'

'I can manage that. Are the lifts open tomorrow morning?'

'Yes, they're open every day during the summer months.'

'Thank you very much for your help.'

. . .

AFTER I HAVE TUCKED Emily up in bed, I telephone Andrew. 'I've decided I do need closure after all. I'm going to visit Paul's memorial plaque tomorrow.'

'You are?' Andrew sounds surprised.

I don't tell him about seeing a man resembling Paul in the woods; I can't face the humiliation of Andrew thinking I've become unhinged.

'You won't go by yourself, will you? It's dangerous up on the mountains alone.'

'You don't need to tell me that,' I snap, and then immediately apologise. 'Anyway, I can't walk properly, so I'll only be visiting the plaque, not the place where Paul fell.'

'Okay, darling. But I'd still rather you don't go alone.'

He's only looking out for me. I now wish I'd taken up his offer of visiting when he was here because the truth is, I have no one to go with. Saskia is working, Manon is too elderly, and I don't know anyone else I could ask. Besides, it's not physically challenging, it's just going to be emotionally difficult, and no one can help me deal with that.

THE NEXT MORNING, there is a clear blue sky, and it's warm. I take it as a good omen. I tell Jacques that I will be off-site for a couple of hours, and I get Sylvie to promise she'll stay in or around the cabin with Emily. I take Camilla's Golf and drive to Lanvière. It's only twenty minutes away, but my knuckles are white as I clutch the steering wheel. I follow the signs to the lift station and park in the car park, which is surprisingly empty. The return ticket for the lifts is expensive, and as I swipe the card ticket and hobble through the turnstile, I pause. Do I really want to be doing this? Will I be stirring up old, unpleasant memories rather than laying them to rest? The last time I got on these gondola lifts was the last day I saw Paul alive. Then it was heaving with eager skiers; now I am the only visitor.

The lift attendant strides towards me and speaks rapidly in French.

'Sorry, I don't understand,' I say.

'I ask if there is a problem?' He looks at me kindly, and I wonder whether he thinks I'm phobic of heights or something.

'No, no. Sorry. I'm just going.' I smile briefly and climb into the next gondola, quickly sitting down facing the valley. The lift rises rapidly and smoothly, in contrast to my heart, which feels as if it's skipping beats. I take several slow breaths and concentrate on the stunning view. This looks a totally different place to five years ago. Today, the vista is of green and grey mountains with just the smallest patches of snow on the peaks. The sun glistens, and I force myself to smile. I'm safe, I'm alone, and all will be fine. I may be safe, but what about Emily? I pull out my mobile phone and dial Sylvie's number.

'Is everything alright?' I ask when she answers.

'Yes, we're having a lovely time. Do you want to speak to Mummy?' Sylvie says.

I can hear Emily in the background. 'No. I'm busy.'

'That's not very nice, Emily,' Sylvie chastises her.

I laugh. 'It's fine. If she doesn't want to talk to me, that means she's happy.'

'Yes, she is. We're having a lovely time.'

'Thank you, Sylvie. I'll see you both around lunchtime.'

Less than five minutes later, the gondola slows down, and we enter the lift station. I climb out into the cold, grey concrete building and, hanging on to the handrail, cautiously walk down a flight of metal steps. Outside, it is significantly colder than down in the village, and despite the sun, I shiver. There are a few people milling around, dressed in shorts or cargo pants, rucksacks on their backs and sturdy hiking boots on their feet. I am out of place here, dressed in jeans and an anorak. Positioned on the side of the building is a map of the ski lifts, and it's obvious that the chairlift directly in front of me is the one that goes up to Col de Pavarois. I walk slowly across the grassy meadow to the chairlift. Once again, I hesitate. I don't even know where the plaque is exactly; I just recall Paul's father mentioning the ski lift. After steadying myself, I walk up to the chairlift and stand in line. There's an older couple in front of me, their faces weathered, dressed for a hike. The woman throws me a quizzical glance as she notices the boot on my foot. I smile awkwardly.

Then it's my turn. I'm relieved to be alone on the chair. It bounces upwards, and the cold air once again makes me shiver. There's a herd of cows in a pasture below, their bells jangling loudly, and for some silly reason it makes me feel less alone. The lift doesn't take long, and I stumble slightly as I get off, trying to walk too quickly. After righting myself, I hobble around the lift, but there is nothing here except a small wooden hut, where a man sits smoking cigarettes, and the metal posts of the chairlift. Where is the memorial plaque? I wander around the structures again but see nothing. Eventually I go over to the lift attendant.

'*Excusez-moi mais parlez-vous anglaise?*' I ask, hoping I've got the basic phrase right.

'*Malheureusement, non,*' he says, shaking his head.

'I'm looking for a memorial plaque,' I say, in the vain hope that some of the words might be similar in French, but he just shrugs his shoulders and gestures that he doesn't understand. This is hopeless.

It simply never crossed my mind that I wouldn't be able to find the plaque. After a couple of minutes during which the attendant is staring at me with a frown, I decide to return home. I feel nothing up here. No connection with Paul. No overwhelming sadness. Not even any of the guilt that plagued me for so long. I debate telephoning Susannah and asking where the plaque was installed, but quickly discount that. Our relationship is fragile, and I doubt she'd understand what I was doing. Instead, I get on the next chairlift returning to the main station. It isn't until I'm back in the grey concrete building that it hits me. Paul's parents wouldn't have had a plaque installed in a place where barely anyone would see it. They wanted their son to be remembered and recognised. Perhaps I got it wrong. It would be much more likely to find something here in this cold, stark building where hordes of people pass through every day in the winter season.

I shuffle slowly through the hall where the skiers walk to approach the gondolas. On the concrete walls are a series of large advertisements for fizzy drinks and driving school instructors, a piste map and notices for the ski school. I don't see any memorial plates. The mechanical noise of the lifts is harsh and loud here, and there's no one around. It reminds me of the evening I went looking for Paul, when the ski station in Lanvière was desolate. I round a corner and then hear heavy footsteps coming towards me. The footsteps are uneven, as if the person has a slight limp. It makes me freeze. I lean against the cold wall, a wave of terror gripping my throat. And then a man comes into view. He's wearing grey overalls and carrying a bag of tools. I'm being such an idiot.

'Excuse me, do you speak English?' I ask once again.

'Sure,' he says with a strong New Zealand accent.

'Do you know if there are any memorial plaques in this building, commemorating people who have died on the slopes?'

'Actually, yes. They're on the wall outside the office. I'll show you if you like.'

'Thank you,' I say. I follow him down a side corridor, and there, on the wall, are three metal plates attached to the grey concrete wall. He hesitates awkwardly for a moment and then mumbles good luck and disappears.

So this is it. The first plaque lists the names of three people who lost their lives in an avalanche in 1994. The second plaque has four names on it. It's the third plaque that I'm here for.

Paul Harris Sellers

That's all it says. Just his name. No date of birth or death. It's a simple bronze plaque with black letters. I run my fingers over his name and realise the lettering is not engraved, as there are no indentations. I feel absolutely nothing. No sadness, no regret, no longing. It's as if I'm looking at a stranger's name. Quite why Andrew thought this might be cathartic, I have no idea. It's not. Looking at his name gives me zero reassurance that the creep who approached Emily and followed us was not Paul. I know that I'm achieving nothing by being here. I'm going to have to take a very different approach.

22

Back in the car, I talk out loud to myself.

'Get a grip, woman,' I yell. Yet all I see in my mind's eyes is the retreating back of the man with the slight limp. Somehow I'm going to have to prove to myself, once and for all, that Paul is dead and the man with the unusual gait wasn't him. I also need to work out who's been talking to Emily and who gave her the teddy bear. Frankly, I haven't got time for this, but for both Emily's and my sakes, I must take control. Perhaps I could talk to the detectives who worked on Paul's disappearance, but I discount that, thinking of how the British police reacted to my imaginary sightings of Paul a few years ago.

As I pass a run-down-looking hotel, I recall how kind Gabriella was towards me during those first few days after Paul went missing. It's not like I even knew her very well. She came to the memorial service, but I haven't been in touch with her since. I remember how she had a friend whose parents lived in Corviez. I wonder if they're still here, whether they might be able to help me. Perhaps being locals, they could talk to the police again for me, just double-check whether there have been any other sightings of Paul, but frustratingly I can't remember the friend's name. Back at the chalet, I do a quick check-in with Jacques and then hurry to the cabin, where I'm relieved to see Sylvie and Emily playing with her dolls. I give Emily a quick kiss and then fire up my laptop.

I do a Google search for Gabriella and discover that she's a solicitor, working for a firm in Reading. Her email address is listed next to her photo, and I fire off an email, asking if she's still in touch with the friend who was from Corviez.

An hour later I get a reply.

Hi Helen, hope you're well. I'm surprised you're back in Corviez. My friend is called Orla Sinerre. Her family still have a place there, I think, but I lost touch with her some years ago. She moved to Australia and I'm not sure where she is now. Sorry I don't have any contact details.
All the best, Gabriella.

I have no idea how to find out where the Sinerres live, or if they've still got a property here, so I walk over to Manon and Guillaume's house and knock on their door. Manon appears with a dishcloth in one hand. She appears slightly frazzled, and I wonder if I've interrupted at a bad time.

'Shall I come back?' I ask.

'No, no. Happy to see you. How can I help?'

'I am trying to track down an old friend. Do you know the Sinerre family?'

'Of course,' she says, although I think I notice a brief scowl on her face. 'Everyone knows everyone here. They're in Corviez.'

'Would you be able to give me directions to their house?'

'I can try. Come in.'

I follow Manon into the small, dark chalet. The walls of

the corridor are lined with numerous photographs, mainly in black and white, pictures of their extended family, I assume, skiing in exotic locations. The kitchen is lined with pine cupboards and the floor covered with terracotta tiles. She tears a piece of paper out of a notebook and uses a biro to draw directions.

'You know the Sinerres?' she asks.

'No. Their daughter is a friend of a friend. My friend has asked me to make contact.'

'They're a very rich and powerful family, in banking in Geneva. I don't know them personally, but everyone knows of them.' I get the sense that there's an undercurrent of dislike that Manon isn't prepared to articulate. It's as if she's warning me that these people wield a power that I need to be wary of. I thank her for the directions and hurry back to the car.

I loathe driving on the other side of the road, particularly on these narrow, windy stretches where everything is so unfamiliar. It's ridiculous because I'm a confident driver at home, but here I'm in someone else's car, and everything is different. Then there's the cumbersome boot on my left foot that doesn't help matters. But I have no choice. I need to know if anyone else has seen Paul, whether the person stalking Emily is him or a stranger. Hopefully the Sinerres' daughter has returned to live here, and being a friend of Gaby's, she'll be willing to help. For all I know, she might have met Paul too, back before he and I got together. And then I'm going to the police. I don't care if they think I'm overreacting; I will do anything to keep my daughter safe.

The Sinerre family chalet looks more like a small castle, with turrets and little spires and wonderfully ornate tiles with carved wooden balconies. The property is set off the road and doesn't have the magical views that Camilla's chalet has, but it has seclusion, with lawns extending around the house and trees hemming it in on every side. I pull up at the front and hobble up the steps. There's a bronze bell contraption with a handle. It rings loudly.

A few moments later, the front door opens, and an Asian lady wearing an apron stands there.

'Hello. I'm hoping to talk to a member of the Sinerre family,' I say.

'They're not here.'

'I'm an old friend of the family and was hoping to see them.' I'm surprised how easily the lie slips off my tongue.

'Monsieur and Madame are at their property on Lac Leman. I'm not expecting them back here for another ten days.'

'Actually I was hoping to talk to their daughter. She's my friend. Is Orla around?'

'No, Orla doesn't live here. She has her own house in Corviez.'

'Any chance you could give me the address?'

The woman hesitates but then clearly decides I'm trustworthy and reels off an address back in the village I've just come from.

'Who should I say is looking for her?'

'My name is Helen Sellers.' Although she probably won't know who I am. I'm not sure that we ever met. 'The late Paul Sellers' wife,' I add.

I PLUG Orla Sinerre's address into my phone and, following Google Maps, turn the car around to head back in the direction I came from. And then my phone rings. When I see Sylvie's name come up as the caller, my breath catches in my throat. I slam my foot on the brakes and pull over onto the kerb.

'Sylvie, is everything alright?'

There's silence.

'Sylvie?' I say again, panic mounting. Still nothing. My God, what has happened? My imagination goes into overdrive. Has that man captured Sylvie and Emily? Is Sylvie unable to speak to me and calling just to alert me that something terrible has happened? Should I call the police? 'Sylvie, are you there?'

And then I hear a rustle and movement. 'What's going on?' I shout. It dawns on me that perhaps the phone is in her pocket, and she's pressed the call button by mistake. I'm probably massively overreacting. I take a deep breath and end the call, ringing her back immediately. The phone rings several times whilst I will her to answer.

At last. 'Sylvie, what's going on?'

'Mummy?'

Emily's high-pitched voice makes me want to weep with relief. 'Darling, is everything alright?'

'Yes.'

'Where's Sylvie?'

'She's just gone out.'

'What do you mean, she's gone out?' I swallow hard.

'She gave me her phone to play with, and she's gone to the neighbours'. She said she couldn't get something to work.'

'But I told her not to leave you! Are you all alone?'

'Don't worry, Mummy,' Emily says with the naïve confidence of a four-year-old.

'Where are you, sweetheart?'

'In the garden.'

'I want you to go back inside the cabin straight away and shut the door. Make sure you don't let anyone in.'

'But, Mummy...'

'Do as I say, Emily, and I'll be home as quickly as I can. It's important, darling. I love you.'

I hang up and thump the palms of my hands against the

steering wheel. What the hell is Sylvie doing? I told her not to leave Emily alone. I knew it was a bad idea to let a sixteen-year-old look after my child. Sylvie's still a child herself. I put my foot on the accelerator and speed away.

I don't get far. Ahead, on the narrow winding road there are workmen, one of them holding a stop sign, a lorry behind him. There's a loud, rumbling sound, and as I look upwards, I see a helicopter hovering. As if my panic wasn't already at full blast, now I feel sick. What the hell's going on? I'm in a desperate hurry. I look at Google Maps, wondering if there's another way back to Corviez, but no such luck. I wind down my window and gesticulate at the man holding the sign.

'What's going on?' I ask in my faltering French. He gabbles away some response, and the only words I can work out are helicopter and tree.

'How long will it take?' I ask.

He throws his hands up in the air and shrugs.

'Five minutes, ten?' I ask, feeling an overwhelming desperation.

'Perhaps. Helicopter expensive so goes quickly.'

'Thank you,' I say, trying to concentrate on staying calm. I count my breaths in and out and force myself to look upwards at the hovering helicopter.

I remind myself that this is not a rescue helicopter. It's a workhorse and nothing to be scared of. A long rope is lowered, and then to my amazement, I see a full-sized pine tree being lifted up into the air. It hangs precariously, and I wonder for a horrible moment whether it might come crashing down onto the bonnet of my car. I tap my fingers impatiently on the dashboard, and then, perhaps five minutes later, the longest ever five minutes, I'm waved through to continue on my way.

I drive too quickly, and when I almost take out a car coming in the opposite direction and am rewarded by the hooting of a horn, I remind myself there's nothing to worry about. Emily is safe in the cabin, and Sylvie is probably back by now. I need to calm down.

Ten minutes later, I swerve onto the drive of the chalet, dumping the car next to a white van and racing towards the cabin. Jacques is standing outside the chalet.

'What's the hurry?' he asks, one eyebrow raised in amusement. The man annoys me so much. I don't answer and rush past him.

'Hey!' he shouts. 'I'm talking to you, Hélène. I need you here on-site. There's a problem in the master bedroom.'

'Sorry, not now.'

'*Bien alors!*' he says. 'You don't have your eyes on the job. What do you want me to tell Camilla? That her fancy English designer is too busy with her little girl to do her job properly? Too many screw-ups, Hélène.' He shakes his head.

I freeze. How does Jacques know that I'm rushing back to the cabin to check up on Emily? Could he be the man stalking my daughter? If so, he's much, much too close for comfort.

'What do you know about Emily?' I ask, coming to a halt and narrowing my eyes at him.

He shrugs his shoulders. 'We have work to do.' He turns and strides away from me. I bite the inside of my mouth, drawing blood. I have never been prone to violence, but right now I could hurl something at Jacques. I grit my teeth and remind myself I need to focus on Emily, make sure that she's safe.

I race to the cabin and wrench open the front door. Emily is sitting at the table, a piece of paper in front of her, crayons scattered across the wooden surface. Sylvie has her back to the door, and she's stirring something on the stove. She turns.

'Is everything alright?' I ask, my voice strident.

'Hello, Helen.'

'Mummy!' Emily says, shoving her chair back and racing towards me, throwing her arms around my legs.

'What happened?' I ask as I stroke Emily's hair.

Sylvie looks up at me with alarm. 'Nothing!'

'Emily said you left her alone to go to the neighbours'.'

Sylvie's cheeks flush red. 'I couldn't open the tin of tomatoes.' She holds up the tin opener. This morning, I left her some bolognaise that I made last night and told her to heat it up with the tinned tomatoes, knowing how much Emily likes it. Sylvie told me she knew how to cook pasta and could easily give her spaghetti bolognaise for lunch. It never crossed my mind Sylvie wouldn't know how to use a tin opener.

'But I told you never to leave Emily alone.'

'I'm sorry,' Sylvie says, her bottom lip trembling. 'But she's safe here, and I couldn't open it. I haven't used one of these openers before. Emily said that your neighbour, Manon, is very nice and suggested I ask her to open the tin for me. I didn't want to disturb the people working on-site.'

Emily releases her grip on me and returns to the table. I sink down onto the sofa, realising I've totally overreacted. Even my little Emily has shown initiative.

'Will I lose my job?' Sylvie asks. She looks so forlorn and upset.

'No, of course not. But you really should have taken Emily with you rather than leaving her alone here. Anyway, it's my fault for not showing you how the tin opener works.' But what I'm really thinking is, have I been naïve expecting a sixteen-year-old to babysit my daughter? This is a young girl who lives at home and has likely never cooked a meal by herself before, so it's unfair of me to be angry with her when she was only following my instructions. 'Do you need help with anything else?'

'No. I'm sorry I didn't know how it worked.'

'It's fine, Sylvie. I'm just a bit on edge at the moment with everything that's going on.' I stand up.

She frowns at me, and I realise she doesn't understand. Her English is excellent but likely doesn't stretch to idioms. 'Don't worry. I need to get back to work, but you two have fun this afternoon, and I'll see you later.'

I walk back to the chalet feeling a little calmer now, wondering which is the better option to ensure Emily's safety. Sylvie or the playgroup? I still think Sylvie is the better choice. At least I can check up on her and Emily several times a day, and I suspect I scared her by my little outburst, so it's unlikely she'll take her eyes off Emily now. I glance at my watch. I'll deal with the problem in the master bedroom, and then I'll head out again. I really want to talk to Orla.

THIRTY MINUTES LATER, Jacques has calmed down. I've dealt with the outstanding issues on-site, and I'm back in the car, heading towards Orla's chalet. It's outside the village, up a winding lane above Corviez. I wonder what she does out here and whether she has a family of her own now. This chalet is more traditional, dark wood with shutters and a slightly abandoned feel, probably due to the overgrown garden. I walk up to the front door and bang on the knocker.

There's no answer. I wait a good thirty seconds and then knock again. I'm just about to shuffle to the side to peek through a window when I hear footsteps and the unlocking of the door.

'Hello,' the woman says, looking at me blankly.

'Sorry to disturb you, but are you Orla Sinerre?'

'Yes, and you are?'

'Helen Sellers. I understand that we have a mutual friend – Gabriella?'

There's a pause, and then she says, 'Oh goodness, I haven't heard from Gaby in ages. How is she?'

'Fine,' I say. 'Well. She sends her best wishes.'

'Any friend of Gaby's is a friend of mine too,' Orla says, laughing. 'What are you doing over here?'

'I have some work. I'm an interior designer.'

I notice that Orla doesn't invite me in; instead, she keeps the door pulled closed behind her.

'Gabriella said you might be able to help me.' Of course she hasn't said that, but it's my best bet for getting Orla on my side. 'You look familiar,' I say. I've definitely seen her somewhere before; perhaps during those awful days of our skiing holiday or after Paul disappeared. That long, curly black hair and those high cheekbones ring a bell.

'We probably attended the same parties in the past if we have mutual friends. Did you go to Gaby's wedding?'

'Yes, I did.' I remember the lovely occasion just a few months before our own wedding.

'Look, why don't we go for a coffee in the village,' Orla suggests. 'We've obviously got lots in common, and you can tell me all about how I can help you.'

'That's very kind,' I say. 'I don't want to disturb.'

'Oh, you're not. I was just pottering. Why don't I meet you at La Coin? It's the coffee shop next to the bank.'

'Oh sure, if that's not much of an inconvenience.'

'Absolutely not. I'll just collect my bag and meet you there in ten minutes.'

And then the door closes, and Orla has disappeared inside.

23

Yesterday, I ignored Orla's instruction to stay indoors and went for a run. I needed to clear my head as much as I needed to check that Helen and Emily were safe. I almost pushed it too far though, and I frightened myself. I don't think she saw me, but Helen shouted out, asking who was there. I've never run so fast. Back at the chalet, I had a quick shower, and when Orla returned, I was putting the final touches to the spreadsheet. She acted as if she'd never said those threatening words, and I let it go, because what other choice do I have? Orla is a blusterer, capricious and quick to anger, but I've never experienced anything other than her soft centre.

Today I'm upstairs in the small bedroom that we have turned into my office. It looks out onto the front of the house, and I'm surprised by the sound of a car pulling up in front of the chalet. The only person who visits us here is the post lady in her van. It'll be a visitor for Orla, so I turn back to concentrate on my business plan's conclusion. When eventually Orla answers the door, I hear two female voices. It takes me a moment to realise I recognise them both.

What the hell is Helen doing here?

I swallow hard and tiptoe across the room to open the bedroom door, hoping to hear the conversation better. What game is Orla playing at suggesting she meet Helen for a coffee? I feel sick now, not knowing what to do. When the front door eventually shuts and Orla walks back into the hallway, she runs straight up the stairs, her eyes on me.

'Get back in the room,' she says in a low whisper.

'What is Helen doing here?' I ask as I back into the room.

'Keep your bloody voice down!'

We're both still as we hear a car door closing and then an engine starting up, the wheels crunching on gravel as the car reverses and then drives away.

'What the hell is going on, Orla?' I ask, grabbing her upper arms.

'Calm down!' she says, pushing me backwards. 'I don't know what she's doing here, but I'm going to find out. You need to stay hidden.'

I shake my head. 'No. Maybe it's time to tell Helen the truth. Maybe all of this deceit is destroying us.'

'Are you crazy, Joel? If you suddenly appear, you'll get arrested for murder and fraud and God knows what else. Stop being such an idiot. Just keep your head down and stay quiet, exactly as we discussed. I've got this.'

'I didn't kill anyone,' I say. 'Our lives are about to unravel. We've lived lies for too long. I think the time has come to face the truth.'

Orla's face is set firm, her eyes hard. 'Over my dead body. Just stay here.'

Then she turns around and slams the door behind her. I hesitate for a moment, trying to work out how Helen found Orla. The conversation sounded perfectly amiable, but what if Helen suspects I'm here?

And then I hear the lock turning in the door, and Orla

running down the stairs.

'Orla?' I shout, striding to the bedroom door and turning the handle.

She's locked me in. Orla has locked me in!

I rush to the window, undo the latch and shove it open, but Orla is already in her car, and then her engine starts up, and I watch with horror as she drives away. My partner, my lover, the woman I have just spent the past five years with, has locked me in this room like a prisoner. What the hell is she playing at?

I glance around for my mobile phone, but it's not on the table. I try my back pocket, scour the floor, check in the pockets of the jacket I flung on the bed, but it's not here. I groan as I try to recall when I last had it. Probably at breakfast. I most likely left it on the kitchen table because it never crossed my mind that I might be locked in! So what now? I walk back to the window and push it open a bit further. It's much too far to jump, I'm fit and agile, but I'm sure I'd hurt myself.

I pace for a few moments and then accept that I'll just have to wait here until Orla returns. I try the door again. Could I break it down? It's solid wood, and when I ram it with my shoulder, it barely moves. I kick it in fury, but all I do is hurt my foot. I go back to my laptop and fire off an email to Orla.

What the hell are you playing at? Come back here and let me out.

I've no idea when she'll pick it up.

After letting out a furious shout, I realise I have little choice but to distract myself with my business plan. I fail spectacularly. All I can think about is Orla and Helen meeting for the first time. Could Orla hurt Helen? Or has

Helen found out that I had an affair with Orla, and will she hurt her? That seems a lot less likely. Orla is the strong one, with the quick chess-master brain, fearless and reckless. But Helen has the potential to ruin everything for us. If she tells the police she's seen me, I will be going to prison, and for all Orla knows, I'll bring her down too. But has Orla got it in her to knowingly hurt another human being? Yes, she skied into that Noemie girl, but that was an accident and an impulsive error of judgement not to stay around to help. It was manslaughter at worst, certainly not premeditated. Surely my Orla wouldn't do anything that horrific?

I try but fail to calm myself. It's totally unacceptable for Orla to lock me in! I would never do that to her; it would simply never cross my mind. I can't still myself, and I'm not sure whom I'm more fearful for: Orla, Helen, Emily or myself. What's certain is that I can't stay cooped up in this chalet doing nothing. After nearly half an hour of mounting fury and fear, I push the window open as wide as it will go and haul myself up onto the window ledge. I'm much too high up to jump, but there is a drainpipe extending the whole way down the side of the building. It's copper and looks sturdier than the plastic ones we had at home in England. I turn to one side and grab the pipe, placing my right foot on a strut that's securing the drainpipe to the wall. My heart is pumping wildly, and I daren't look down. The palms of my hands are slippery as I grab the drainpipe and swing my left leg around. I let one foot down, seeking a foothold. I can't look, so I just let my weight drop with my leg. It holds. I do it again. And then I lose my footing. I flail wildly, trying to hang on, but it's no good. In that split second, I try to remember how to fall. I know that as soon as I hit the ground, I must land on my side and immediately roll over. But it's all so fast. The air swishes past.

Blackness.

24

I arrive before Orla and sit at a table on the terrace, looking through the drinks menu. There's fencing around the terrace with window boxes overflowing with red geraniums, and even though the view is onto the main street through the village, looking onto uninspiring, concrete apartment blocks, there's still a pleasant ambience. The waitress comes over and asks me what I'd like. In faltering French, I tell her I'm waiting for a friend. After ten minutes, Orla still hasn't turned up, and I wonder whether she has decided she's got better things to do than have coffee with a random friend of a friend. The waitress appears again, so I order a sparkling mineral water and decide that if Orla hasn't arrived by the time I've finished it, I'll leave.

'I'm sorry, so sorry!' Orla appears in a whirlwind of white linen, flowing dark curly hair and a cloud of floral perfume. 'The phone rang just as I was on my way out,' she says breathlessly. 'It was a call I've been waiting for all day. So frustrating how that always happens.' She sits down and puts her designer sunglasses on the table next to her phone and leather wallet. 'I'm glad you didn't wait for me to order a drink. Can I get you another one?'

I decline. She clicks her fingers at the waitress in the way overly privileged people tend to do. It always grates with me. The waitress doesn't seem to mind and strides over with a smile of recognition on her face. Orla orders a double espresso.

She tilts her head to one side and stares at me. Her big, black eyes, and something about the way she looks at me, is unsettling.

'So, you're a friend of Gaby's,' she says.

'Yes. I don't know if you remember, but my husband, Paul, who was an old university friend of Gaby's, went missing on the mountains here five years ago.'

Orla's hand rushes to cover her mouth, and her eyes widen. 'Oh my goodness. Now I know who you are. I'm so sorry for your loss. Everyone knew about the poor Englishman who went missing. I assume he was never found?'

I frown slightly because she'd know, wouldn't she? And if she was a friend of Gaby's, then she'd certainly know.

'I've been living abroad for a few years and only returned to Switzerland recently,' Orla explains.

'No, he was never found.'

'I'm sorry to hear that. What can I do to help?' Orla puts her sunglasses on and then removes them again. She seems restless, but this doesn't surprise me. People deal with premature death in a myriad of different ways, and some people simply don't know how to handle it. And in many ways, Paul's situation is even worse because it's awkward. People don't know whether to pass on their condolences or their commiserations or perhaps say nothing at all. There's no script for when someone vanishes.

The waitress brings over Orla's coffee. She doesn't

acknowledge the waitress but takes a sip despite the fact it must be burning hot. Her red lipstick leaves a mark on the edge of the small white cup, yet she doesn't flinch from the heat.

'The thing is,' I say, sitting back in my chair, 'as unlikely as it sounds, I think Paul might still be alive and living here.'

'What!' she exclaims. Her coffee cup wobbles violently, but she catches it just in time before it slips off the saucer. 'Surely not! Why do you think that?'

I realise how crazy I sound and wonder what Orla thinks of me. 'I've seen a man who looks just like him a couple of times, and some things have happened that I can't really explain.'

'Goodness. What do the police say?'

'I haven't told the police. I don't have any concrete proof, it's just a hunch, and I think they'd send me packing.' I don't tell Orla that I'd notified the police twice in the UK, thinking I'd seen Paul, when it turned out I didn't. My police liaison officer tells me it's common to think we've seen people we love and lost, even if they're not there. It's one of the many stages of grief. 'Can you help me track him down?'

'Gosh, I wouldn't know where to begin.' Orla seems truly startled by this request, but I suppose it is a strange one.

'Perhaps I could send you a photograph of Paul. It would be great if you could ask around, your friends and family, and maybe show his photograph to shopkeepers and restaurant staff? Anyone you come across, really.'

'You really think you saw Paul here in Switzerland?'

'Yes. I'm pretty sure I've spotted him twice. I know it sounds crazy. He had a very distinctive walk and–' My voice peters out as I begin to doubt myself.

'Um, yes, I can do my best, but perhaps Paul doesn't want to be found. I mean, wouldn't he have come home to you if he had just got lost?'

I sigh, because of course Orla is right. If it was Paul talking to Emily and if it was him when we were in the woods last night, it's obvious he doesn't want to make himself known. Perhaps he sustained a head injury on the mountains and has some sort of amnesia and doesn't know how to approach me now. If an intermediary could explain that I'm not angry, that I just want to help him, then that would be perfect. But of course I am angry. I don't want him back, I'm happy with Andrew, but I do want resolution for me and Emily.

'I just need to know, Orla. It's an impossible situation.'

'Maybe you imagined it? I mean, it's very unlikely, isn't it? The authorities here are very good at finding lost people on the mountainside, and if they said he's dead, then I fear he probably is.'

'I realise it sounds absurd, but I have a hunch about it. I can't explain logically. I just want to be sure that it wasn't him I saw.'

She nods and asks, 'Are you in a new relationship?'

I smile. 'Yes, and as soon as the seven years is up and we can officially declare Paul dead, we're going to get married, and Andrew will formally adopt Emily. Unless Paul's alive of course, in which case I'll demand a quick divorce.'

'I'm glad you've found happiness despite everything,' she says, putting her sunglasses back on. 'So, tell me about the project you're working on.'

I explain the basics of the design brief for Camilla's chalet, and I wonder for a moment whether Orla knows Camilla, but she gives no indication of doing so.

'I have lots of friends in need of an interior designer,' Orla says. 'I might be able to get you more work. I assume you don't just do chalets?'

'Oh no. This is the first one I've done. I can turn my hand to any style.'

'Definitely worth knowing,' Orla says.

'Do you work?' I ask.

She throws her head back and laughs. 'Yes, and it's what has taken me away for the past years. I work in my father's investment bank. We have portfolios we manage all over the world. Wealthy people trust the Swiss because for generations we've kept their identities anonymous. Unfortunately, in today's day and age with all the technology, that's become harder, but we still do our best.'

'What exactly do you do?' I ask. It sounds very clandestine and glamorous.

'Just select the best investments for our private clients and make sure their money is working for them. It's not nearly as fun and creative as what you do.'

That might be the case, but from the look of her expensive watch with a black face surrounded by sparkling diamonds that match the large glistening drop diamonds in her ears, it will certainly be better at paying the bills.

'Let's swap phone numbers and stay in touch.' She glances at her watch. 'I've got a call I need to get back for, but it was lovely to meet you, Helen, and I'll certainly do what I can to see if Paul really is alive and in Switzerland. You know, this is a very small, tight-knit community. The chances of him being here and not being spotted are about zero, so I don't want you to get your hopes up.'

I smile tightly at her because I suspect she's right. It really isn't logical for Paul to return to the very place he disappeared. But at least I have another local on my side now, and she seems very well connected.

I LEAVE the coffee shop feeling positive, and knowing Emily is safe with Sylvie, I drive back to the chalet.

'Helen, the electrician has some questions for you about

the light fittings in the utility room,' Jacques shouts at me from one of the balconies as I walk up the drive. That's annoying. I wanted to check on Emily and Sylvie.

Half an hour later, after I have resolved the electrician's questions, I walk through each room, making sure that everything has been installed to the highest standard. The master bedroom has a brass chandelier that looks slightly wonky. I'm just walking down the stairs to ask the electrician to straighten it when I hear a female cry. I stop still.

'Helen!' There's a shout. I rush outside to the small area of grass between the chalet and the cabin. Sylvie is running towards me with tears streaking her cheeks. She's waving her arms wildly.

'What's happened?' I ask, fear gripping my throat.

'Emily is gone! She's missing! I can't find her anywhere.'

25

I t's every mother's worst nightmare. We prepare ourselves for this, think about how we might react, what we might say, but until it happens, you can never know.

It feels as if my innards are being ripped open, yet I have to be the grown-up here. Sylvie is still a kid, and I'm in my workplace, so I can't scream or sob.

'When did you last see her?' I ask, grabbing Sylvie's arm.

She cries so violently, her words don't make sense. 'You need to pull yourself together and tell me!' I say.

'Ten minutes ago, maybe! I've been looking for her.'

'Were you playing hide-and-seek? She loves hiding.'

Sylvie shakes her head. 'She was playing with her dolls in the garden.'

'At the back of the cabin?' I ask, my heart sinking. It backs onto the Bisse – a public footpath.

She nods. 'And weren't you there with her?' My tone is accusatory, and Sylvie sobs again.

'I went to the toilet, and then she was gone.'

'But I told you not to leave her alone!' I race into the

cabin, screaming, 'Emily!' I'm met with silence. 'Darling, if you're hiding, you need to come out now because I'm scared.' But this place is essentially four walls with a little internal box for a bathroom. There's nowhere for a young child to hide. I run out the back and onto the Bisse, screaming her name, my voice shrill with panic. Has that man taken her? Is it Paul?

In moments like this, you don't think logically. It's all instinctual. I know it's unfair of me to shout at Sylvie, because of course she should be allowed to go to the toilet in peace. I realise I must call the emergency services, but I don't even know the number here. I need help, and the first number I find is Saskia's. I press dial, willing her to answer, but the phone rings and rings, and eventually her voicemail kicks in. My breathing comes in short gasps, and my voice doesn't sound like my own.

'Saskia, Emily has gone missing, and I don't know what to do, who to call. Please ring me back. It's Helen, by the way.' I hang up. Of course she'll know it's me. But what now? The lovely Swiss neighbours – Manon and Guillaume. I run towards their chalet, skidding on the steep grassy bank that I take instead of the steps, and I hurtle towards the door, rapping hard on it. I wait a few seconds and then rap on the door again, but there's no answer. They must be out. What now?

'Emily!' I shout again, ridiculously wondering if I'll see her little face smudged up against the window, shouting to be let out. I see nothing, so I stride away. There's total silence; even the birds have stopped singing.

I take out my phone and call Orla. After all, she's bilingual and knows everyone here.

She answers immediately. 'Helen, it was lovely to get to know you this afternoon.'

'Emily, my daughter, has gone missing. I need to call the police. What's the number?'

'Oh my God, Helen. When did this happen?'

'What's the number for the police?'

'It's 117. I'll come over as soon as I can.'

'Thanks,' I say, immediately ending the call.

I RUN BACK towards the cabin. Sylvie is still standing there. 'Go inside and tell all the workmen that Emily's gone missing. Search the chalet. I'm calling the police.' She nods and runs towards the chalet. Sylvie has a strange run, more like the skip of a little child, rather like how Emily runs. I stifle a sob and hit 117 on my phone.

'My daughter has gone missing. I think she's been taken.'

I explain to the emergency services where we are and beg them to hurry. It's only when I finish the call do I think of the last time I had dealings with the police here. About how it didn't have a happy ending.

'What's happened?' Jacques comes rushing out.

'My daughter has disappeared. She was playing out here.'

Jacques turns and runs back inside the chalet, and before I fully comprehend what's happening, he has organised all the tradespeople – the electricians, plumbers and decorators to put down their tools – and he groups them, sending some along the Bisse to the left, some to the right and a couple up the mountain. As they all hurry off, he makes a phone call.

'Okay,' he says as he finishes the call. 'I have told the local mayor, and he will make sure that everyone looks out for Emily. He will call Mademoiselle Marie at the playgroup because perhaps Emily went there.'

'She knows not to go off with strangers or to wander away by herself. That's the reason I employed Sylvie, and we had words about it only this morning. She's been abducted. I'm sure of it.'

'Abducted!' Jacques' initial reaction is shock, and then he tilts his head slightly, and I wonder if he thinks I'm crazy or whether he's a very good actor and knows exactly what's happening because he's the perpetrator. 'This is a close-knit community, Helen. People look out for each other here,' he says.

That attitude seems so naive to me. Bad things can happen anywhere, even in paradise.

SHOUTS of Emily's name echo across the mountain while my stomach clenches and my lungs fail to inhale enough of the fresh mountain air. I pace up and down, every so often adding my shout to that of strangers'. Eventually, I hear a siren getting increasingly louder. Two gendarmes arrive, and they follow me into Camilla's empty chalet.

'Do you speak English?' I ask.

'A little,' the older of the two men replies.

'My husband, Paul Sellers, disappeared in the mountains above Corviez five years ago. He was never found, and now I think he didn't die. I think he skied into Noemie Moser and then disappeared, but now he's come back and abducted my daughter.'

'I'm sorry, but that I don't understand. Can you speak more slowly?'

'I think my daughter has been stolen,' I say too loudly.

The two men look at each other, eyebrows raised.

'These are the mountains, madame. People walk away, they fall, they get lost. This happens often. We find them.'

'But you don't!' I exclaim. 'You didn't find Paul.'

And then I burst into tears.

26

PAUL – NOW

Harsh sunlight pricks my eyelids, and I force them open. I groan as I sit up. My head feels sore, and the world spins around me as I glance around. I'm sitting in a large bed of lavender, which clearly cushioned my fall. It smells nice, but it's prickly, and I'm sure I'm covered in bruises. I rub the back of my head and find a big bump. I must have been concussed for a few seconds, but as I blink and turn my head slowly, the world comes back into focus. Cautiously, I move all my limbs and flex my neck. Everything aches, but nothing really hurts. I'm pretty sure that I have broken nothing and that I'm extremely lucky. I stand up slowly, glancing up at the top window, which is wide open. I've fallen a long way.

It takes me a few moments to remember why I climbed out of the window. Helen came to the chalet, and Orla has gone to meet her. That churning sense of doom returns. Surely Orla wouldn't do anything stupid? If she did, could I still love her? I'm really not sure. She's taken the car, so I'm going to have to walk or take the free bus that shuttles around the village, but at this time of year, I'm not sure how often it comes. Neither will be a quick option, but I have little choice. And I realise I have nothing on me, no phone, keys or wallet. I wipe myself down and step cautiously towards the front door, hoping Orla might have left it open. It's locked, as is the back door, and all the downstairs windows are firmly closed. It's as if my lover purposefully turned our house into a prison.

I set off down the hill, walking along the verges, trying to stay in the shadows as much as I can. How long will it take to walk to where Helen is staying? Perhaps forty-five minutes if I go quickly, but my head is throbbing, and waves of nausea come over me. I don't want to vomit. I keep to a slow but steady pace, watching out for the passing traffic, wondering if I'll pass Orla driving back to the chalet. She'll be furious when she discovers I've gone and that she has no way of contacting me.

I was optimistic on my timings, and it's over an hour before I'm walking along the Bisse, nearing the chalet that Helen is working on. At least the nausea has settled, and I feel vaguely normal. I glance towards the driveway of the chalet, and there's a police car parked up in front. I swallow bile. What has happened? Has something happened to Helen or Emily, or is it just a construction accident? Could Orla have had anything to do with this, or am I being totally unfair by imagining the worst of the woman I've loved for the past five years? As I watch the chalet from the cover of a pine tree, I let out an audible sigh when I see Helen step out of the house, followed by two policemen. Her face looks red and tear-stained, and then there's a shout from high above me in the forest.

'Emily!' a man yells. His call is echoed by someone else shouting Emily's name from further away.

No! What has happened to Emily? Have they lost her? Has something happened to my daughter? But I can't go charging down there to ask because I'm not meant to be here.

I can't even ask the people who are obviously out here looking for Emily, because I'm a ghost.

I step further back into the forest and crouch behind a deciduous bush. I've made some truly terrible decisions. I wonder again if I should have stayed with Helen. Perhaps we could have worked things out; perhaps the birth of Emily would have brought us closer together and we would be living happily, maybe even with a second child by now. How did I allow myself to be bewitched by Orla for so many years? But then I think of the amazing times Orla and I have had over the past few years, the exotic places I have visited thanks to her, the easy life I've had. Yes, Orla is a mercurial character, but that's what makes her so exciting. Is she really a bad person? Perhaps she was just panicked into locking me in the room, it's not like either of us could have imagined Helen would turn up at our door, and perhaps Orla thought I might rush back into the arms of the mother of my child. If so, she's wrong. My love for Orla is all-consuming. But there's still this primal urge to protect Helen and most of all to protect our little Emily. Perhaps when Orla has a child, my yearning to be around Emily will lessen, but for now I just feel sheer panic, as if I have let my daughter down. Maybe she wouldn't have disappeared if I had stuck around. I wonder for a moment if she is out there on the mountainside looking for me. I never told her that I was her daddy, but perhaps she had some deep instinct. Or more likely that's wishful thinking, that need to be wanted.

Helen looks terrible. She's gesticulating, and the policeman shakes his head. I wish I knew what's happened and where Orla is now. I wonder if she's back at the chalet, searching for me. Oh, this is such a mess, and I simply don't know what to do.

'Madame, you need to sit down and tell us slowly what's happened,' the policeman says. 'My name is Patrick Keller, and I'd like you to start at the beginning.'

'My daughter, Emily, has gone missing,' I say, trying not to choke on the words. 'I think she's been abducted.'

'Abducted?'

I want to scream. These men don't speak good enough English, and my French is rubbish. How am I going to make myself understood? Time is of the essence, and they need to take action. Now.

'My neighbours. They were out earlier, but they might be back now. They speak English, so perhaps they can translate.' Even though I barely know Guillaume and Manon, they have been so kind to me. 'Come,' I say, beckoning them to follow me. I rush up the steps and onto the Bisse, hurrying towards the neighbours' house. I pray that they've arrived back home in the past few minutes. I run up to their front door and knock. There's still no answer.

I take out my mobile phone and jab in Manon's number, but the phone rings out. No, no!

And then Jacques appears on the Bisse. Although I dislike the man, I could throw my arms around him now. 'Can you translate for me?' I ask. 'They don't understand what I'm saying.'

'Of course.'

Jacques talks rapidly to Patrick Keller, who responds equally fast, so I zone out.

'He's suggesting that Emily has wandered off by herself and perhaps got lost.'

I shake my head violently. 'No, she'd never do that. Emily knows not to go off by herself or accept a lift with strangers.' But a little voice niggles at the back of my head, because Emily did talk to that stranger. 'I was trying to tell the policeman that my husband disappeared in the mountains here five years ago and was never found, presumed dead.'

Jacques' eyes widen, and he tilts his head to one side.

'A man has been talking to Emily, someone left her a present at the playgroup, and on the day of the Inalpe festival–' I hesitate. Should I tell the policeman that I think I've seen Paul? Everyone is positive he's dead, and they'll surely think I'm some nutcase. On the other hand, if there's just the remotest possibility that I might be right, I have to mention it. Emily's life could be at stake here. 'Look, I know this sounds crazy, but I think I saw Paul, my husband, at the Inalpe festival and again here in the woods. I think he might be alive and living here, and he could have abducted Emily.'

'Really? Why would he disappear and then reappear?' Jacques asks the question I can't answer. Nevertheless, he speaks in French to Patrick Keller again, who asks me for Paul's full name and the date of his disappearance. But I can see in both men's eyes that they just feel pity for me: the delusional woman who thinks her dead husband has come back from the grave.

The policeman walks away, so we follow him back to the chalet's garden.

'He's making some phone calls,' Jacques explains. 'Liaising with mountain rescue and looking through the old files.'

I nod. 'I need to tell Andrew what's going on.'

It's only then that I notice Sylvie. She's perched on a cut-down tree trunk, her face in her hands, crying. I walk over to her and put a hand on her shoulder.

'I'm so sorry,' she sobs. 'I wasn't paying attention. It's all my fault.'

'No, it's not your fault, Sylvie,' I say, trying to be calm because what I'd really like to do is scream at her. Ultimately, it's my fault because I shouldn't have left my four-year-old with a sixteen-year-old who is still a child herself. 'I think you should go home and try to calm down.'

'You'll let me know as soon as Emily is found?' she asks, rubbing her eyes with the back of her hand.

'Of course.'

I sit on the step outside the cabin and call Andrew. Until now, I've tried to keep my emotions in check, but just uttering the words, 'Emily is missing,' to Andrew sends me into a spasm of terror and tears.

'I think Paul has taken her,' I splutter. 'It must have been him behind everything, and it's all my fault. I shouldn't have left Emily with Sylvie, and now my little girl has gone.'

'Calm down, Helen,' Andrew says, which only makes me feel even more agitated. 'I think your mind is playing tricks. You're under so much stress.'

'You think I'm imagining that Emily has disappeared!' I yell.

'No, but the likelihood it's Paul is close to zero. We've

talked about this so many times before. Emily's probably at the playgroup looking for that teddy bear, or perhaps she's with the lovely neighbours.'

'You don't believe me, do you?' If Andrew doesn't believe me, then I'm truly lost. He has always been my greatest supporter, but perhaps our perfect relationship has been an illusion, a desperate replacement for my husband and Emily's birth father.

'Of course I believe she's missing, but I'm sure there's a reasonable explanation. Have you checked with Guillaume and Manon?'

'There's no answer at their house.'

'Guillaume wears a hearing aid. He might not have heard you knocking.'

It's typical of Andrew to have noticed something like that. 'Get the police to look at their house and the playgroup,' he suggests.

'I will.'

'You need to stay positive, darling. I will get to you as quickly as I can. I'll drive if I have to.'

'No, please don't. I'll only worry. Get a flight when you can.'

'I will get the earliest flight possible. I'm just looking now, and realistically it might have to be first thing tomorrow. But in the meantime, keep me posted. I love you, Helen, and I love Emily.'

'I know you do,' I murmur. 'And I'm not crazy, Andrew.'

But he's already hung up.

PATRICK KELLER RETURNS WITH JACQUES, who once again acts as translator. 'Can you give a description of your ex-husband?'

I describe the man I saw at the Inalpe festival because I'm

not sure what Paul looks like now, but I show him an old photograph of Paul that I have on my phone. 'Can you ask the police to go to the playgroup, just in case Emily has gone there?'

'Of course,' Jacques says.

The next thing I know is that the policeman is handing me a business card and saying he's leaving.

'He can't leave! Why isn't he out there looking for Emily?' I ask, desperation making my voice shrill.

'That's what he'll be doing. He says that they will be sending people out to look for her, and a helicopter. He will go to see Mademoiselle Marie at the playgroup and then will go back to the police station to speak to his team. He wants you to stay here and call him if Emily turns up.'

'I'm going to look myself,' I say.

'No. Patrick Keller says please stay here. If Emily comes back by herself, she'll need you to be in the cabin, and the police will stop by later.'

'You mean I've got to stay here all alone, doing nothing?' My voice is becoming more strident. 'I need to be out there on the mountainside looking for my baby!'

'I'm taking you inside and making you a drink. Come on.' Jacques places a hand on my back and guides me towards the cabin. The policeman walks off in the opposite direction.

'What would you like?' he asks as he glances around the room.

'Nothing, really nothing.' I pace backwards and forwards. 'I need to go back to Guillaume and Manon's house just in case Emily's there. Andrew reminded me that Guillaume is deaf. Perhaps he didn't hear me knocking.' I walk to the door and open it.

'But the policeman said you should stay here,' Jacques says.

I turn and stare at him. Does he know more than he's

letting on? Does it suit him that I remain in the cabin? Perhaps he has hidden Emily somewhere or he is Paul's accomplice? I know that's a ridiculous thought, but I really need to consider everything right now.

'You stay here. I won't be long,' I say, and stride out of the cabin. As I walk up onto the Bisse, I can hear shouts of Emily's name, and even though I have my doubts about Jacques, I'm grateful that he's sent Camilla's workforce out to search for Emily. I say a silent prayer to God, begging him to keep Emily safe and to bring my little girl home right now.

I bang on Guillaume and Manon's door once again, and there's still no answer. I step backwards and notice that one of the upstairs windows is wide open. Isn't it strange to go out and leave the window open? Surely the crime rates here aren't that low? Something doesn't feel right, but I can't put my finger on it. I walk around the chalet and see that their car is gone, and two other upstairs windows are wide open. It really doesn't feel right.

'Guillaume! Manon!' I shout.

The air is still. I try to peer in through one of the windows, but it's dark inside, and I can't see a thing. I return to the door facing the Bisse and cautiously turn the handle. To my dismay, the door opens. I rather hoped they were out and I was worrying about nothing. I step into the small kitchen. There are two empty cups of coffee on the drainer.

'Manon!' I shout, standing very still.

Cautiously, I walk through the dark kitchen to the hall beyond.

And then I hear it. A groan.

I step into the wood-panelled living room. It's even darker in here and cluttered with furniture, and there's a strange metallic smell. I glance down at the carpet.

And scream.

28

I feel sick. What is going on? What's happened to Emily? I step further into the forest and hear a man shouting Emily's name quite close to me. I scramble up between the trees until I see him just above me. He's wearing a red T-shirt and jeans and is holding a mobile phone in his right hand.

'Excuse me, but what's happened?' I ask.

'A little girl has gone missing. We're looking for her.'

'Has something bad happened to her?' I ask.

'I don't know. We hope not.'

'How long has she been gone for?'

'I'm sorry, I don't know.'

Beautiful little Emily has disappeared, and I think I know who has her. *Oh, Orla,* I murmur to myself. *What have you done? Please don't harm my baby.* Yet what can I do? It's not like I can knock on Helen's door and say, *Hello, darling. Sorry I've been gone for all these years, but here I am now to help you in your hour of need. Come with me. I'll take you to Orla.* Yet, I have to find Orla, if only to set my mind at rest that she hasn't done anything terrible. I turn back to the stranger.

'I'd like to help look for the little girl, but I left my phone at home and need to tell my wife that I'll be late back. Is it possible for me to borrow your phone to make a very quick call?'

The man looks at me asquint and, after a brief hesitation, steps downwards and hands me his phone. I know it's a risk calling Orla from a stranger's phone, but I must eliminate her. If she answers, it will be such a relief.

I dial her number, but it rings and rings and rings. When her voicemail kicks in, I end the call and hand the phone back to the stranger.

'No answer,' I say needlessly.

Oh, Orla, what have you done?

If Orla has taken Emily, I know exactly where she has gone. To the cabin high up on the mountainside where I hid all those years ago. Yet here I am several kilometres downhill, with no money and no means of transport. I'm going to have to do something radical. I slip back down to the Bisse and hurry off in the opposite direction to where Helen is staying. I then walk down to the road. There are several chalets here, some of which are rented out to holidaymakers, many of whom visit Corviez in the summer to go mountain biking, taking advantage of the many trails through the forest.

My heart is thumping as I tiptoe up the drive to a large chalet. There are people on the balcony, and there's the scent of cooked meat coming from a barbeque. I sidle around the house and to my relief see three bikes leaning against the wall. I just hope they're not locked. I can hear laughter coming from above me. Desperately hoping the bikes' owners are otherwise engaged, I dart forwards and grab the largest of the three. People are so careless with their bikes, and to my relief, it's not locked. I wheel the bike to the front of the house, keeping very close to the walls, underneath the high-up balconies. And then I wait. I know I'm going to have to dash forwards, fully exposed, and just hope that no one is watching. My stomach clenches, but I think of Emily. I have to do this for my daughter. Swinging my right leg over the bike, I pull myself up onto the saddle. I count one, two, three under my breath, and then I go for it, pedalling the hardest I've ever pedalled, praying that no one shouts out, no one sees me leaving, and no one calls the police.

When I reach the bottom of the short drive and turn left onto the road, I want to cry with relief. I've stolen something for the first time in my life, and glancing at this bike, I'm sure it's not a cheap one. As I pedal hard up the road, I realise I've chosen a good bike. It's an electric bike and will make it so much easier for me to climb the steep road high up the mountain. I play around with the controls, turn on the motor and, to my delight, realise that this bike has some serious power. The harder I turn the pedals, the greater assistance I get from the motor. I really have got lucky.

29

I t takes me a moment to realise that the red marks on the carpet aren't part of the design. It's blood. Splatters and pools. Manon is lying motionless on the floor, her head almost under the wooden coffee table, her legs askew.

'Oh my God, what's happened?' My head feels light, and I grab the back of the sofa as I try to stop myself from fainting.

As my eyes adjust to the darkness, I realise there's so much wrong about this scene. A chair is upside down. A glass vase lies shattered on the carpet next to Manon's stockinged feet.

'Manon?' I say as I drop to the floor next to her. 'Manon! Open your eyes!'

To my utter relief, she does. They flicker open and then close again. 'Manon, you need to stay with me. I'm going to get help. You're going to be alright.' I just hope she can hear me and that she understands. I take my phone out of my pocket and with a shaking hand type in the numbers off the business card that Patrick Keller, the policeman, gave me just minutes ago.

'Hello, this is Helen Sellers. You need to come here

straight away and get an ambulance. My neighbour has been injured, and it's very urgent. I think she's been assaulted.'

'Your little girl?'

'No. My neighbour, Manon.' I realise I don't even know her surname. 'Someone has attacked her. You need to come now. Bring paramedics, urgently.' I give him Manon's address to pass on to the paramedics.

'Okay, I come.'

'Manon, can you hear me? Is Emily here? Have you seen her?' Manon groans but doesn't answer. I hold her hand, but my first aid skills are non-existent, so I dare not move her. 'Where's Guillaume? Is he alright?'

She groans louder and tries to shake her head. I can't work out why my questions seem to distress her, and then I wonder whether Guillaume is also hurt, or even worse. Is Guillaume bleeding to death upstairs? I move as if to stand up, but Manon clutches my hand harder, and I'm loath to leave her. It dawns on me then that I might also be in danger. Is her attacker still in the house? Should I try to get us both out?

'Manon, I'm going to look around the house. Help is on its way, and I'll be right back.' I unclasp her hand and stand up. Her face is waxy, and I'm terrified she's going to die, but my priority has to be Emily. I have to make sure that my little girl hasn't been caught up in this horror.

The chalet is small with just the living room, a dining room and kitchen downstairs. I tiptoe up the stairs, my heart hammering. On the landing, everything is quiet. I push open the first wooden door. It's a bedroom with a double bed, neatly made up with sheets and blankets, and wardrobes built into the wall. There's no one here, and nothing looks as if it's been disturbed. The second door leads to a family bathroom, while the third door must be Guillaume and Manon's bedroom. It's untidier in here. The bed is made, but the top drawer of the chest of drawers positioned against the wall opposite the bed hangs open, a pale blue shirt hanging out. The window is partially open, and the curtains flap gently in the breeze.

'Emily,' I whisper, but there's no answer, and now I'm sure that this house is empty other than Manon and myself. Where is Guillaume? I wonder. Is he safe? There's a small empty box discarded on the floor. I bend down to pick it up, but it slips through my fingers when I realise what it is. It's a box of bullets. *A box of bullets!* What the hell is that doing here?

I race back downstairs and crouch next to Manon. 'Manon, do you have a gun?'

She doesn't answer, and for a horrible moment, I wonder if she's dead. I gently pick up her wrist, and relief floods through me when I feel a faint pulse. *Please hurry up*, I silently beg the emergency services.

I assumed her injuries were from being beaten, but has she been shot? This is so far beyond anything I have ever experienced. I've never even held a gun; it's just not the norm in England. Yet I recall someone telling me that it's compulsory for every man to attend military service in Switzerland and that most men keep their guns at home. It's the only explanation I can come up with for a box of empty cartridges to be lying on their bedroom floor. But Guillaume is a pensioner, he must be early- to mid-seventies, and why would he have a gun?

And then, to my utter relief, I hear the faint wailing of a siren. 'Help is coming,' I murmur to Manon, praying that she can hear me.

Five minutes later, the small chalet is swarming with people. Two paramedics are attending to Manon while Patrick Keller and a policewoman have led me into the kitchen.

'My colleague, she speaks excellent English,' Patrick Keller says.

'I'm Thérèse Bayent, and I work with Monsieur Keller. What happened here?' I nod at the policewoman.

'I don't know. I was looking for Emily, and when I got no answer after knocking on the door, I was worried because their bedroom window was open. I found the door unlocked and Manon severely injured. Upstairs, there's an empty box of bullets on the bedroom floor.'

'We will investigate, but that is not so unusual. Many people here have guns. It is legal.'

'Are you still looking for Emily?'

'Of course.'

Suddenly there's a commotion, and a paramedic rushes into the kitchen, talking quietly to Patrick Keller, who in turn whispers to Thérèse Bayent. I think for one horrible moment that Manon might have passed away, but no.

'Madame wants to talk to you urgently,' Thérèse Bayent says.

'You mean Manon?'

'Yes. The paramedics are unhappy because she is very poorly, but she insists.' I follow the paramedic back into the living room, where Manon is lying on a stretcher. Her eyes flicker open.

'Guillaume. You need to find him,' she whispers in a voice so faint I can barely hear her. 'I told him not to. I begged him. It's not right. I'm sorry.'

'What! What do you mean?' But Manon's eyes have closed, and the paramedic puts an oxygen mask over her head.

'They need to go now,' Thérèse Bayent says. 'They must get her to the hospital.'

'But she was trying to tell me something. It could be

something about Emily. What does she mean that she begged Guillaume not to? It doesn't make sense.'

Thérèse Bayent shrugs her shoulders, and I want to swipe her. This is my daughter we're talking about, and from what Manon said, I can only deduce that Guillaume has something to do with Emily's disappearance.

'Their car is missing, and the upstairs windows were wide open,' I say.

'Okay, so we need to find Guillaume's car and try to track him down.'

Thérèse Bayent talks rapidly to her colleague, and I recognise the occasional word. *Helicopter. Car. Chalet.* Patrick Keller strides away quickly.

'What's happening?' I ask.

'We need to find Guillaume to make sure he's safe. My colleague is putting out a bulletin over the car radio to look out for his car and perhaps mobilise a helicopter. We have details of the make, model and registration number. Maybe we can search their cabin high up on the mountain.'

'Their cabin?'

'Yes. Many people here have a little chalet in the high pastures, often inherited from their ancestors. They stay there in the summer sometimes for holidays.' Thérèse Bayent looks at her mobile phone and sends a message. She seems so calm, yet we're in the middle of a horrific emergency, and I want to scream at her to inject some urgency into this investigation. My daughter's life could be at stake.

'We need to do something!' I say, my voice shrill.

'We will,' she says, without looking at me.

I pace backwards and forwards in the small garden for a couple of minutes, and then to my relief, Patrick Keller returns. After a quick conversation, Thérèse Bayent tells me that they will search Manon's house now, looking for the keys to their cabin. I try to follow them inside, but Patrick Keller turns to me and holds out his hand.

'This is a crime scene, madame. You cannot come in.'

I'm at a total loss, feeling utterly futile. I scramble up the bank on the other side of the chalet and shout Emily's name, but I'm met with silence. I shout again and again, and as if my voice is echoed, I hear a male shout in the far distance, also calling for Emily. At least people are still out there looking. Keller and Bayent come back out of the house, removing white shoe covers and peeling rubber gloves off their hands.

'Did you find anything?' I ask as I hurry across the garden towards them.

'No, there were no keys on their key hook. We're going to the cabin now,' Thérèse Bayent says.

'I want to come with you,' I demand.

'*Non*, that's not possible.'

'I insist. This is my daughter who has been abducted. You've got to let me come.' My voice is strident. 'Please!' Keller and Bayent glance at each other, and Keller shrugs his shoulders.

'Okay, you can come, but you stay in the car,' Thérèse Bayent says. I nod in agreement.

I sit in the back of the police car. Patrick Keller drives, and I wish he'd go faster and put the sirens on. Why don't they understand that this is an emergency, possibly life or death, and I'm terrified? My phone pings with a text, but it's just Andrew asking for an update. I can't tell him about Manon, he'd be too worried, so I just ignore it and put the phone back in my pocket. The car drives steadily up the mountainside, through the extensive forest, until we emerge into a skiing village. We drive through and head further upwards. Eventually the trees thin out, and the road turns into a track. The views are stupendous here, with the hillside dropping away dramatically, but I can't look. I just want to get there, to this cabin that they say Manon and Guillaume own. To make sure that my little girl is safe, and to find out what Guillaume has done. As the trees thin out, it's as if we're driving through a vast meadow of wildflowers, much like I saw at the Inalpe festival, and it seems wrong that the multicoloured blooms are nodding their heads in the breeze when my whole world is upside down. We pass small wooden chalets, mostly with their shutters closed, but a few look lived in. There are no electricity poles up here, and I notice that many of the cabins have solar panels in their gardens or attached to their roofs.

Keller brings the car to a sudden halt behind a smaller, pale-wood cabin.

'We leave the car here and walk on foot. You stay here.'

'No–'

'That was the deal,' Thérèse Bayent says. 'It's too dangerous for you. If he has a gun...' She lets the words fade away. They both get out of the car, close the doors quietly, and prowl up the grass bank towards a small cabin about a hundred metres above us. It's warm in the car, and I want to wind down the window, but the engine is switched off, so I can't. Instead, I open the passenger door and get out. The air smells wonderful up here, and the views are exquisite, but I really couldn't care. I need to know whether Manon's injuries have anything to do with Emily's disappearance, and the urge to find my little girl is over-consuming. I'm damned if I'm going to stay in the car.

Once the police officers are over the top of the grassy bank, I follow in their footsteps. I keep low to the ground in the hope that if they glance downhill, I won't be spotted. It's hard going because my breath is so shallow; terror, I suppose. As I near the cabin made from ancient, dark wood, I see that it's a traditional chalet shape with a steep-pitched roof. There are shutters on the windows, which are closed, giving the place an abandoned feel. I duck down behind a large rock as

I watch the police officers disappear inside the door. I wonder if it was open or whether they broke it to get in.

Now is my chance to explore. Clambering up the side of the bank, I realise it's not abandoned at all. There's a small vegetable patch with tomatoes and marrows growing, and propped up against the left-hand wall of the chalet there's a little shrine. It looks like a road-side memorial left by the relatives of people who have died in road traffic accidents. There's a simple cross, a statue of the Virgin Mary standing inside a carved grey stone, along with trinkets and freshly cut flowers. As I peer closer, I can make out the words:

Noemie Moser 2003 – 2018 Petite ange, ton regard restera à tout jamais dans nos cœurs

I sink to my knees as I stare at the memorial. *Noemie Moser. Little angel, you remain always in our hearts.* Why is that name so familiar? And then I realise with a jolt. Noemie Moser was the young girl who died on the slopes a couple of days before Paul disappeared. Paul and I argued over her when I accused him of acting strangely when he heard of her death. My hand rushes to cover my mouth. Why is there a shrine to Noemie outside Guillaume and Manon's cabin?

'What are you doing here?' I stumble backwards and scramble to stand up. Patrick Keller is staring at me with narrow eyes.

'Noemie Moser. What has she got to do with Guillaume and Manon?'

'She was their granddaughter. She died,' Thérèse Bayent says.

'I know. She was killed five years ago when someone skied into her and then skied off.'

'And how do you know this?'

'Because it happened just before my husband, Paul,

vanished. At the time, I wondered whether he had something to do with it.'

'Did you ever tell the police that?'

'No, because it was pure speculation.'

'My colleague checked our files, and although your husband was asked to come to the police station to give a statement about Noemie Moser's death, he never did. It was assumed he fell to his death before he could do that.'

'Didn't anyone think that was suspicious?' I ask.

'Naturally there were some locals who thought it was a bit of a coincidence that there was a hit-and-run on the slopes and two days later Paul Sellers had a tragic accident, but this is a small town. People talk. There was mention of death by suicide because of guilt.'

'Do you think the Mosers felt that way?'

Thérèse Bayent shrugs her shoulders. 'Perhaps this was a rumour spread by them, that your husband killed himself out of remorse. I'm afraid I don't know.'

'Did you find anything in the cabin?'

'No. It is empty, but the door was unlocked. Someone might have been here recently. Guillaume's car is here.'

My eyes follow her finger, and I see his car, the back door left open. There's something very wrong about this scene. Slowly my thoughts begin to come together. If Guillaume, for some reason, realised that Emily is the daughter of the man who killed his granddaughter, could he have taken Emily out of revenge? Is that what Manon meant when she said that she told him not to and that she was sorry? But how did he come to that conclusion? I try to remember whether I ever explicitly told them that my husband disappeared on the mountains five years ago, shortly after their granddaughter died. I can't remember.

I stand up, but my throat is raw, as if it's full of thorns, and my heart feels as if it's going to leap out of my chest. I turn to the police officers.

'There are two people who might have Emily. My husband, Paul, who disappeared, or Guillaume. If he thinks that my husband was responsible for Noemie's death, perhaps Guillaume has taken Emily out of revenge?'

Patrick Keller makes a pff sound as if I'm some delusional woman, but I know I'm not. I stare up at the blindingly bright blue sky. One of those two men have Emily; I'm sure of it.

Keller and Bayent exchange a look, one I've seen many times before. It's a mixture of pity and the unspoken thought that I'm talking nonsense. I've got no time for their doubts.

'You need to do a proper search of the cabin,' I say, knowing they won't appreciate me telling them how to do their job. I'm right. Bayent raises her eyebrows.

'Madame, you need to go back to the police car and stay there; otherwise we will call for backup to remove you. Do you understand?' she says, quiet fury tinging her words.

I nod. Slowly, I turn around and walk with some difficulty back down the steep bank towards the car. I glance backwards and see Keller and Bayent disappear into the cabin. I know they're trying to do their jobs, but there's a lack of urgency in their attitudes that makes me livid. I reach the gravel drive and have my hand on the car door handle.

And then I hear a shout.

30

PAUL – NOW

Sweat is pouring off me as I ride the bike, standing up and pumping the pedals as I climb the steep roads. I am fit, probably the fittest I have ever been, but I have never worked my body so hard. The urge to reach Orla before she does something terrible is propelling me on, firing every molecule in my body. If I were competing in some great cycling race, I'm sure I'd win because it's extraordinary what adrenaline can help achieve. In my mind's eye, I see Orla dragging Emily into the cabin, and I can't imagine what she'll do next. My Orla isn't a killer. She wouldn't physically hurt Emily, surely? But she does seem unhinged at the moment, and if Emily doesn't do what Orla demands, then who knows?

The trees give way to fields, and I pass the first of the small summer cabins. No cars have overtaken me although a couple of hikers I passed were staring, no doubt at my puce face, drenched body and steely gaze. I'm not even dressed to go mountain biking. Eventually I reach Orla's family cabin. I drop the bike onto the long grass and creep up to the side of it, expecting to see Orla's car. But there's no car here. Of course not. Orla is too clever to leave her car in open view. The shutters are open, as they always are in the summer, and my heart is pumping when I stand up and peer through the window. I haven't been back here. This place doesn't hold good memories for me, and when Orla suggested we have a romantic picnic here a few weeks ago, I came up with some excuse. It looks exactly the same. The furniture, the fabrics, everything is as I remember it. I tiptoe to the door and turn the handle. It's locked. What if Orla is inside with Emily? What if Emily is gagged? There's a woodshed next to the door, fully stocked with evenly cut logs. I take one, and using all my strength, I jam the log against the door, once, twice, three times. The lock gives way with a splinter, and the door swings open. I stumble as I crash inside.

'Orla, are you here?'

My eyes take time to adjust to the darkness, but I fumble around inside, pulling the daybed away from the wall, swinging open the door to the toilet. I swivel around. This place is empty. It smells musty and unused. She's not here.

I sink onto the daybed where I slept all those years ago and put my head in my hands. Have I been on a wild goose chase for nothing? Have I been a total idiot again? What will I tell Orla when they discover their cabin was broken into? I'll have to suggest it was some late-night hikers who needed to bed down. I groan. I'm such an idiot.

After turning on the cold tap and drinking the ice-cold water, I walk out of the cabin, wedging the door shut so it doesn't look as if the lock has been broken. I stand there for a moment, staring at the mountains across the valley, hoping for some inspiration.

There's a car creeping up the winding track, and as I squint to focus, wondering if it's Orla, my heart sinks. It's a police car. I swear under my breath. Has the bike got a tracker on it? Has the owner reported it missing? They're worth a lot of money, electric bikes like this one, so it's very likely the police are out looking for it and the idiot who stole it.

I need to get out of here. Now.

I glance at the dense forest to the left of the cabin, the forest from which I emerged five years ago. And then I run. My initial steps are full of panic until I rationalise with myself. It's not unusual for people to be out running in the mountains. If I move steadily, as if I am on one of my regular runs, I won't look suspicious. I head off into the forest, glancing back over my shoulder only when I'm under the shadows of the trees. Then I hear an engine being turned off and the slamming of car doors. I jog for a while, following a path that might be man-made, or perhaps it's been worn down by the hooved feet of antelope.

That's when I hear it. A faint shout from a young girl.

I strain to hear it again, but all I hear are the crickets, the birds and the distant sound of an airplane.

'Get off!'

Yes, it's definitely a young girl shouting, and she isn't far from here – perhaps fifty metres or so below me. *Is that Emily?*

'Orla!' I shout. 'Orla, let her go!'

Now there's complete silence. I dart down, jumping over tree roots and fallen branches, my trainers slipping on moss, waiting to hear voices. I hear nothing.

'Orla,' I yell, 'I know you tried to hurt Helen. I know you're jealous of her and you've taken Emily, but it's you I love. It's always been you. Come on, Orla. Let her go!'

31

I strain to listen again, trying to work out where the male voice came from.

'Orla, let her go!'

I stagger backwards, leaning against the car. It feels as if I've been punched in the stomach because I know that voice. I have absolutely no doubt now. Paul is here, but why the hell is he shouting at Orla? This doesn't make any sense.

'Thérèse!' I shout, hoping that the policewoman might hear me, but I can't see the cabin from here. 'Police!' But I sense that my voice is being carried away in the opposite direction, and there's no hope of Keller or Bayent hearing me if they're inside.

In that split second, I decide. I can't wait for the police. It's up to me to work out what's going on, and if Paul has Emily, then I must save my little girl. The shout came from the forest to the right of me, and despite the boot on my foot, I run. The grass gives way to trees, tall pine trees crowded together, the ground covered in sparse grass and fallen pine cones and twigs that crunch under my feet. I have no idea where I'm going. All I can hear is my rapid breathing and the cawing of crows from high up in the sky. I listen hard, hoping to hear Paul's voice again but, at the same time, praying that I don't. What is Orla doing here? Have I got it all wrong, and does she have Emily? If so, why?

I rush forwards again, but my foot catches the root of a tree, and I yelp as pain spears through my already sprained ankle. I can't focus on that; I need to find Orla or Paul. I pull myself from tree to tree, moving further into the dense forest, the scent of pine so at odds with the fear pumping through my veins. Then I see light just below me, a clearing where the trees are further apart, and I think I catch a glimpse of a person.

'Emily!' I shout as I emerge into the brightness. 'Oh my God, Emily!'

My little girl is standing there, but a thick arm is clasped around her neck. It takes a moment for me to realise that it's not Orla and it's not Paul. It's Guillaume. He has my daughter.

'Mummy!' Emily cries. She tries to wriggle out of Guillaume's grasp, but he's much too strong.

'Stay there!' he shouts at me. But I don't listen. I scramble forwards.

And then there's a gunshot. It's so loud, it rings in my ears. Emily is sobbing, gasping. I stand stock-still.

Guillaume has a gun. He stretches out his right arm and points the gun directly at me, his left arm restraining Emily. My little girl's face creases, tears flow, and her hair is mussed up. *What the hell has he done to her?*

'That was a warning shot, Helen,' he says, any traces of the sweet old man I thought I knew having dissipated.

'Please let Emily go,' I say, my voice barely a whisper. 'If you just let her go, we won't say anything. You can just disappear into the forest.'

He waves the gun at me, and I take a step backwards. My

knees are trembling, but I need to stay strong, to be brave for Emily.

'It's alright, darling, I'm here,' I murmur. 'You're going to be absolutely fine. Guillaume is angry with me, not you.'

'Mummy!' Emily sobs, and my heart cracks.

'Stay there,' Guillaume says again.

'Please just let her go.'

'You are married to a murderer. He took my son's daughter, the most beautiful girl in the world, and now it's an eye for an eye.'

'No!' I exclaim. 'It doesn't have to be like that. Emily has nothing to do with Noemie's death.'

'So you knew!' He waves the gun wildly in my direction, and I wonder whether this is it. I'm going to die in front of my beautiful little girl, right now.

But then I glimpse movement in the trees a few metres above Guillaume. I can't help my eyes widening as I see Paul emerge from behind a tree. I wasn't mad. I didn't imagine it. Paul may have a neat beard and moustache, his hair lighter than before, and a trimmer figure, but he is instantly recognisable as the man I married. He puts his index finger in front of his mouth, indicating for me to be silent, to not give away the fact that he's there. I try to stop my eyes from following him, from not expressing the utter shock of seeing the man I married alive, right here, five years after his supposed death. He tiptoes to the left and then downwards, and I know that my job is to keep Guillaume talking, to stop him realising that Paul is right behind him.

'Guillaume, I'm so sorry for what happened to your granddaughter. It must have been devastating.'

He grunts.

'He was too much of a coward to face up to what he did.'

'What do you want from us?' I ask. I can see Paul in the periphery of my vision, but I keep my eyes fixed on Guillaume and Emily. 'Please just let Emily go and do whatever you need to to me.'

'Did you know what your husband did?'

I shake my head. 'If he skied into Noemie, I'm so sorry. I can't imagine the heartache your family has suffered all of these years.'

'When I realised who you were, it was too much. Much too much,' Guillaume says.

Paul is so close to Guillaume now, but as he takes a step to the side, Emily turns her head, and she sees him. Her eyes widen, and I can tell that she recognises him. I assume he's the man she's been talking to in the woods, the person who left her the teddy bear. It all happens in an instant. Guillaume swings his head around, and Paul launches himself at Guillaume. The older man releases his grip on Emily, who races towards me. I fling my arms around her, scooping her up, holding her head against my shoulder so she can't see what's happening. And then another gunshot resonates through the silent forest. Paul crumples to the ground, and I stifle a scream, keeping my hand on Emily's head, moving backwards, trying to protect her from the horror unfolding in front of us.

There is no way that we can escape, but I pray that Guillaume's next shot will take me out, and as I fall, I can protect Emily. And then it comes. A brutal shot with a sound that rebounds from tree to tree to tree.

But I'm still standing. Emily is trembling in my arms, her hands tightly clasped around my neck.

I freeze.

'It's alright, Helen. You are safe.'

The voice is familiar, and then I see Thérèse Bayent step out from behind a tree trunk, walking towards me. Patrick Keller is putting his gun into its holster and leaning down next to the fallen bodies of the two men. He gently examines both of them. Thérèse puts her arms around Emily and me and whispers to my daughter, 'You are the bravest little girl I have ever met.' I glance at Emily, who smiles, but my eyes are drawn back to Patrick Keller. He gently shakes his head.

'*Mort*,' he whispers. 'Both dead.'

32

HELEN – NOW – TEN DAYS LATER

The mud patch between the cabin and the chalet has been covered with fresh turf, and the scent of barbecued burgers wafts across the lawn. There's a trio playing jazz, a saxophonist, drummer and keyboard player, and the jolly music adds to the carnival atmosphere. There must be fifty people here, the women wearing pretty designer summer dresses, and the men in open shirts and smart trousers. Everyone has a glass of champagne in their hand, and they're mingling happily.

Andrew flew to Switzerland the day Guillaume and Paul died. Time stopped that afternoon, and I have no idea how he managed to get here so quickly. He was adamant that we should go home immediately, but the police wanted to talk to me, and I surprised myself by insisting that I wanted to stay. It felt vital to finish the project despite everything that had happened. And I wanted to know what Paul had been doing these past five years, why he made the decisions he did.

I walk into the kitchen, where Andrew is chatting to Saskia and Matteo. I'm so proud of this chalet, and even Camilla couldn't stop grinning when we handed her the keys. It's stylish and totally meets her brief. Yes, it was tight finishing to her new deadline, especially because much of the past week was spent talking to the police and trying to unravel everything that happened. I glance into the next-door room and can see that Emily is playing with a couple of her friends from playgroup. I know she might need therapy at some point, but it's as if the trauma of her abduction by Guillaume never happened. As she knew Guillaume as a friendly face, she didn't sense any danger, I think, not until those last few minutes when he held her at gunpoint. But for now, she's just a happy little girl, delighted that Andrew is here and looking forward to going home.

I visited Manon in hospital a couple of days ago. The poor woman is broken, less so physically, as her wounds are fast healing, but emotionally, I'm not sure she'll ever recover. She was in a private room, a bandage around her head, Steri-Strips on her cheek. Her face was so pale and deeply wrinkled, it was as if she had aged a decade since I last saw her. I placed a large bouquet of flowers on the windowsill and sat on the blue plastic chair next to her bed.

'I'm so sorry, Manon,' I said, taking her hand. Her skin felt like parchment paper.

'Our family changed forever when Noemie died,' Manon said quietly. 'She was our only grandchild. Her mother, our daughter-in-law, couldn't forgive herself. She was just a few seconds behind Noemie when they were skiing, but she didn't see what happened. Her marriage to our son broke down, and our son couldn't cope. The grief was too much, and he became dependent on drink and drugs. He also died.'

'That's terrible,' I said, blinking hard to keep the tears at bay.

'It broke Guillaume. To lose our granddaughter and our son, it was just too much. He had a nervous breakdown, but the last few months I thought maybe he was getting better.

But then he discovered who you were, who your husband was, and it shattered him. I told him that the past was the past and he had to let it go, but no. He took your beautiful, innocent child, and I feared he wanted to kill her. I tried to stop him, but he beat me. You know Guillaume is such a gentle man, but he cracked. He was no longer himself. The irony is that he didn't know that Paul was still alive. If he had, then you and your little girl wouldn't have been hurt.'

'We weren't hurt,' I tried to reassure Manon, and I just hope that long term Emily will be alright. She heard the gunshots, but I made sure that she didn't see the two dead men on the forest floor.

'You know the day of the storm when that roof tile fell down,' she said in a haltering whisper. 'I think Guillaume pushed the tile.'

'But you both helped me; you took me to hospital.'

'I know. But later when we got home, I found a pile of soaking wet overalls in the garage. Guillaume refused to tell me why they were sodden.'

'Did he try to undermine me by cancelling the orders for the chalet?' I asked. 'Was he trying to get Camilla to boot me off the renovation project?'

Manon frowned. 'No, I don't think so. He wouldn't have done that.'

We were both silent for a while. I remember the bathroom store saleswoman saying a woman had called them, so unless Manon was involved, she must be telling the truth. I wonder who did it or whether it was a weird but genuine mistake.

'You know, Paul may have killed Noemie, but I don't believe in retribution. Paul Sellers didn't deserve to die,' Manon said.

It was heartbreaking leaving the elderly woman there in

hospital, knowing that her life was in tatters. I told her I'd stay in touch, but she gently shook her head.

'You're a good person, Helen. Concentrate on having a happy life with Andrew and Emily. Our paths won't cross again.'

I left the hospital in tears. I've shed a lot of those these past few days.

I'm in total conflict over Paul. Yes, he gave his life to save our child, but does that make up for what he did? For the cowardice he showed in skiing into Noemie and then running away for five years. For the heartache he gave me and his parents.

THERE'S the ringing of a high-pitched cowbell and the squeak of a microphone. We move outside to join the people standing on the lawn. Camilla is standing next to the band, wearing a white strappy dress and vertiginous sandals. Her husband, a portly man with sandy hair, stands next to her.

'Thank you, everyone, for coming today. As you know, this is the pre-party because the big event is on Saturday when my beloved husband here' – she winks at him – 'turns fifty. But we wanted you all to enjoy our beautifully renovated chalet before the party, just in case it gets ruined!'

Saskia and I glance at each other. She raises an eyebrow, and I grimace. We're not invited to the fiftieth birthday party, and it's just as well, as it would be galling to see all our hard work go to waste.

'I'd like to thank everyone involved in the project. All the tradespeople and Jacques, but particularly Saskia, our incredibly talented architect, and Helen, our amazing interior designer. Please raise your glass to the people who made this dream house come true.'

The guests let out a cheer, and I blush as I feel the eyes of these strangers on me. Camilla steps away from the microphone, and the music starts up again.

'I need to get moving,' I say to Saskia as I glance at my watch. 'I'm taking the lift up the mountainside.'

Saskia raises her eyebrows, but I don't hang around to explain. Andrew is staying here to look after Emily, and I'm going to do this alone.

AN HOUR LATER, I'm up in the Lanvière lift station, striding to the cold corridor where the plaques are. I take a screwdriver out of my pocket and quickly unscrew the metal plaque from the wall. There's a lighter patch of concrete now where the plaque used to be. Shoving the screwdriver back into my pocket, I walk back towards the lift and see a large, black plastic rubbish bin. I push open the swing lid and drop the plaque inside.

'Goodbye, Paul,' I say under my breath. I wonder whether his parents will visit one day and have another plaque made, one with dates on it. I suspect they won't because deep down they must know the truth about their son.

THE NEXT DAY we're packing up. I'm so relieved to be catching a flight home later this afternoon. There's a knock on the cabin door.

My heart sinks slightly as I see Thérèse Bayent standing there.

'Can we have a quick conversation?' she asks.

I nod, leading her to a bench at the side of the garden.

'I thought you would like to know what your ex-husband, Paul, had been doing these past five years.'

'Yes.' I brace myself.

'We have interviewed Orla extensively. According to Orla,

she and Paul were deeply in love. Using a forged passport and the false name of Joel Silver, they travelled the world. They returned to Switzerland just a few months ago and were hoping to start a family. She admits she was jealous of you and when she discovered you were here, she tried to undermine your work. She admits to cancelling your orders, but of course, that isn't a crime. However, it is likely she will be charged with fraud, for assisting Paul, perhaps even as an accessory to manslaughter. She claims she had no idea that Paul had skied into Noemie, but they were planning on eloping anyway.'

'Do you believe her?' I ask.

Thérèse pulls a face. 'That's for the courts to decide.'

I don't mention that I sent Orla a message, but she never replied.

HALF AN HOUR LATER, with our bags at our feet, we're standing in the driveway, waiting for a taxi to take us to the railway station in the valley.

'Are you alright?' Andrew's arm snakes around my waist, and I lean my head on his shoulder.

'I was just thinking how beautiful it is here,' I say. 'Despite everything, the mountains really are magical.'

'I totally agree.'

'I was also thinking that we should come back to the Alps and perhaps teach Emily to ski. What do you reckon?'

'When does the new project start?' Andrew is referring to the design project that Saskia wants me to help her on – a stunning new chalet being built just adjacent to the slopes.

'Not until late spring next year, but if the snow is still here, perhaps we could have a holiday beforehand.'

'Are you really happy about coming back here?'

'Yes. It's not the place. It was just a series of tragic events that could have occurred anywhere.'

Andrew and I have discussed what we're going to tell Emily. Right now, she is oblivious to the fact that the man she spoke to on the Bisse was her birth father and that he tried to rescue her and subsequently died. One day we're going to have to tell her the truth, or at least a version of it. How can you ever tell your child that her birth daddy was a murderer, a cheat and a fraudster? Andrew says we have a few years to refine our story, but for now we just have to protect our little girl.

Fortunately, from our telephone conversations, Paul's parents agree that Emily is too young to be told that her daddy died twice. Susannah has already told me that they will be telling the world that Paul died a hero, protecting his young daughter. I haven't mentioned that they're conveniently forgetting his first 'death' and that their son was also a killer.

Perhaps in a few years' time, I'll seek out Orla. I want to know whether she and Paul were really in love and how she managed to hide Paul. I wonder whether all that deceit was truly worthwhile. But for now, I'm going to leave her alone with her grief. Gaby says that she's broken, that she may well go to prison herself. But Orla isn't my problem. I have a wedding to plan and a new chalet to design.

A LETTER FROM MIRANDA

Thank you very much for reading *Forget Me Not*. This book is for my sister, Juliette, who shares my love of the mountains and pink sunsets.

I've set this novel in Valais, Switzerland. It's one of my favourite places in the world and somewhere I'm lucky enough to visit often. Ever since I was a little girl, I dreamed of living in the mountains in a tiny, dark wooden chalet with bright red shutters. That dream has partly come true (minus the dark wooden chalet with red shutters!) and every day I look out of the window at the awe-inspiring Swiss Alps is a blessed day. So naturally I had to share this wonderful location in a book.

The place names in *Forget Me Not* are invented principally because I don't want to write about horrible things in a place I love! However, I have taken my inspiration from many of the traditions of the canton of Valais. There is an extensive network of bisses throughout this area of Switzerland and there are countless wonderful walks following the bisses around the mountainsides. The Inalpe festival happens in many villages in the canton of Valais in June, when the Hérens cows are taken up to high pastures, while the Désalpe happens in the autumn, when they're brought back down. The little cabins I describe are often called Mayen. They're small buildings set into the high pastures, traditionally built with stone bases and the upper part in larch planks. These days, local families use them as summer holiday homes.

I hope the descriptions of Valais encourage you to visit this beautiful part of Switzerland. It's an ideal holiday destination, not only in the winter for skiing and snowboarding in some of the best resorts in the world, but also in the less visited months. In early summer the mountainsides are covered in a breath-taking display of wildflowers. Apricots are one of the many local delicacies. By autumn, the vines are heavy with grapes, ready for the harvest. Swiss wines are magnificent but often not exported. You need to visit to taste them and of course they go perfectly alongside the delicacies of fondues, both meat and cheese varieties. Okay, enough – I'm not part of the Swiss tourism board!

I would like to thank Orla and her family for being the successful bidders for the naming rights in this book and helping raise a lot of money for charity in the process. A special call out to Sarah Hall and Nathan. Emily appears in this book (although a much younger version!).

Once again, a huge thank you to my awesome editor Jan Smith. As I've mentioned before, the writing process with the Inkubator Books team is incredibly collaborative and despite our remote locations, I never feel alone. A very big thank you to Brian Lynch, Garret Ryan, Stephen, Claire, Alice and the rest of the team.

My books simply wouldn't have the reach they do without the generosity of the book blogging community who review my thrillers, do cover reveals and share their thoughts with readers.

Thank you so much to all you book bloggers and a particularly big thank you to Carrie Shields (@carriereadsthem_all). Many thanks to Zooloos Book Tours along with everyone who takes part.

Lastly but most importantly, thank *you* for reading my books. Reviews on Amazon and Goodreads help other people discover my novels, so if you could spend a moment writing an honest review, no matter how short it is, I would be massively grateful. Finally, let me know if you visit Valais!

My warmest wishes,

Miranda

www.mirandarijks.com

ALSO BY MIRANDA RIJKS

<u>Psychological Thrillers</u>

THE VISITORS

I WANT YOU GONE

DESERVE TO DIE

YOU ARE MINE

ROSES ARE RED

THE ARRANGEMENT

THE INFLUENCER

WHAT SHE KNEW

THE ONLY CHILD

THE NEW NEIGHBOUR

THE SECOND WIFE

THE INSOMNIAC

FORGET ME NOT

<u>The Dr Pippa Durrant Mystery Series</u>

FATAL FORTUNE

(Book 1)

FATAL FLOWERS

(Book 2)

FATAL FINALE

(Book 3)

Made in the USA
Las Vegas, NV
17 November 2022

59708182R00156